Jenny Pattrick is a writer and former jeweller whose nine published novels have all been NZ number one bestsellers. With her husband Laughton she has written children's songs and musical shows, many of them performed professionally by Capital E National Theatre for Children. She has chaired the boards of many arts organisations, including QEII Arts Council of New Zealand. In 1990 she was awarded an OBE for services to the Arts. In 2009 she received the prestigious Katherine Mansfield Fellowship. Jenny lives in Wellington.

# HARBOURING

# JENNY PATTRICK

BLACK
SWAN

BLACK SWAN

UK | USA | Canada | Ireland | Australia
India | New Zealand | South Africa | China

Black Swan is an imprint of the Penguin Random House group of companies, whose
addresses can be found at global.penguinrandomhouse.com.

Penguin
Random House
New Zealand

First published by Penguin Random House New Zealand, 2022

1 3 5 7 9 10 8 6 4 2

Text © Jenny Pattrick, 2022

Design by Cat Taylor © Penguin Random House New Zealand
Illustrations on page 8 and page 234 by Cat Taylor; image on page 132 courtesy of
Wellington City Council via wellington.recollect.co.nz
Cover image © Magdalena Russocka via Trevillion Images, reference MRA127668
Back cover image: Heaphy, Charles, 1820–1881; Allom, Thomas, 1804–1872; C
Hullmandel (Firm); Smith, Elder & Company. Part of Lambton Harbour, in Port Nicholson,
New Zealand, view from the corner of Willis Street and Lambton Quay looking along the
length of Lambton Quay, April, 1841, Alexander Turnbull Library C-026-001-b.
Author photograph by Deanna Walker
Prepress by Image Centre Group
Printed and bound in Australia by Griffin Press, an Accredited ISO AS/NZS 14001
Environmental Management Systems Printer

A catalogue record for this book is available from the National Library of New Zealand.

ISBN 978-0-14-377667-3
eISBN 978-0-14-377668-0

penguin.co.nz

The demigod Māui sent his line, baited with the jawbone of his grandmother, deep into the sea. His hook caught in the fish which formed the roof of sea-god Tangaroa's dwelling. With great strength Māui hauled this fish to the surface. He called it Te Ika a Māui — Māui's fish. The narrow tail of the fish lay to the north, the fins protruded east and west. The head — Te Upoko o te Ika (the Head of the Fish) — with its gaping mouth pointed south. That gaping mouth — a beautiful harbour — has been variously known as Whanganui a Tara, Port Nicholson, Pōneke and Wellington Harbour.

Benthyg dros amser byr yw popeth a geir yn y byd hwn: Everything you have in this world is just borrowed for a short time.
— *Welsh proverb*

Whatungarongaro te tangata; toitū te whenua:  People pass away; the land remains. — *Māori proverb*

For Laughton.
First and last.

Much has been written about the colonial settlement of Wellington, mostly from the point of view of the leaders — the Wakefields, the colonial government, the landowners, the tribal chiefs. This novel attempts to imagine the lives of those at the bottom of the heap at that time — both Māori and Pākehā.

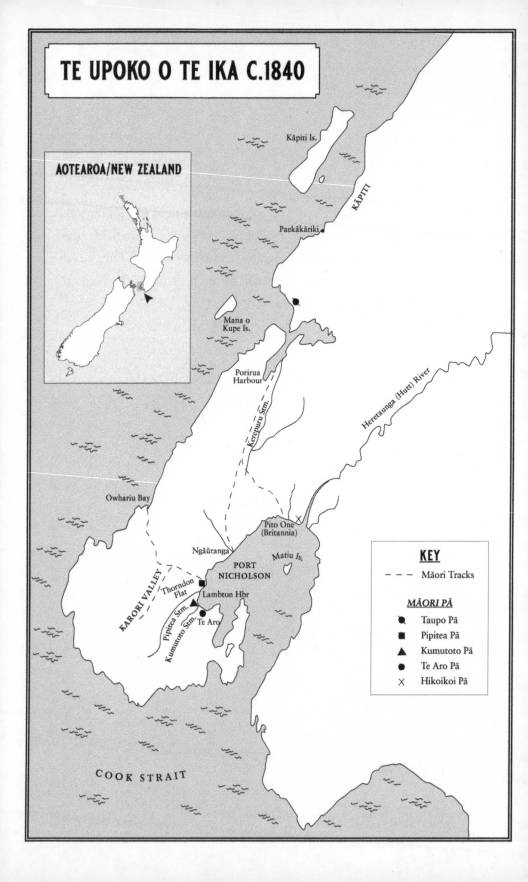

# TE UPOKO O TE IKA C.1840

AOTEAROA/NEW ZEALAND

Kāpiti Is.

KĀPITI

Paekākāriki

Mana o
Kupe Is.

Porirua
Harbour

Kerepuru Stm.

Heretaunga (Hutt) River

Owhariu Bay

Pito One
(Britannia)

Ngāūranga

Matiu Is.

KARORI VALLEY

Thorndon
Flat

Lambton Hbr

Pipitea Stm.

Kumutoto Stm.

Te Aro

PORT
NICHOLSON

COOK STRAIT

## KEY

– – – Māori Tracks

### MĀORI PĀ

Taupo Pā

Pipitea Pā

Kumutoto Pā

Te Aro Pā

Hikoikoi Pā

# Part One

---

# Journeys to the Head of the Fish

# TRADE GOODS

## HUW PENGELLIN

*NEWPORT, WALES, 1839*

Word came to me at the foundry. How the Colonel traced me, bless his boots, I never knew, but trace me he did. Boss appeared to me out of the din and fire and brimstone of the furnace room where I was shovelling the last of the day's spills into a pile for smelting tomorrow.

'Message for you, lad. Call at my office after you finish.'

That set me wondering. The wife? Gareth in trouble again? Baby sick, or worse? Messages don't come two a penny to the likes of a foundry worker. I scraped and swept with a will, in a fever to know. Whistle blew and I was up the steps to his office within the minute. I held no love or respect for the boss — an Englishman of course; he cared not a jot for his workers. We were dispensable ants to him. An accident or a death among us and he would shrug. Plenty more desperate for work out on the streets. I was careful to smile, mind — daren't let my true feelings show. If I lost this hellish job, we might as well curl up our grimy toes and wait for death.

Boss handed me a piece of paper. 'Message from some fancy feller. I told him he'd have to wait till shift end, and he went off in a huff. Tried to tell me it was urgent. Foundry work is urgent, I told him. You want to meet my worker? Do it in his own time, not mine.'

Just one more word from that fat slug and I would have crowned him, I swear. I snatched at the paper and ran off, clang, clang, my boots down the iron treads, outside into the grey light. What fancy feller? And where was he now?

The note was brief. *Colonel Wakefield has a task for you. I am at the White Hart Inn, Tredegar Street, until six o'clock. — J. J. Small.*

My shout set the pigeons on the clock tower flapping. Part pure joy and part anguish. Tredegar Street was in Pillgwenlly. It lacked only five minutes to the hour: I could not reach the hotel in time. Sure I could not. But would die in the attempt.

All my tiredness gone, I raced down over the cobbles, never mind the smog and black, belching chimneys, past the market, closed for the day, and headed for the river. Wait, wait, I prayed to Mr Small, whoever he might be. Stay another five minutes. The clock struck six, and I was still on wrong side of river. Take a last pint, mister, I am on my way. Over the River Usk I pounded, heart bursting, and into the area they call Pillgwenlly. Tredegar Street, yes, but which way? Right or left? 'The White Hart!' I shouted to a smart gentleman, who gave me a startled look and pointed. There it was in front of my very nose. Please God and all His Archangels the man had not left.

Inside the door I wasted no time. 'Mr Small? Is there a Mr Small in the house?'

The bar was crowded. All heads turned towards me. I can make a decent cry when pressed, as the Colonel well knows. 'Mr Small?' What a picture I must have cut. These were commercial men in their tidy suits and ties. My face would have been black from the furnace, my hands grimed, shirt-sleeves dirty and no coat to cover them; not even a cap to my wild hair. No way to meet someone in the Colonel's employ. I began to fear Mr Small, if still present, would turn on his heel at the sight of me. I drew a cloth from my trouser pocket and wiped my sweating face. 'Mr Small? I am Huw Pengellin, the Colonel's man!'

For a moment there was silence in the pub, and then a tall fellow close by rose, looked me up and down, nodded and drew me into a corner. He carried two pint pots with him and set one before me. I could have cried with joy; like as not I did.

He waited politely until my labouring breath steadied and my shaking hand was able to raise the pot. He watched me drink, not smiling, nor frowning either. A strange, quiet fellow. Surely he would be wondering why the Colonel wished to give me a task.

I tried a smile. 'Forgive my appearance, Mr Small. As you will understand, I was in a fever to answer the Colonel's call. I can scrub up quite respectable and pass for a regular fellow. Colonel Wakefield will vouch for that.'

Mr Small nodded thoughtfully and took a pull at his pint. 'Colonel Wakefield tells me you are a good procurer.'

This startled me somewhat. I hoped this was not some illegal or indecent plan. The Colonel was no angel and loved a wild adventure. 'Procurer of what exactly?' I asked cautiously.

Mr Small allowed a prim smile. 'Of a variety of materials and goods for his men, I understand. He says you served under him in Spain and were always able to find his Lancers whatever was needed, even when the king's army failed to provide.'

Our conversation continued without yet mentioning what 'procurement' the Colonel had in mind. I believe Mr Small was assessing my character. He asked about my reason for leaving the British Legion (lack of pay, a pregnant wife) and my present circumstances (pitiful, though I cast them in a slightly more rosy light, choosing not to describe our wretched manufactory hovel or my indebtedness).

Finally, he came to the point. 'You have heard of the New Zealand Company?'

I had not.

'The Colonel is engaged in a new enterprise. His brother— You are acquainted with the name Edward Gibbon Wakefield?'

Of course I was. My Colonel had spent time in prison as a

direct result of his brother's unseemly and grasping behaviour. The Colonel's good name had been besmirched. His men said that this was the reason for his signing on as a mercenary in a foreign army. I held no candle for the older brother, but kept my peace.

'The elder Wakefield is at the forefront of a movement to colonise New Zealand. I am in the employ of the Company. Mr Pengellin, we are greatly pressed for time. A ship will presently leave for New Zealand equipped with a great quantity of trade goods intended for the purchasing of land for colonisation. The Company has made a start purchasing these goods, and of course provisions for the journey, but now we must move with all haste.' Mr Small took from his pocket a folded piece of paper and spread it on the table. The lettering was not the Colonel's flowing hand — I suspected the bespectacled man was a secretary or some such. 'Can you help with these supplies? You will be paid for your services.'

I would have said yes no matter if the order paper included monkeys and peacock feathers. I scanned the list. 'Blankets, yes; iron pots, no problem; muskets, of course. Two thousand fish-hooks? A lot, but possible I reckon. Double-barrelled fowling pieces? Three hundred might be a tall order, but I will find them if they exist. Axe-heads and mirrors — these are manufactured here and in Cardiff. Frock-coats, shirts, waistcoats — yes, yes, yes . . . Top hats!'

The list went on. Jew's harps surprised me. Why on earth? On the whole, though, I was astonished at the quantity required, not the goods themselves.

Mr Small nodded. 'A large quantity, yes. We intend to buy extensive lands from the natives. And settle that most beautiful land with good, God-fearing colonists. Rich and poor. All walks of life. A veritable English society transplanted to the far side of the world.'

I had heard the views of the Colonel's brother on colonisation. The failed Canada expedition, which the Colonel would have joined and offered me a place, too. And the failed Australian venture. I tapped the sheet. 'Is the money for these goods secure?'

'It is. Mr Wakefield is most persuasive. Many important share-holders have joined the Company. You have heard of Sir William Molesworth? Lord Durham? The Honourable A. G. Tollemache? They all hold shares in large parcels of land and will themselves join the colonies.'

Truth is, I wanted to be persuaded. The Colonel's brother was a big-mouth in my opinion, full of fancy ideas, and an abductor of young girls to boot, but perhaps this venture might go ahead. 'How will I be paid? Do you have a purse for me?'

He looked at me coolly. 'You will be paid according to your success. The overall budget for barter goods is five hundred pounds, of which two hundred and eighty pounds, ten shillings and six pence is spent to date.' He looked at me expecting surprise, I thought, at the scale of the enterprise. I *was* surprised — both impressed and cautious — but held my peace. He continued without glancing back at the paper, which did impress me. This man had a better head for accounting than my Colonel. He cleared his throat. 'Which leaves two hundred pounds, nineteen shillings and six pence still available. You will be paid one per cent of the value of your purchases.'

I have a quick mind for money matters. One per cent would serve me well enough, but two would be capital. 'If you are in haste, Mr Small, I think the Company might stretch to two per cent? If I deliver on time.'

He narrowed his eyes. I feared I had pushed too hard, and cursed my wretched appearance. A dapper man may more easily drive a bargain, any fool knows that. But after a moment's hesitation he nodded. 'If delivered on time and in full, two per cent. Purchases to be billed to the New Zealand Company. And sent direct to the docks. The barque *Tory* is the ship. Captain Chaffers the captain.

Addresses here.' He handed me a second sheet of paper with several important names attached, all vouching for and underwriting the company. 'She sails in May. That gives you three weeks and four days.'

I almost choked on my porter. 'Mr Small, I will need to travel to procure these. I am completely without funds. Surely I will need to set out tomorrow if the time is so pressing?'

I wished the man would show some emotion. He was impossible to read. But I would need some reassurance if I was to walk away from the foundry.

Mr Small seemed at last to make up his mind. He stood, reached into a small case he carried and drew out a purse. 'Five sovereigns for your travel and keep. Colonel Wakefield is a generous man. He says you are to be trusted. *I* say you must account for every penny. The Colonel wants you to know that Dr John Dorset, whom you know from the Spanish campaign, will be on board as Company doctor. Also two others from the Lancers.' He paused, as if reluctant to go on. 'Also, he invites you to join the expedition, specifically to keep an eye on the trade goods and see they survive the journey in top condition. Which tidy condition, I feel obliged to say, you do not seem to display yourself at this moment.'

My head whirled with so much information. With the porter, too, I dare say. I must have looked an idiot sitting there bare-headed and dirty. All I could manage was a nod.

'We will be taking on hands in Plymouth early next month. Please deal directly with the Colonel if you decide to embark with us.' He turned as if to leave, but then hesitated and sat again, speaking quietly. 'Mr Pengellin, you need not be too particular about the quality. The natives are ignorant of anything to do with iron, glass, cloth. As long as the goods look smart and shiny they will serve. Red blankets or tartan are favoured, as are brightly coloured waistcoats.

If the axe-head blunts after a few blows the natives will be none the wiser. But,' he raised an admonitory finger, 'the natives are fighting men and are already familiar with guns. All the muskets and fowling pieces must function properly.'

With that he rose, declined to shake my proffered hand, and left by the door I had entered.

For a moment I sat, staring into my pot, grinning, I suppose, like a madman. Then, too late, the questions came tumbling. My once rosy-cheeked wife; my elfin son — what of them? I rose, shot out the door into the darkening street. The fellow was already a distance away, walking smartly, his cane swinging and his head down against a flurry of rain.

'Mr Small! Sir!' I stumbled over the slippery cobbles, ignoring the icy weather. 'Mr Small!'

He paused, and turned, frowning.

'Sir, I have a wife and child. What of them?'

'That is your concern. Not mine. Nor the Colonel's. Good evening.'

'She is a handy wench. Could she not come, too? On the expedition? Cook, maybe?'

He showed some spirit at last, but not to my advantage. 'Mr Pengellin, that is an entirely ridiculous suggestion. The *Tory*'s complement will be exclusively male. This is a survey ship, not an immigrant one. Those will come later.' He held out a finely gloved hand. 'If you wish to withdraw from our arrangement I will trouble you for my purse.'

'No, sir. No. We have agreed on it. I am the Colonel's man. We will manage, sir.'

With that he proceeded into the rain and left me standing.

# FIVE GOLD SOVEREIGNS

## MARTHA PENGELLIN

*NEWPORT, WALES, 1839*

I sat there in the doorway of our little hut — pig-pen, more like — looking down the row for my Huw. Little Alfie fussing on my knee and the light fading. Winter dragging on. How I longed for a bit of sunshine. April, which should be spring, still bitter cold; smoke from the manufactory chimneys blotting out what feeble rays might please themselves to warm us. One by one the workers dragged themselves up the lane — even the ones who'd stopped for a pint — and disappeared into their doorways.

Twenty-five identical huts, shoulder to shoulder, dirty, leaking, stinking, rat-infested hovels which the boss called 'fit accommodation'. Fit for the likes of us desperate enough, hungry enough. The outhouse, which served us all, overflowed when it rained, which was one day in three. When Huw and another worker went to complain, the boss made a sorry face, but explained that times were hard for him as well, the price of steel low, markets in the doldrums, and so on. Boss always had some excuse. When things improved he would see to it, he promised. Meantime our little ones fell sick and died.

But where was Huw? As dark fell I feared he would not come. My man is not cut out for life in a manufactory. Not after his months adventuring in Spain with the Legion. His lovely spirit was fading, anyone could see that. No more bedtime stories about fairies and giants, nor a kiss and cuddle for me at night. Had he run off and left us? Or, worse, been injured at work and no one bothered to report it? Well, I could not sit all night waiting. Swallowing what little pride remained in my poor body, I put our little bit of supper in a tin against the marauding rats and waded through the mud, down the row to Maud's. Knocked on her door. They were at supper, all five, crammed around the lamp and as dour as a pack of donkeys.

'Have you seen my Huw?' I asked Thomas. 'He has not come home. Was he hurt, did you notice?'

Thomas paused in his chewing and shook his head. He is not one of the world's great conversationalists, maybe on account of Maud's chatter. 'He ran off at whistle, beat us all out.' Then went back to his chewing.

I waited for more, but none was offered, so said my thanks and backed away from their pitying stares. But oh, when I trudged back there he was, my Huw, in a fervent at our door shouting my name! He had no shame that man, hopping and shouting for all the world to hear, but I did love him for it. How long since I had seen that light in his eye, the quick smile, the way his feet would beat a dancing rhythm, keeping time with some mad idea in his head? Three months in the foundry had quenched that fire, but here it was again, blazing.

'Martha, love!' he shouted. He tucked a stray lock of my wretched unruly curls back into my bun, then kissed me full on the mouth, the wanton man, 'Here you are, my darling! Come in, come in and hear what I have to tell.'

Alfie chuckled to see his daddy and held out his arms. Huw tossed him high and caught him. 'Fly, my little dragon! Fly, baby draig!', and tossed him again. Huw, who sees elves under every stone and dragons flying high in every cloud, wanted to call Alfie Draig, which means dragon in our language. I wanted Colin, which is nice and sensible, like his mam. In the end we settled for Alfie, which means he will speak with and advise the elves. It suits him well enough. He has bright eyes and an impish smile.

'Huw, Huw, he will fall!' I laughed as Alfie flew in the air again, but sure I was happy to see the two of them. Yesterday Huw had dragged home and sat wordless until bedtime. Today he was all sunlight. Soon we were laughing together and chewing on our bacon butties. Whatever could have brought about this transformation? But Huw would not say until he had eaten, drunk his mug of tea and set himself down on the bed, which served as couch as well as sleeping quarters.

'Watch my hands,' he said to his little son, who could understand no word but followed with his little black eyes as Huw, in the weaving way of a magician, drew from his pocket a little pouch and spread the shining contents on the blanket. Five gold sovereigns! More than Huw would earn in six weeks. Quick as a blink, Alfie reached out to pick one up, and then tried to stuff it in his little mouth. We both rushed to retrieve the precious gold and then deal with Alfie's tantrum. Dear God in heaven, the whole row of families would be wondering what had got into the Pengellin hut!

The very presence of the gold cast its glow on Huw's mood. He made a great fuss of settling Alfie and tucking him into the wooden crate that served as cot. Sang him a little made-up song about an elf who wanted to learn to fly. I waited. For now I could see a shadow lurking under the excitement. Huw was gathering himself for a difficult explanation. I said a quick prayer to sweet Jesus: let there be a way out for us; a new life. This present one is drowning us all three in despair.

I turned down the oil lamp, lit a stub of candle and waited. 'Huw, sweetheart, will you ever spill this great good news or leave my poor heart beating out of its cage?' I dragged him down by me, and we sat close, our Spanish blanket draped across our knees against the clammy air. Once it would not have stretched to cover us both; when we married I was his 'broad, bonny lass', strong as an ox, my skin freckled as a thrush's egg. Now my poor dress hung loose over breasts that did little to tempt a man. The rug tucked over us all too comfortably.

'Well,' said Huw at last, the glow from the candle turning his dear face into a changing landscape like moon behind cloud. 'I have been offered work with the Colonel.'

He told me the story, and I listened, weighing the good news against whatever it was that he was holding back. He had three weeks' work buying up goods, and then what? Finally, he came to it. My man was offered passage to some strange, wild country. On the other side of our great world. To New Zealand. He would be away — far away — for half a year at least if he took sail with the Colonel. Three or four months on the sea even before he arrived at some distant far shore. And what of his wife and son?

I waited in silence. Huw was always the one to dream up a solution; often with the aid of mythical creatures who rise out of some lake and foretell his future. I am the one to make that dream a reality. Or not. Both of us knew that the work at the foundry was Huw's worst solution so far in our short married life. The Spanish war a close second.

Huw held my hand, turned the little gold ring that he had brought back from the war. 'Here is a plan,' he said, his brow furrowing with the effort to persuade me. 'I have not it all worked out yet, but listen, Martha annwyl, we have a chance at last.'

His plan was that he would sail with the Colonel to a country no one had heard of. Then Alfie and I were to come as immigrants and join him there, where we would make our fortunes in a gentle and blessed land at the bottom of the world.

'That's your plan?' I said.

He gave me a rueful smile. 'Sweetheart, I said I did not have it all worked out, but don't you see—'

'And what meantime? We can't stay here if you leave the foundry.'

He swallowed. 'Gareth would put you up.'

I can fire up a tidy temper when needed. 'Huw Pengellin, you know full well I will go nowhere near your brother with his hot eyes and roving hands. Don't you dare make such a foolish suggestion!'

He had the good grace to lower his eyes. 'Just for a short time. He can afford to house you. And feed Alfie. Surely you can manage—'

But I had had enough of his silliness. Even so, I must admit that some small ray of hope had crept in to warm me. I was as desperate to be away from Newport as he was. But if Huw's idea might be made to work, it would be my doing, not his. 'We know nothing about this immigration,' I said, 'or whether this plan will falter like the other Wakefield endeavours. Here is what we will do, Huw. You will give me one of those gold sovereigns—' He started to protest, but I placed my hand firmly over his. 'You are a genius with your accounting if you have a mind. I will take the sovereign and go up with Alfie to Dai and Liddy's farm. The sovereign will pay our way until I find work.'

My brain was racing now. If Huw could find out about the immigrant ships from his precious Colonel; if he could use his influence to get me aboard; if my brother Dai and his Liddy could manage to house us for however long that might take; if Huw could leave the ship when he arrived and join us as an immigrant . . . Too many ifs, perhaps. But we were despairing and desperately poor. You clutch at straws.

I took his purse and drew out a sovereign. 'Do not on any account mention to Gareth that I am heading his way.'

Huw nodded, ashamed now that he had even thought it.

# THE STANDING STONES

## MARTHA PENGELLIN

*PRESELI HILLS, WALES, SPRING 1839*

I found Bryan the carter down at market next morning. A grin split his wizened little face to see me, which cheered me, what with me feeling anxious and unready for adventure, and my Huw already disappeared on his grand shopping endeavour. Bryan leaned against his cart, pipe alight, old Nobbin his horse already in traces; I was just in time.

'Bryan, man, could you take us on up to the farm?' says I. 'And here are six fresh scones for you to take back to May.' Bryan's farm is two over from the family land which Dai had inherited, so we would not be taking him out of his way.

'Eh, lass, keep your scones,' says Bryan, scratching his stubbly chin. 'May will have fresh in oven when I step across the stoop, sure.'

So we set off out of Newport, Alfie asleep in my arms, bless him, and Bryan grumbling on about the new toll gate in the Preseli Hills.

'On a side road, mind! They do not maintain that road. Never have. By time we have paid toll in the hills and then again on main road into town, it's hardly worth bringing corn to market. Might better just store and eat it. Then, bringing lime back to our fields, toll to pay again. And again.' He slapped a sack in the cart. 'Can't grow nothing without lime. Four pence each way for cart. Penny ha'penny for old Nobbin here! That Bullin's a greedy bastard.' Bryan spat over the side as we rattled along.

'Who's he, then?'

'Thomas Bloody Bullin. The English toff who bought the toll

taxes all round here. Every week a new toll gate. He's supposed to keep the roads tidy, but the mud is just as deep, toll gate or no. Your Dai complained to some fellow in authority, but naught come of it. Dai says all us Preseli Hills farmers should march into town and raise a fuss.'

I smiled at that. My brother does love a cause to fight.

Ah, dear God, what a pleasure to climb out of the smoke and fog. Here was spring at last and a bit of sun to warm our backs. Daisies and forget-me-nots winking from behind the rocks, and white May blossom gracing the hedgerows. Tears stood in my eyes. No doubt Bryan imagined they were anger or sorrow at his toll-gate grumbles.

Late in the day we came on over the hills. Bryan would have taken me to the farm, but I knew that meant he would have to drive past Gareth's holding. That great bully's eyes were sharp.

'Drop me here, Bryan,' says I. 'I fancy a walk over the way. I'll give those stones a little pat hello and then surprise Liddy.'

The sun was low and lovely over the valley. The scent of dewy grass and sheep-shit rising. There was a queer lift to my heart, seeing those great stones standing against the sky. For all my fear of what might lie ahead, I also felt a sense of freedom, after the dank stink of those foundry huts. In the distance a ground mist creeping through trees. I picked my way with care, my skirts damp, one boot leaking already. Where reeds grow tall you can be sure soft bog underlies them, and a woman laden as I was that day could be trapped in the mud for a day. I whistled a ditty to divert Alfie, but he whimpered to be let down.

We came to the ring of stones stabbing up through the earth, ancient ancestors buried beneath, they say. I stopped and let the boy have his way. He toddled among them, chattering as if he knew the souls lying under, and I smiled at last. I had walked here myself as a child and talked to them, as my mam and her mam before her had always done. Huw says King Arthur himself is lying beneath, and his famous sword drawn from these very stones. He might be right. I prefer to think of our own ordinary people buried there.

And now I could see down to Dai's little holding — only a few fields and a handful of cows, but a lovely sight. The cottage where I grew up; where part of my heart will always lie. I said a quick prayer to the ancestors. Gareth would condemn me for a pagan. Let him rant away in Chapel, but the old words are a simple comfort and do no harm. These ancient stones belong to us.

That big bully never saw me arrive. He would rage, I knew, when he heard I was here and not staying with him, but I doubted he would come for me.

Well, I was wrong on that count. Come he did. Dai's little holding at the foot of the Preseli Hills was too close.

There was Liddy straightening up from her digging and waving as she saw me come down, Alfie stumbling on ahead on his unsteady little legs, bless him. He was as fond of Liddy as I am. I could see Dai in the far field, sowing wheat, perhaps, or readying the soil. I was glad to have a first word or two alone with Liddy: get her on-side.

Liddy is as slim and wiry and pretty as I grew up stout, freckled and plain. Her garden drew admiring praise throughout the valley. The cabbage and potato and carrots she managed to coax out of that stony soil won prizes at the local fair, not to mention her rhubarb and strawberries and apples. They might not do so well with the wheat and barley, but they eat well enough, the chickens and house cow providing when meat is short.

Well, they made us welcome. Bless the two of them. But there had been an anxious glint to my brother's eye when he came in tired and muddy and saw the little cottage so crowded, with Alfie and their two girls scampering, me and Liddy preparing the meal, and the dog underfoot; hardly room for him to reach his chair.

'Times are not so good, Martha,' he warned.

But Liddy would not let him go on, the dear heart. 'Look what she has brought, love: a gold sovereign! And she will not be here long. They are off to a country called New Zealand, can you believe?'

I found it hard to believe that part, but had to hope that Huw would find a way.

'Would you not come, too, Dai? You and Liddy and the girls? If times are so hard.' But even as I suggested it I knew that Liddy would not leave her garden, nor Dai the farm.

# A SHARP TONGUE

## HINEROA

*KĀPITI COAST, c. 1823*

There was a time, before I met Huw Pengellin, before Pākehā came, before even Ngāti Toa invaded, when I belonged to a tribe and a hapū, when my mother and father were both of chiefly lineage, and I, young though I was, could proudly recite my whakapapa. Then my full name was Te Hine Tāroaroa: the tall woman. Now I can claim none of those connections. I became a no one.

But the memories survive. Those cannot be erased by war and slavery.

When my first Matariki arrived, our tohunga looked up at the stars, looked at my open mouth and pronounced that I would be cursed with a sharp tongue. So my mother told me some years later. We were walking together in the tall bush looking for herbs to heal my brother's infected foot. She spoke with a smile.

I turned to face her and poked out my tongue for her inspection. 'Was he right?' I asked. 'Is it sharp?' I rolled my eyes for good measure. I was perhaps seven or eight years old then — a peaceful time. Before the terror.

My mother laughed and pulled at my tongue. 'Not that kind of sharp. But he was right, āe. Our tohunga is a wise man who makes clever guesses. He knew I was outspoken and guessed I would pass that talent on to my daughter. Ah!' She pointed to a clump of kawakawa bushes. 'Pick me some of these — branch and leaf — a big armful, Hineroa, while I cut this bark here.' (I still keep my name — Hineroa, tall woman — although I have been called many other names since.)

When we had our arms full and were returning to the kāinga she spoke again of the tohunga's words. 'Some might say it is a curse to be outspoken — especially if you are a woman. I have earned black looks and worse, true. But Hine, listen to me. Sometimes the elders speak with loud voices, but what they say may not be well thought out. If you disagree with a foolish speech or action, it is wise to be brave and to disagree, even if it earns you a blow. Your words may plant a seed.'

'But is it true? Do I have a sharp tongue like you?' I asked.

'You do. Only yesterday you shouted at your brother when he held his blade wrongly and sliced his leg.'

'And then he hit me!'

'Āe. There is the curse. But your words were wise, and perhaps he will remember next time!'

We walked down out of the bush, into the sunshine. Some of the young men were bobbing for eels in the shaded pools of the stream. My mouth watered.

My brother danced on the bank and held up a long, wriggling fish. 'E, sister, look! And we have three more! Feast tonight!'

Rere loved to make a song or a dance over anything. Maybe he was slow to learn his fighting moves. He often earned a cuff from our father for his clumsiness or his lack of concentration. But his great pleasure was to make us all laugh. To imitate the sound of the ruru or the kererū; to tell us scary stories of taniwha lying in wait among the flax in the swamp; to jump down from a tree branch with a wild yell and set the little ones screaming. Sometimes he seemed more like a sister than a brother.

That day his silly dancing annoyed me. 'Three is not enough for a feast!' I shouted. 'Keep fishing!'

This earned me a stern look from my mother. 'Who are you to taunt those boys? They are finding food for the hapū. Listen to me,

Hine. Save your sharp tongue for important matters. Now let us find pūhā and raurēkau to steam with those fine tuna.'

Why, now, do I remember that day? That forgotten advice? Many times since, I have failed to curb my tongue, and many times have I suffered terribly for my boldness.

Many Matariki have passed since that time. Back then I possessed a mother and father and lived in peace with my tribe. That place bore the name Kāpiti, though now it has a new name — Paekākāriki, which means the perching place of the green parrot. My mother was daughter of a chief and was famed for her knowledge of healing. A wise and gentle mother who rubbed away my tears when the rough boys teased me for my height. (Even at ten years old I was taller than was proper for a girl.) She would take me by the hand and teach me the good plants and berries, the poisonous ones, and when karaka berries might be picked and cooked.

I think back to that time as if it was some kind of paradise, like the one Adam and Eve lived in before she ate the apple. Our blessed land was wedged between sea and high cliffs. The soil was good: a little sandy, needing the richness of seaweed and leaves from the trees which climbed the hills above our settlement. The bush descended, growing less tall, gradually thinning out as trees met the shifting sand dunes which blew inland year after year. There were swamps full of eels and shellfish in the shallow sea at low tide. Kūmara and the new white-man potato, brought by whalers, grew well.

It was not paradise, of course. There was sickness and hungry years and fighting between tribes.

But nothing compared with the bitter, ugly war that descended upon us from the north. Te Rauparaha and his nephew Te Rangihaeata and the Taranaki tribes arrived. Invaded, I should say. Not a simple war party coming to right an ancient wrong or a warrior demanding revenge for an insult to his family; we were used to these from time to time. No. Ngāti Toa and Ngāti Raukawa and Te Āti Awa spread over our settlements in their hordes! They wished to take all our lands, to settle like a plague of rats where our ancestors were buried. Where the stories of our people belonged.

Why did they come? This I have only recently understood. They came because they themselves were driven out from *their* ancestral land by Waikato tribes. But also because they wanted the benefits that white men brought. That wily Te Rauparaha guessed that white men would come to our lands.

Our men — even our women — fought bravely. To begin with we drove them away. But more came, and more. My mother said our fighting men were superior. My father agreed. But the invaders had guns, many many guns. This was a new kind of war to our tribe. We had no muskets. Te Rauparaha brought those fire sticks from the north. White men's guns. We knew nothing of such things. Their noise and their stinging bullets unnerved our fighting spirit. We were proud to fight hand to hand with taiaha and mere. But the invaders stood at a distance like cowards, and shot our chiefs, wounding them so they were not able to stem the rush when it came. We were driven out like Adam and Eve into the wilderness.

Up in the hills, we survivors took shelter and gathered to plan. Our tribe was Muaūpoko. In those days — maybe fifteen or twenty Matariki past — there were many Muaūpoko hapū on the Kāpiti coast. We had strong pā. On Kāpiti Island a mighty pā. That island was our stronghold. A place of retreat. We were feared for our fighting skill. My father and the allied chiefs from Pukerua and Waikanae and Ōtaki united to drive the invaders back. Down from the hills, down through the bush they crept silently one night to burst upon the sleeping Taranaki tribes led by Te Rauparaha.

At first, our plan was successful. Te Rauparaha was driven back; also his fearsome nephew Te Rangihaeata. We celebrated. There was a feast of human flesh, for in those days it was a customary end to a successful battle. But the great impregnable fortress of Kāpiti Island, which had been a place of refuge to us in other times, was taken by Ngāti Toa. That was a terrible blow to my father and the other chiefs. We were driven back. Our spirit was broken after losing the island. Te Rauparaha and his chiefs stayed there — licking their wounds, said my father sourly — and gathered strength for some weeks. They say he purchased more muskets from the whaling stations on the island.

I do not like to remember the night they returned. Too many warriors; too many muskets; far far too much death. My father killed. My mother (for she fought, too) captured.

When my father's body was thrown on the umu for the victory feast, my mother broke away from the huddled remaining captives of our hapū. She stood proud to sing a high, keening lament for him. Then, tears streaming down her face, blood from her clawing nails coating her chest, she turned to Te Rangihaeata.

'You from the north! You Ngāti Toa! Shame upon you; you cowardly warriors! You who hide behind guns and fight from a distance. Shame! Look around you. Is there not land enough to support us all? Why must you drive us out? Look elsewhere for your new gardens, your new fishing grounds. What further quarrel have you with Muaūpoko? There was no reason for this battle. You have already exacted payment for your dead chiefs. That obligation has been righted. We should now be living in peace.'

My mother pointed at Te Rangihaeata and then at Te Rauparaha. 'Shame! Shame!'

With my father beaten in battle she had no mana. No honourable future. She had nothing to lose by letting her sharp tongue loose. As she had advised me, she saved it for an important moment. It earned her no praise. That evil chief Te Rangihaeata (I can say evil now; I

no longer need to hold back my thoughts) raised his mere high as she
stood unflinching. He motioned to a young chief to strike the blow.
My mother's fine, proud head was split. She fell. I hid my eyes then,
for the chief gestured to two young warriors to remove her head
and cut out the heart. I do not know where her body was taken or
whether she was eaten.

She made no sound. My father eaten in the victory feast, as my
brother and I, now captive slaves, watched. I saw, in the light of the
many glowing fires, my brother seated some distance from me. Over
and over again he beat his fist on the ground. Tears ran in rivers down
his grimy face. None of the other captured men cried. They watched
stony-faced as was required. Not Rere. He was always different. His
captors noticed his distress and taunted him. Behold the baby-face!
Son of a chief and he cries like a woman! They bestowed on him the
worst insult — 'toenga kainga' — remnant of the feast. Not even
worthy of being eaten.

I think Te Rauparaha hated to be beaten. And we Muaūpoko
had for a time driven him back. For that he and his chiefs set out to
destroy our many hapū; to wipe away our customs and occupy our
lands. They took many slaves. My brother was given as slave to a
Ngāti Toa hapū further south and made to weed kūmara gardens
and cut flax for them. Women's work. He would have hated that.
They sold what we grew or toiled over for more guns.

Auē! Our people have never recovered. Where is my tribe now?
My people? Scattered like sand blowing over the dunes. We are a
people enslaved.

Where was my brother, Rere? It would be many years before I
saw him again.

I tell you this: when your land is taken, when you are considered
as lowly as the rats and dogs that are also eaten, when you are
traded for a gun, or (as I was later) for two cook pots belonging

to a missionary, then it is most difficult to hold up your head and remember you are the daughter of a once proud fighting chief and a mother once revered for her healing knowledge.

# WHALERS AND WAKA

## HINEROA

*KĀPITI ISLAND, 1824–1830s*

I do not include Te Rauparaha's sister, Waitohi, among those to receive my curses. A wise and clever woman. After the battle which killed my father, she saw me softening leaves in a gourd of hot water to put on one of our warriors' wounds. (We were all slaves now — mōkai — but a live slave can be useful, so healing was allowed.) Waitohi stopped to watch. Flies were gathering about the wounds.

'What is that leaf you use?' she asked.

I told her that I didn't know the name but that my mother used it to keep flies away from open wounds. 'If your son had not killed her, she might tell you,' I said.

That earned me a slap, but not enough to knock me over. Her sharp eyes showed amusement, not anger. 'Show me then, little loudmouth,' she said. 'Show me the bush. I think it does not grow up north in Taranaki.'

I led her to a bush hanging over a little stream and pointed.

'Pick me some!'

Waitohi was used to giving orders and used to being obeyed. For an hour or two she led me into the forest and had me gather examples of all the herbs and cures I could remember.

'You might be useful on Kāpiti,' she said, frowning. 'There will be more fighting and more wounding before next Matariki arrives. Come with me.'

Perhaps I was eleven years old then. Or ten. People always took me for older because of my height. For the next two Matariki I stayed on the island, scraping flax with the other mōkai and gathering herbs when fresh wounds and sores needed healing.

Waitohi was not in any way frightened of Te Rauparaha. Often she would disagree with her brother. 'You should rest your warriors,' she might say when he became restless to set out and conquer more tribes further south. 'Build up your fighting men first.'

Also, she was the one who decided which tribes from the north should settle in which places. Ngāti Toa got Kāpiti Island and the best parts of the mainland, Te Āti Awa and Ngāti Raukawa went where she said. She was indeed powerful. I never saw her go against her son's wishes, though. Te Rangihaeata was a fierce and cruel man. I learned to curb my tongue whenever he came onto the island.

But then Waitohi moved to live on the island called Te Mana o Kupe, and I lost my protector.

———

There is a small island off great Kāpiti Island called Tokomapuna. A rocky, windswept place. I was sent there by Te Rauparaha to care for and pleasure one of his special Pākehā, Thomas Evans. A big, wide-shouldered fellow who loved to laugh and drink strong liquor and fight anyone who crossed him. His gang of whalers lived on Tokomapuna during the whaling season. I was still young, not quite a woman. Maybe Te Rauparaha sent me there because he didn't like it that I was taller than him. Thomas already had a chieftain's daughter for a wife — I was just an extra.

Those whalers were mostly ill-mannered, bad-tempered, hard-drinking fellows who used me when they felt like it. But there was one, Jimmy the Goat they called him for his little tufty beard, who took a fancy to me. Jimmy was clever and fearless with the harpoon, so since I was no beauty nor easy in my laughter or flaunting — 'Surly-Girly' they called me — after a while they left me to Jimmy. I stayed in Jimmy's hut and helped prepare food for the gang or picked shellfish off the rocks.

That would have been a sad and broken time for me but for one thing: Jimmy the Goat had a Bible in his hut which he could read. He took it into his head to teach me on stormy days — there were plenty of those — when the whaleboats could not go out or the mother whales avoided the shore-waters. Jimmy was pleased that I learned so quickly. He tried to show off my skill, but the gang were not interested. Thomas himself could read, but most of the others had very few letters.

'Go on,' Jimmy would say, as the crashing waves shook the hut and the candle guttered, 'read me this part. "Jesus and the loaves and fishes".'

And I would read to him. I burned to see my own language written on paper like that. Sometimes I would take a stick and try to write te reo in the sand. Some words were easy: 'hapū'; 'iwi'; not 'Muaūpoko', though — the name of my poor scattered tribe. How could that be written?

———

One clear night Thomas Evans noticed a fire over on the mainland shore. He climbed as far up the rocky peak of our little island as he could get.

'Here's trouble,' he said. 'Hey, Surly-Girly, see if those long legs can climb to the top. Tell me what you see.'

There was no wind that evening, the sea a dark mirror to the stars. Even in the dark my body remembered the best handholds and craggy ledges, for I was sometimes sent up to watch for the plume of mother whales who came close to shore to calve. And oh, what a sight that night! There on the mainland shore firelight twinkled. Many, many fires. Too many to count. There must have been hundreds gathered, and to what purpose but to regain Kāpiti Island!

My heart pounded in my throat. What news should I take back? Surely this was a Muaūpoko war-party. Reinforced by many friendly hapū. If they were successful in wresting this stronghold from Te Rauparaha, what would my life then become? Once a slave, always one. No one from my tribe would want to give me a place around the fire. The gods had cursed my parents with bad luck. I would also carry that ill-fortune. I would remain a nobody, destined to serve at the whim of whoever owned me. But still . . . The thought of Te Rauparaha and his relatives being beaten by my former tribe was a thought to warm my belly.

I climbed down and ran to the little gaggle of huts. When Thomas questioned me, I tried to hold his stern gaze. 'There are several fires. From their position I think they will attack the north of the island, not here.'

'How many fires? Can't you count, Surly-Girly? How many?'

'Not too many,' I said, but I think he saw through me. He was a clever man and a good leader despite his rough ways. 'Up you go, Jimmy the Goat, quick as you may. I don't trust this girl of yours.'

So it was Jimmy who brought back the news which earned me a beating and a broken finger. 'We had better warn the boss,' growled Thomas, leaving me lying while he and some others ran a whaleboat into the sea, and rowed with a will to warn Te Rauparaha, who would not be able to see the fires ashore from his pā.

Jimmy picked me up and splinted my finger. He was a kind man, but angry then. 'That was ill-done, Hineroa,' he said as he bound up my finger. 'You belong with us, and we belong with the chief. Don't forget that again. Our livelihood depends on his goodwill.'

Those of us left on Tokomapuna watched in the dark. No sign for a while. And then, as the sky lightened above the hills to the east, we saw them coming. Hundreds of waka, black against the pearly water, heading to the north of the island as I had guessed. So many! Surely they would be successful.

We heard gunfire; saw the first wave of waka drive towards the far shore; heard their shouts. But the action was out of sight to us. A second and third wave of waka surged forward. I feared the paddlers would now be too exhausted to engage in warfare. Perhaps they were successful, though, for I saw no waka falter nor change direction.

But Jimmy grinned and pointed. 'Here comes our man. Now we will see.'

From the shore a little north of our island we saw our whaleboat, filled with Te Rauparaha's warriors, set out. Others ran along the shore track, guns over shoulders, mere and powder-horns banging against thighs. Several other waka taua laden with warriors followed the whaleboat.

'Our man will not be beaten,' crowed Jimmy.

'It is his guns not his skill that wins wars,' I muttered sourly, even though I knew by then that he was a brilliant warrior. I would never sing his praises, though. Besides, I was too sore.

Ngāti Toa won. Many dead. Much feasting. I was sent back to Te Rauparaha, beaten again for my disloyalty, and then given to a Te Āti Awa chief on the mainland in exchange for three kete of kūmara. My new work for many years: grow more kūmara and potato for trading with the Pākehā. Trading meant acquiring guns as far as Te Rauparaha was concerned. I was glad to be away from Kāpiti.

Te Āti Awa chiefs began to listen to the missionaries. But during those years I trusted no one, earned my reputation for bad temper, and kept close the secret of my ability to read and speak the Pākehā tongue.

This was my life for many years until the day I met Huw Pengellin. Twice I bore children. The boy was taken away, sent back to Kāpiti Island and raised as a Ngāti Toa warrior. I never saw him or knew what happened to him. The girl was considered weak and left out in the open to die.

# CEFFYL PREN

## MARTHA PENGELLIN

### PRESELI HILLS, WALES, SPRING 1839

O n a Saturday, Liddy would take some of her vegetables and pickles to sell at the village market. It was only a few pennies she earned in these hard times, but it was a chance to chat with the other women and hear the news. That first Saturday I went with her. We spread the few goods on a bench and sat in the sun. Oh, it was a pleasure after Newport. How had I ever agreed to that plan? Well, we were desperate, that's why.

One of my old friends from Chapel, Arial Conti, walked past with her head down, but something must have caught her attention for she turned, her face suddenly come alight. 'Martha Pengellin, is that you, dear heart? Have you been hiding under some stone up in the hills, then?'

To tell the truth I didn't recognise her at first. She had always been the prettiest in the village and the sauciest, but here she stood grey-faced and thin, her clothes lacking attention and her bonnet ribbons in tatters.

Liddy saw my confusion and whispered, 'It's Arial Thomas who was married off to that Cadoc Conti, remember?'

Then I could see it, but Lord how she had changed. None of us had been happy at the wedding — Arial so young and Cadoc twenty years her senior. A rough man, known to be bad-tempered with most, fellow or lass alike, but a hard worker who owned a decent few fields on the sunny side of the valley. Arial had four sisters and three brothers all alive on the one tiny farm. It was a marriage of

convenience, we all knew it, but at least she would not starve. Or so
we had thought.

I made room for her on the bench, but she would not settle. She
looked this way and that, plucking at a hole in her jacket. 'The men
are out on a Ceffyl Pren hunt. Did you not hear the shouting?'

Now we heard it, off down the road a mite and coming our way.
Sometimes the Ceffyl Pren punishments are harmless — a bit of
mischief and good for a laugh. But the way Arial was acting you
could be sure this one was more serious. I had not been in the village
long so did not know the gossip, but Liddy knew, clear enough. She
took hold of Arial's arm and drew her behind the bench where a
bush would shade her from the approaching men.

'Come on, sweetheart; you don't need to be seen. Look away, do.
Martha, mind my leeks, will you?'

Round the bend they came, six or eight of them all in women's
garb, their faces blacked with soot. The tallest of them was Gareth, I
would lay a bet on it. 'Ceffyl Pren! Ceffyl Pren!' they shouted, which
means 'wooden horse' in our tongue. They dragged a ladder behind
them on which was tied a young fellow. He had been rolled in the
mud by the look of him, chicken feathers stuck in his hair, but it was
Bryn Evans, sure it was — a nice fellow, blacksmith's apprentice and
set to take over from old Evans, his uncle.

Gareth — it was him alright — was fair bouncing with a devilish
enjoyment, waving to the market bystanders. 'Judged guilty! Guilty
indeed!' he shouted out in our own tongue, as is proper for Ceffyl
Pren. 'Guilty of laying his hands on a good man's wife!' He grabbed
a handful of cabbage leaves from under a stall and brandished them
on high. 'Out with your rubbish! Pelt the offender! Ceffyl Pren!'
With an imperious gesture — the big show-off — he halted the
cavalcade to give us time to pelt the guilty fellow. But no one else
was laughing much. Bryn was generally liked. Several turned away

or bent over their vegetables, embarrassed it seemed by the black-faced, long-skirted, prancing lads.

Poor Bryn turned his head away, trying to hide from us. Gareth was angry now; the fun was turning sour. He grabbed Bryn's desperate face and turned it towards us. 'Bryn Evans! Look you! Loose with another's wife!' He whipped the cabbage leaves back and forth across the boy's face.

Now there was a shriek from behind me. I should have known. Arial Conti, brave woman, broke from Liddy's restraint and stormed through the market, knocking cabbages and potatoes flying — Liddy's good leeks, too, before I could guard them. She grabbed Gareth's handful of leaves and flung them back in his face. 'Is that you, Gareth Pengellin, hiding in your mother's skirt?' She yelled the words in English so that all could hear, Welsh and English. 'Bully that you are!' Slash, slash with her palm across his astonished face. 'You would do well to clean up your own mucky barn before you cast a stone at another's!' Oh, she was a sonsy tiger in her rage, all the quiet misery gone from her face. She turned to the other black-faced boys. 'Off with ye, then; you've had your silly fun. Ceffyl Pren is over.' She turned her fierce eyes on the crowd. 'Who will untie him now? Does he have no friend here?' She stood for a moment to be sure that hands were forthcoming, then stalked away. Wise woman. A step too far to untie him herself.

Gareth never noticed me sitting quietly by the leeks with the children.

Later, Liddy told me the gossip as we walked home, carrying the unsold vegetables. It was plain to see how hard times were. Old Cadoc, it seemed, was no use in bed. Arial, still sharp and wayward in those days, let his shortcomings be known to some of the lasses, and so the gossip spread. Cadoc, when he heard the whispers and laughter, as sure you will in a small town, shut Arial in the house and beat her. Starved her, too, until she learned to behave herself: turn up to Chapel at his side; keep her eyes low; serve his meals without carping.

'We all thought her spirit broken,' said Liddy, 'but of late there's been a change in her. Some say she and Bryn are meeting secretly.' She grinned. 'If they are and she manages to get a babby in her poor belly you'd think Cadoc might be pleased, but with him, who knows? And Gareth ranting on in Chapel . . .' She stopped at a wee stone cottage. Putting a finger to her lips to quiet my chatter, she tiptoed to the door. There she quietly laid the unsold leeks and onions. 'Their crop failed last summer and now they can't even afford lime to dress their tiny plot. The toll-gate charges are ruining the likes of them. And others.'

'You are a good woman, Liddy,' I said, smiling and linking arms with her.

'Well,' she said, 'a good gardener anyway.'

The children were running ahead. What a joy to see Meg and Holly take Alfie's hands and swing him along, his little legs going like windmills. Already he had colour in his cheeks and a bit of fat on his scrawny arms. We had both lost weight in Newport. Growing up I had been taunted for my chubby cheeks and freckles, but foundry life had wasted me; I had become almost as gaunt and tattered as poor Ariel.

'We'll soon have you back to your old plump self,' Liddy had said when I arrived.

'Plump?' said I, pretending outrage.

She had laughed. 'Well-covered then. A bit of flesh suits you, Martha. Sure, Huw likes you a bit cuddly, doesn't he?'

We walked back home, arms still linked. Suddenly the thought of leaving my valley filled me with an unbearable sadness — *hiraeth*, we say in our tongue. My mother's hearth-stone by the fire, which she had brought from her farm when she married my father. The cottage built by my grandfather. I stopped, unable to go on, tears falling.

'Martha, Martha!' said Liddy. 'Whatever is it?'

But for once I had no words.

# REBECCA MEN

## MARTHA PENGELLIN

*PRESELI HILLS, WALES, 1839*

Two weeks later Gareth arrived at Dai's cottage. He stood in the doorway stamping the mud off his boots as we were at table.

'No, no!' he roared at Liddy. 'Sit down, sweetheart, I've not come to eat. Here, take this piece of ham for your butties tomorrow.'

He had come for a word with Dai, but stopped in his tracks when he saw me. Try as I might, there was no place to hide.

'Martha Pengellin, is that you?' Gareth never talks in a quiet, conversational manner. It is all loud laughter or barking anger. Even his most innocent remark comes out at a roar. 'How long have you been here and not called to see your brother-in-law?'

I would not talk to him. He knew full well why, and so did Liddy. Dai knew only half of it. There was a silence in the room, broken only by a burst of laughter from the bedroom where the children were whispering; woken, no doubt, by Gareth's bullocky ways.

For a full minute Gareth stood there, filling the room with his bulk. Those blazing eyes, which can incite a congregation to ecstasy or fear, boring into me. I rose, too, and glared back. He would neither cow me nor draw me in; not ever again.

At last he cleared his throat and turned to Dai. 'We are going to attack the toll gate tomorrow. Are you in?'

Dai nodded. 'I am.'

'We will go in the manner of Ceffyl Pren.'

Dai smiled at that.

Gareth roared with laughter as if he had invented the idea, which he had not. Dai told me later that red-headed Thomas Rees had the idea.

'So, sister-in-law, I may have need of your dress,' said Gareth with a queer, sly smile. 'There is none else in the district will fit me.'

I walked away to see to the children. 'Go to hell, Gareth,' I said. 'I have none to spare.'

———

Perhaps I was wrong to be so angry with Gareth. He and Dai and the other men did well enough over the toll gate. They gave us women a good laugh as they rehearsed in Thomas's cottage down the valley.

'Oh, my dear children,' piped Red Thomas, sweeping his wife's skirts back and forth like a strumpet, 'what is this before me? I cannot get past.'

'Why it's a toll gate, mother.' That was my brother Dai, who looked the image of a pretty girl in Liddy's Sunday best. I darted forward to tie his ribbons properly. Liddy would be anxious about her only tidy dress.

Red Thomas gathered Dai to his side, moaning in his queer, high voice. 'But, my dears, what shall we do? I cannot get to market.'

Gareth said his lines in a growl; he was not as good at the play-acting as the others. 'Shall we break it down for you, Mother Rebecca dear?'

'Shall we help you, Mother Rebecca dear?' piped the other men, giggling and primping.

Oh, it was a tonic in those bitter times to see the men enjoying themselves for once. Usually it was all damn the English, damn the weather, God damn the price of corn and so on, brows lowered from morning till night.

And when they set out into the dark that night, they stepped lightly, faces smeared with soot, their muddy boots odd under their wives' skirts: a game it was, though the purpose was serious.

We women sat together, waiting in Thomas Rees's house, fearful now. What if Mr Bullin had got word? What if his bailiffs were waiting at the toll gate? Thomas had warned us: 'Afterwards, men: go straight home, take off your pretty robes. Wash the soot from your faces and into bed. And wives: now don't you keep chattering on in my house, mind. Off with you back to your own homes. It must all seem quiet and normal.' But we stayed on for a bit, taking comfort from each other until Sarah pinched the candle.

I walked back over the fields in the moonlight. Liddy was home with the little ones. I kept thinking of Huw. No word at all. The sovereign I had brought was used up by now and no work found. Dai, who admired Gareth, would no doubt suggest Alfie and I move in with him. I couldn't keep taking food from their mouths, and Gareth would feed us well. But he would try to exact payment as he had before. That man knew his Bible; could call hell-fire down on fornicators and extortionists, quoting chapter and verse at our Chapel meetings. Dear God, didn't I try to throw the same verses back in his face when he came at me, but he was deaf and blind when the heat was on him. Strong as I was, I could not fight him off. Afterwards he might look away, mutter that I had led him on, that like as not Huw was dead on some foreign battlefield. It was his duty, he claimed, to take me and care for me. No, I thought, as I walked back to Dai's tiny cottage, if it comes to that I will take Alfie and go to the poorhouse back in Newport.

———

Dai crept in near daybreak, grinning like a madman. 'Oh, boyo, what a victory! You should have seen it, Liddy. Twenty of us, I swear, with our pitchforks and spades. We tore down the gate, set fire to it and the roof of the toll house; sent Bullin's man packing with his tail between his legs.' He slumped into a chair while Liddy unlaced his bonnet and then washed the black off his face. 'It's a grand plan, see? No one can tell for sure who was there. We'll tear it down again if they rebuild.' He rubbed a tired hand across his face. 'When word gets out there'll be riots all over. Rebecca Men, we are now, after Rebekah in the Bible.'

His poor tired head hit the table and he was asleep, just like that, with a silly grin still on that dear face. But up again two hours later and out to the fields. Red Thomas had cautioned them: everything must be normal. If the bailiffs come looking they should see every man innocently at work. It was indeed a grand plan.

———

Dai forgot about the note until he stumbled back from work that night. Bryan had brought it up from someone at the market. It was from Huw. 'Dai, Dai, read it to me quick!' I shouted. 'Oh, what does the man say?'

Neither Liddy nor I knew our letters. Most women in our village the same. We spoke two languages, mind, which the English could not. Too often Huw was away, or maybe I was too busy with other matters to ask his help. In our village where we spoke our

own language and most never learned to read it — even the men —
there seemed little point. Now I cursed the fact that I had to ask my
brother to read to me. The letter was in English. My Huw could read
and write a fine hand in both English and Welsh.


*Martha annwyl, good news. I have been successful in
my purchases and earned my commission. Dai will
shortly receive two sovereigns for your keep. Now
here is my plan. I have spent some of my commission
on goods of my own — saws, axes, nails and the like
— and plan that we may set up a little shop in New
Zealand. The Colonel is pleased with my purchases. He
has put in a word for you with Mr and Mrs Abernethy
who are travelling as passengers on one of the first
immigrant ships. They have bought a quantity of land.
Which is strange when you think that the goods to buy
that land are still sitting in the* Tory's *hold in London!
Mr Abernethy says his wife will need a washerwoman
and will take you with her as labourer attached to her.
I doubt a washerwoman's quarters will be comfortable
on board. It will be very crowded, but you are strong,
sweetheart, and we will meet in New Zealand. I sail
shortly. Your barque, the* Oriental, *captained by
William Wilson, will sail some months later. Please kiss
little Alfie for his daddy. Stay strong, love. Do not be
too afeared. Think of it as a grand adventure. In truth
we have no choice but to take this chance.*
    *Huw Pengellin*
    *PS I have bought a little medal of Llŷr to keep
me safe on the sea. A fellow sells them on the street*

*outside the White Horse Inn in Pillgwenlly. The very*
*place where our fortunes changed! It is a sign, Martha,*
*that all will be well. Be sure to buy one from him*
*yourself and one for Alfie.*

I had to smile. Huw lays such store in the gods and their power. I
lack his confidence. I doubt Llŷr would rule over seas the other side
of the world. Better to learn to swim, I would say to him.

# A NEW LANGUAGE

## HUW PENGELLIN

*ON BOARD THE BARQUE* TORY, *JULY 1839*

It was not what I expected — shipboard with the Colonel. Not at all. In the Spanish war we sat around the fire at night, all of us — Lancers, foot soldiers, quartermaster like me — and laughed together. Colonel would kick a log into the fire, light a fresh cheroot and tell a tale as the sparks flew up. The simplest groomsman might pipe up with a story to stop us in our eating — knife halfway to mouth — until we heard the end. He was a strict leader, the Colonel, and a brave soldier, but a bit of a father to us for all that.

Shipboard was another matter entirely. I was to answer to Captain Chaffers, a fearsome fellow. The Colonel and the other cabin passengers were in awe of him to a man. Captain ran the ship with an iron fist, ready to call for the lash if you strayed from his orders.

Passengers like the Colonel and Dr Dorset, and the science men Heaphy and Dieffenbach, didn't mix with us below decks. They had cabins and drank every night with Captain, and ate fresh meat while the pigs and chickens lasted. I had fancied Colonel and I would be easy with each other since I was to look after his trade goods, but we hardly spoke a word all those long, tedious three months at sea. He would give me a nod sometimes if we passed up on deck, but the look on his face was distracted. Was he trying to remember who I was, or did some other preoccupation gnaw at him? Maybe he felt as out of place shipboard as I was. Or even as fearful as I of the great heaving, open ocean.

When the weather turned foul, I was expected to help the seamen as best I could, but truth was they were a grim-faced lot and despised me for my clumsy ways. Crossing the Channel to Spain was a very different kettle of fish from the open ocean, especially the wild storms we encountered around the Cape. I could not manage up the yards as the other hands did, and was reduced to slipping and sliding, hanging onto some rope or rail while Lowry, the first mate, shouted at me.

If it wasn't for Rere and Te Whaiti the voyage would have been a sad, sorry affair for me.

Rere was a New Zealander — one of the crew and as handy up aloft as I was a hindrance. Our first night at sea he grinned at me, indicating that I should sling my hammock next to his in the 'tween deck. Perhaps he lacked friends. I noticed, as the voyage continued, that the rest of the crew, though respectful of his strength and agility, never drew him into their rowdy, bawdy off-shift gaggles.

Rere was tall, brown as a chestnut, his shock of black hair pulled up into a topknot which he would not tar as most of the crew did with their pigtails. Each night he let his hair loose, combed his fingers through the tangle, picked out any foreign material, as fastidious as any woman, and then tied it back up neatly. Often a feather or the bone of a bird inserted for decoration. Always he washed his hands before eating. The other sailors laughed at his fussy habits but to me it was a lesson, if you like — I was not so careful about my person as Rere. 'Good day,' he said to me that first night as we swung side by side, 'I am Rere.' He spoke some other words which may have been English or his own language and leaned over to shake my hand. A polite formal greeting unlike the back-slapping informality of the deck-hands.

'I am Huw from Wales,' I said.

He grinned. 'Heu. Heu. My friend?'

From that first night we became friends, spending time together whenever he was off-shift.

Most of my tasks involved hours spent in the 'tween deck or down in the stinking hold with the precious cargo, which was to buy half of New Zealand, it was said. The hold was where I met the other New Zealander Te Whaiti, a chief, who was to be our interpreter with the natives. Not so tall or strapping as Rere, but with curving tattoos from nose to chin. Rere was perhaps a little afraid of him. Te Whaiti dressed smartly like the cabin passengers and was expected to eat and drink and talk with them, but often walked alone on deck or came below with me. The three of us were of an ilk — not quite belonging to any group.

Te Whaiti had several boxes of his own goods stowed beside the trade goods — presents from his time in London — and he liked to keep an eye on them. 'Watch out for pilfering,' Colonel Wakefield warned me when I came aboard at Portsmouth. 'Some of the hands are not to be trusted.' Which was sound advice. I surprised one seaman using a crowbar on a crate of blankets. My shouts brought the second mate and earned the fellow six lashes, which did not improve my popularity on board. Te Whaiti cheered though. It was his box being tampered with. Often we would air blankets together, shake out jackets or trousers, oil the muskets — he had three of his own and was proud of them.

Gradually I picked up some of the native words. That gave me the idea, which would stave off the tedium and loneliness of that long voyage: I would learn this New Zealander language. Surely that would be of benefit to me when we arrived and set up our little shop? I have always had a quick ear for foreign tongues, and I liked the rolling, liquid way their words came out when my friends spoke together. In Spain there were a couple of Italians among the Colonel's lancers, and their way of speaking sounded similar to me.

Rere thought it a great game. He started naming parts of his own body, dancing with delight and slapping his thigh when I repeated and remembered. Then we moved to the sea, the sky, the sea-birds, the weather. Always we exchanged words, his and mine. He was almost as quick as me, and as soon as my ear tuned in to his way of speaking English, I realised he had already absorbed many English words.

The cabin fellows — including the Colonel I have to admit — couldn't seem to pick up Te Whaiti's name properly, which annoyed him. 'Nayti!' they would call, or 'Neti, come over here!' They had drifted into a lazy habit with his name, I reckon, and couldn't be bothered changing. Once I heard Te Whaiti correct the Colonel but it made no difference. Most times he would respond to the name, but anyone could see he was uncomfortable with the patronising way they talked to him, speaking too loudly or repeating a question over and over. He was no fool; he had picked up some of our language and behaved like any fine gentleman. But they seemed to want to think him inferior.

That young pup Jerningham Wakefield, Colonel's nephew, was particularly poor in his treatment of Te Whaiti. I overheard him lecturing my friend on the great boon about to be offered to his people. Jerningham was sitting up on deck — a fine day for once — with his journal open on his knee, writing away. When Te Whaiti happened by, Jerningham called him over. 'See this word? Can you read it, Nayti?'

Te Whaiti looked at the scribble carefully. 'Some. Not much.'

Jerningham read with vigour, waving a hand airily. 'I have written this. "The natives of New Zealand are about to witness and experience all the benefits and blessings of an educated Christian society such as the citizens of the British Empire presently enjoy!" Ha! What do you think of that, Nayti? Wouldn't you like to write and read as I do? Wouldn't the members of your tribe praise a chief who could read as well as I do?'

Te Whaiti looked at Jerningham without expression. He nodded politely and walked away.

Later, when I was alone with Rere, I asked him because I was curious: 'Would you want to learn to read?'

He shook his curly black head. 'No, Heu, no need. There is no writing in my language. No books.'

'Kāo pukapuka?' I knew those words.

He slapped his thigh and laughed. 'Āe, Heu, āe. Kāo pukapuka.'

'Not even the Bible?' I knew that missionaries were already over there. Surely they were busy with their pens and slates and teaching?

But Rere had no time for the missionaries. He rolled his dark eyes and wagged his head. 'Too much do this, do that. Too many rules.' I loved the way he showed what he felt with his whole body. And was secretly pleased because he showed this only to me. He was always free with me. With the rest of the crew he kind of folded himself up, answering in carefully thought-out little phrases, his face showing nothing. As far as I could see no one else spent much time learning his and Te Whaiti's language. Maybe Dieffenbach did.

We took pleasure in finding connections. His people had a similar belief in the unseen world as we Welsh. His fairy folk — tūrehu — were like our tylwyth teg — except that Rere's fairies were evil spirits and white-skinned. Ours were sometimes helpful.

'Do you have taniwha?' he asked, in a whisper. 'They sometimes make us afraid, but usually they protect. Very big!'

'Have you ever seen one?'

'No, Heu, they hide in the river or the sea.'

To me, they sounded like our afanc. I spread my arms and pretended to burst from the water with a roar. 'Ours live in the water, too.'

'Have *you* seen one?'

'No, but we believe they are there, like you do.' It gave me great pleasure to think that Rere's country had magical folk, too. One day, perhaps I would see or at least feel the presence of a tūrehu or a taniwha. I would have continued, but Rere sighed.

'No more Welsh, Heu. English is hard enough.'

I saw less of Te Whaiti, him being a cabin passenger. But he valued greatly his prized boxes of goods and when he came down to check on them we would talk — increasingly easily as the words took root in my head. Colonel's brother E. G. had taken him to many gatherings, and encouraged him to recite his little learned speech about how noble and welcoming his fellow New Zealanders were and how gentle the climate.

Te Whaiti laughed telling me this, reciting word for word his patter, for which he was paid in clothes and goods. 'Mr Wakefield said to me, "No talking about fighting." I made a fierce face and said, "What about how nice tangata tastes?" Mr Wakefield just smiled and said, "Only happy things, my good man, only happy stories." '

One calm tropical day (Where were we, I wonder? No way to tell), Rere and I were sitting on the boxes in the 'tween deck. I asked him if he had tasted tangata, which by now I knew was human flesh.

He shook his head, suddenly cast down it seemed.

'Did you see others eat tangata?'

For some time he said nothing, and I thought best change the subject. When I looked at him, tears were rolling down his cheeks. I put my hand out to him, but he brushed it away and, standing, held forth in the most dismal keening chant, half-sad, half-warlike, tearing at his shirt and stamping his feet. The change in him was astonishing. Here is the real Rere, I thought. All his polite manners are a thin skin laid over a deep and perhaps unhappy man.

I sat with him until he calmed. He looked at me at last, his face bloated, eyes red, and shrugged. Grinned. Wiped his nose on his shredded shirt.

'Would you tell me your story?' I asked quietly, hoping to learn about the real man.

'Kāo, Heu, kāo. It cannot be told.'

'Another time?'

He shook his head. From that time his mood began to darken. We still spoke in his tongue. We still laughed. Often I saw him on deck at night. He seemed to be smelling the air, always looking ahead as the *Tory* charged through long rollers, day after day, night after night, sails full of the steady wind they called the roaring forties. I learned the name of his mood later from Hineroa. Whakamā. But it was many months before I knew his story.

---

I saw no sign of land that whole voyage. Once the fellow up in the crow's nest called out and pointed. Some island famous for pirates. Captain ordered arms to be worn. Not my trade goods muskets; *Tory* carried her own. Colonel gave me the nod to watch the boxes at all times until we were past the danger. Which we did with no sign of a pirate ship that might have lifted the tedium. Arms locked away again, and on across the great South Pacific Ocean. *Moana*. Food reduced to hard tack and salt beef. Rere, though, spent hours trying to catch flying fish, and would eat them raw when he did.

'Pai, pai!' he would urge me, and sure enough it *was* good. The raw flesh tasted sweet and succulent. Why do we always cook fish, I wonder? Maybe I was just starved for something fresh.

At last New Zealand came in sight. Colonel paid me some attention now. He called me into his cabin and spread my list before him on the table. 'Now, Huw, we do not want the natives to know how large our treasure chest is. There is much land to be bought. The guns, in particular, must be brought up in separate lots when I call for them.' He was in high good humour, puffing away. He must have had a few hundred cheroots packed away in his trunk to last the voyage, for I never saw him without one in his mouth. 'I trust the goods have all travelled well?'

'They have, Colonel. All in top condition. You can count on it.' It warmed my heart to see his smile and feel his little pat on my hand.

'We are all going to make our fortunes, Huw,' he said. 'Count on it.'

I ventured a question. Money matters are a fascination to me, as the Colonel well knows. 'The Company has sold sufficient shares for the venture?'

He twinkled at me with the air of a magician producing a rabbit from thin air. 'I do believe so. My brother says we are bound to succeed this time. More than a thousand shares raised at one hundred pounds a share.'

'But,' said I, hoping for more revelations, 'this venture would cost a pretty penny — the ship, the hands, the provisions?'

'Yes, yes, of course. Twenty thousand pounds, I believe. But think of the profit once we have secured the land! That is the key. Every share entitles the investor to one town acre in the new settlement and *one hundred* country acres!'

I whistled — as he expected me to. 'No doubt you have shares?'

'Of course. A few. My brother has more. But others — serious investors in the venture — have far more.'

I would have gone on probing, but he was ready to get back down to business.

'Well, Huw, can you sort the goods into batches? Several sets if you like.' He tapped the list. 'A box of blankets, one of mirrors, one of axes, one of pots, and so on. Divide the muskets and fowling pieces into . . .' He pushed out his lips and blew a perfect smoke ring. 'Say four or five lots. We don't know how many chiefs we will be dealing with. Nayti is not very useful on the subject.'

I had a bit of a problem there. Not enough boxes. Some of the goods were in two large crates. The lead for making musket balls, for instance. 'Leave it to me, Colonel. There must be some empty boxes somewhere after all these months. I'll talk to Cook. Dieffenbach brought specimen crates, too. I'll manage.'

'Good man, good man. What a grand venture we are on, Huw. Not often you have the chance to see history made.'

He was in expansive mood; ready to chat to his men when things were going well. He confided in me then why we had been in such a rush to buy the goods and leave England. Turned out the British government was sending out a man called Hobson to take over New Zealand for the Crown. Once he arrived and got the natives on-side, all land would belong to the Crown. Groups like the Wakefields' New Zealand Company would then have to buy any land from the Crown. 'No doubt at inflated prices,' said Colonel. 'No doubt inferior land. We must get in first. Take possession of the best land.' He chuckled. 'And this fine barque, the *Tory*, has brought us here in excellent time. We have pipped them, you'll see.'

Rere, in contrast, looked the picture of misery as soon as land was sighted. We had sailed between two headlands and set anchor in the most beautiful bay I have ever seen. But the sight gave no pleasure to my friend. He had been growing quieter and quieter as journey's end approached. By now we could talk a little together in his tongue. We sat on deck, watching a long-boat rowing out from shore. Not a native waka, said Rere. 'Waka tohorā.' I learned later he meant a whaling boat. Dark green forest grew right down to the water, which was as deep and clear as any I have seen.

'Are you not happy to be home?' I asked. 'Surely your people will give you a great welcome?'

Tears stood out in his eyes. He turned away and mumbled something I couldn't catch. His canvas trews hung on his frame — had he lost weight? Was he ill? Or was it some misery transferring itself to the cut of cloth? He turned back to me. 'I am no one,' he whispered in his own tongue. 'Not a son of a chief like Te Whaiti. I am not free.'

Colonel Wakefield came striding across the deck resplendent in full military uniform, followed by Te Whaiti who wore his finest suit. In the past it would have had him strutting, enjoying the feel of the fine wool, adjusting his cravat just so, and smoothing the waistcoat over his trousers. That day even he looked uneasy; both my friends low spirited.

The Colonel slapped the chief's shoulder. 'Look smart, Nayti, now is your time to shine.'

'Colonel,' said Te Whaiti, looking down at the deck, 'this is not my people who live here.'

'But they will surely speak your language?'

Te Whaiti nodded. 'Yes, sir.'

'Well then, come along.'

And off they went, rowed ashore by a motley group of whalers and natives. I was to stay on board and guard the goods, along with most of the grumbling sailors, all of us issued with arms. A great disappointment after all that voyaging. How I craved to sit ashore with the Colonel around a fire, and eat fresh pork and drink fresh water! The little stream I could just glimpse running through the trees and out onto the golden sand tantalised me almost to madness. I dreamed of lying in that clear, sweet water, gulping it down and letting the months of salt wash out of my clothes and body.

I fingered the medal of Llŷr, which always hung around my neck. 'Release me from the sea,' I whispered. 'Let me walk on the land.' I felt no presence, though. Perhaps our gods could not reach me in this distant land. That thought filled me with dread. I held tight to the rail and fixed my eyes on the gentle trees and the glinting stream until the dizziness faded. Dear God, what had I come to?

Late in the day a waka paddled out, laden with cooked pork and sweet potato, so those of us on board were not forgotten. Captain Chaffers made sure we all had our share — after he and Lowry had removed the best for the Captain's table.

Oh, but I was itching to set foot on solid land. That much I learned on the voyage: I am a landlubber born and bred. But look, we were sat in that beautiful bay or sailing up and down between headlands for three long weeks! Colonel searching for broad valleys and good anchorage; me sorting, counting, boxing, tying into bundles, writing lists. Neither of us satisfied. He found plenty of anchorage but scarce any flat land; I was short of boxes and tubs. There was a gross and a half of Jew's harps, for heaven's sake, but no set of containers small enough to sort them into. You try tying two dozen Jew's harps into a neat bundle and you will understand my problem. Same with the scissors; fish-hooks even more tricky.

Te Whaiti spent much time down in the hold with me, caring for his own goods, but he had no need to sort and divide them, did he? All his own. Nevertheless, down in the dumps, the poor fellow. Colonel was not pleased with him, nor the natives on shore it seemed.

'They laugh at me, Heu,' he said sadly. 'Won't listen to my speech. Colonel is angry; says I told untrue things; Tiki Parete says I am no important person.' His brows lowered. 'His wife is Te Āti Awa. They are not friendly with my tribe. She says I am a bad thing. I cannot tell you her words.' He was clearly annoyed that the Colonel would prefer to talk with people from another tribe.

Tiki Parete came on board at the end of three long weeks, so I got to see the strutting fellow. Dicky Barrett was his English name — a white whaler with a high-born native wife. Round as a barrel of his whale oil he was, and dressed in an odd assortment of stripes and canvas with a round hat on his cheeky head. I didn't take to him, but the Colonel was pleased to have Barrett as interpreter instead of Te Whaiti. My friend had sailed all this way to be of service and was now cast aside.

The whaler had news that missionaries were on their way from the north to buy up land in the harbour across the strait: Port Nicholson — the very place the Colonel had decided would be the best to buy. So it was all bustle and fuss and up with the anchor, while all manner of natives came aboard — Dicky and his wife and family — to sail with us.

Colonel called me up to his cabin. 'It seems we will be dealing with three chiefs: two when we make anchor in the harbour, and another up the west coast a way. But we need to keep some back and hidden for later transactions. Can you have two sets ready for tomorrow or the next day?'

Jesus bless us, I was not near ready. 'I have fifty items to sort, Colonel, and much of it in sets of six as you suggested . . .'

He was in no mood to listen. 'Keep all below and out of sight. After I have negotiated an agreement I will want two equal sets brought up smart. Captain Chaffers will have two armed sailors guarding the goods at all times, but you are in charge and responsible.'

Well, I had my hands full then. Two equal sets of fifty items, I ask you! Small and large, some of it heavy like the ball cartridges and slabs of lead, and much of it fiddly like soap and shaving brushes, not to mention the bloody Jew's harps. Double-barrelled fowling pieces a worry, too. We had a scant thirty in all. Some of them a poorer quality. And Te Whaiti put more stock on his two fowling pieces than all his other treasure. My guess was that the chiefs would not be pleased to receive only five each. But what could I do?

To be honest, I had to hope that the chiefs or their underlings would not be too fussy in counting out fifty pencils or measuring one hundred yards of cotton duck. You try measuring and dividing yards of cotton while crossing a wild bit of ocean, not to mention keeping it fresh and neat. Thank goodness for Rere, who was a great help. If he winkled away an odd comb or looking glass I turned a blind eye. Not the red night-cap, though. I had only eighty and could not spare any, so I relieved him of it — but gently. He grinned then and winked: the first spark I'd got from him in days. What was bothering him? Te Whaiti's mood I could understand — he was supplanted by the cocky Dicky Barrett. But I had expected Rere to be overjoyed at the sight of his homeland.

I'm not one to panic, but that crossing into Port Nicholson had me sweating. Dicky's family all singing — or was it moaning — rattling around at any rate, in the 'tween deck. Sweet Jesus, I would be glad to see the end of those Jew's harps. Two of my bundles came apart with the heaving waves and we had the wretched things twanging away wherever we set foot. How did they settle on such a trade good anyway? I asked Te Whaiti.

He shrugged. 'I sailed to your side of the sea on a French sailing ship. They told me I could come and meet the king of their country. Me and my friend together. But, Heu, all they wanted was two more seamen. Those sailors had Jew's harps and showed me how to play. They gave me one. I think Colonel's brother, Mr Edward, saw me and thought all my people liked Jew's harps.' He picked one out of the bilge water and put it in his mouth and got a decent enough twang going, but then threw it back underfoot. 'But, you know,

Heu, in England I see many banjo and guitar and trumpet. Much better sound. Jew's harp is piece of rubbish.'

I laughed at that, and felt less worried if some of them stayed rusting in the hold.

One minute we were heaving and bucking, the next in blessed calm water. I had to leave my goods and run up the ladder for a peek at this wonder — a great harbour surrounded by dark, tree-covered hills. Blue sky and a tidy breeze to set us sailing ahead. To the north, what seemed to be an expanse of flat land. I could not resist a shout of pure joy. Here I would make my fortune, and my sweet Martha with me. I could feel it deep in my bones. Do you know how it is when a feeling like that comes over you? It is like the Lord Jesus is at your back and smiling down. And behind Him all the old gods of mountain and river and lake and tree, nodding a welcome with their hands raised in blessing. They were here with me after all! I near would have jumped into that calm sea and swam ashore, but of course I could not swim.

Instead, back down below, me, no doubt a silly smile on my face, back to my bundles and boxes.

# THE CHARTIST MARCH

## MARTHA PENGELLIN

*PRESELI HILLS, WALES, AUTUMN 1839*

While our men were busy with their destruction of toll gates, I was putting together whatever I could gather to take with me to those far-away islands. Dai gave me ten shillings of Huw's money. What would I need most? The New Zealand Company had a great list, but who could afford six pairs stockings or as many blankets? Surely they would not count how many we actually had of each? The letter said we must look after ourselves on board and make do with a space six feet by ten for a married couple. I measured this out on Liddy's courtyard. Room for a mattress and maybe a box or two.

I bought five yards of strong cotton duck and an extra blanket, a big packet of tea and same of sugar, a small sack of flour. Liddy gave me packets of seeds and wool from their sheep, which I spun into yarn. What else? Did the Company supply the mattress? Surely they would feed us? Or would Mrs Abernethy provide for her washerwoman? Oh, I was in a fervent of indecision and had no one to ask.

I had cutlery and crockery enough for the three of us and a big iron cooking pot. My precious china teapot — a wedding gift from Ma — I stuffed with a ball of wool and wrapped in my only tablecloth against the crashing of storm. If we were at sea for four months I would need to have all my clothes and Alfie's to hand. Soap! I begged some mutton fat from Liddy, from which we made four bars of washing soap. Liddy suggested a few day-old chicks, but I knew they could not survive so long without greens and mash;

I would be pressed enough to keep Alfie in food and drink. But I did stow some potatoes to plant on arrival. Liddy said Captain Cook fed his crew lime juice against scurvy, so she made me a big bottle of hawthorn berry syrup, which was to prove a boon later on. My purse now held two shillings and sixpence. I would spend no more.

My head was so full of this planning — exciting and terrifying in equal measure — that I failed to notice a change in the men. A dangerous and foolhardy change. Not until I was close to leaving did I realise that there was a new battle-light in my brother's eye. The men were puffed up, see, from their success with the toll gates. Gareth whipping them on. It was political now. If direct action could rid them of the tolls, Gareth ranted, why not take to the streets on behalf of the Chartists? I would have stood up at Chapel and argued, but of course we women did not raise our voices, except to sing.

Chartists are peaceful people, I would have said. Their way is not destruction and violence. They march in peace. Dai talked often of the Chartists and counted himself one of them. They wanted all men to have a vote in Parliament, not just the moneyed few. They were against Members of Parliament having to own land; and voting should be in secret to put an end to bribery. They wrote their six demands down on a Charter and collected signatures from all over the country.

Gareth would pound the table when he came over to see us — thank the Lord not too often, as he was diverted by his new crusade. 'They march and they march, but what good does it do? Tell me, boyo, what good? Their petition is accepted politely by Parliament and that's the end of it. Nothing achieved; all smoothed over by milksop words.' Gareth took on his high lady-voice. 'Thank you gentlemen, bless you gentlemen; we will certainly consider your Chartist suggestions.' Then pushed out his lips and blew a rude noise, which made the children laugh.

'It is no laughing matter!' he roared. Which silenced and frighted them. He had no understanding of children, Gareth, none at all, the silly bugger.

Dai would frown and nod and agree. 'But what can we do, Gareth? We cannot go and burn down Parliament in our dresses. This is too big for we Rebeccas.'

But Gareth and Red Thomas and many others were for marching on Newport to take on the government or somesuch. I gathered that one of the Chartists, or maybe a gaggle of them, was held prisoner in Newport. John Frost was the leader from a village across the hills a way. Every Sunday Gareth would have a new plan to voice to the Chapel folk. John Frost himself came over out of the mist one Sunday to speak. I was sick and tired of the ranting. But the men were fired up.

'Thousands will join us,' cried John Frost. 'From the east and the west, we will all meet at Newport. Are you with us, men?'

'Amen and hallelujah!' cried Gareth, leaping to his feet, his fist pumping the air. 'Preseli Hills are with you, man!'

But not all were caught up and blinded by the feverish cant. Liddy, for one, was worried that Dai would be drawn in and get himself in trouble. I, too, should have talked more sense into my brother.

———————

We gathered to wish them well as they marched away, off to Newport, Dai with them. Scythes and picks and staves over their shoulders. Tarred faggots for burning down— What? Did they think they could set fire to the whole of Newport? They were desperate, see, winter coming on and a failed harvest wilting in the fields. It was not really the political Chartist movement, but hunger and poverty that galvanised our men. And the puffed-up speeches of the leaders. Every bird loves its own voice, as my mother used to say.

Liddy and I returned to the farm, the village and the fields silent. Liddy was crying. I think we both knew disaster was in the making.

Old Bryan the carter brought us news two days later. 'The whole countryside all about is aroused,' he said, shaking that matted grey head of his. 'Every village they passed through joined in with their crude weapons and their cheers. They filled the road down to Newport. I could see no end to their column. And they say more are due from the west. What do they know, Martha dear, of the Chartists? What business is it of theirs?'

'Dai believes they are right, sure he does.' Liddy quick to defend her man.

'Well, they will come to no good and our countryside will be worse off in the end, mark me, so.' Bryan shook his reins and clattered off into the empty village. His cart empty, too.

The dark clouds gathered above as if they knew trouble was afoot, and a cold wind swept down from the hills. It is a terrible thing to wait for news when you fear the worst.

And worst it was. The next day the first of the villagers came straggling back, weapons gone, hungry, bruised in body and spirit. Soaked they were, the lot of them, and shivering, for it had rained the whole week.

'What possessed us?' asked John the baker. 'What could we do against the armed police and the authorities?'

'They knew we were coming,' said another poor, bedraggled boy. 'We had no chance, Liddy.'

'But what of Dai?' cried Liddy, beside herself. 'Is he alright? Was anyone killed?'

'Never saw Dai. But many killed, they say. We were not at the front, see. The road was choked with us Welshmen, carrying our clubs and staves. Miners with picks. Shovels even. We ran off when we saw how the odds lay. Never got near the hotel. Westgate Hotel, that's where the battle took place, but we were nowhere near.'

John put his arm around the boy, who was weeping now. 'We were bloody fools. Burning the toll gates was one thing; Newport is a big city. Idiots, right enough. Thing is, we were too many, Liddy. Ten thousand, they say. How can ten thousand spring a surprise? News had got out, sure, and soldiers brought in.'

———

Was it a day later? Two or three perhaps? News finally came that Dai was dead and buried along with twenty-one others in Newport. Gareth arrested.

'They'll hang him,' Bryan pronounced gloomily. 'Treason, they say. Treason is a hanging matter. Hanged, drawn and quartered is traitors' punishment.'

Liddy was shrieking by now, the girls clinging to her skirts and howling. Alfie joining in, of course. I had to drag her away back to the farm, away from the carter's gloom and doom.

And there, on the doorstep, was the letter I had been praying for. I put it aside. Neither Liddy nor I would be able to make it out and anyway, this was not the time.

'We will think about that in the morning. Tonight is for Dai.'

The five of us sat, solemn as owls, around the little table. Liddy could not swallow the soup that I ladled out.

'Mam,' said Meg through her tears, 'I can milk the cow. She is gentle with me.'

'And Daddy showed me how to hoe weeds,' sobbed Holly, who had often accompanied her beloved father to the fields. 'I will do it now.'

Liddy held out her hands and they went to her, clinging one each side. 'Ah, my sweethearts.' But she looked over at me in despair. We both knew she would not be able to manage. My brother had been built as sturdy as I was, and worked every daylight hour to coax a living from the soil. Liddy for all her skill in the garden was small and light-boned. She would never manage a plough in the stony soil.

'Where's Alfie?' said Meg, looking up suddenly. 'Did he go to bed all by himself?'

Meg, though only six, was the responsible one — always an eye out for the youngsters. I went quickly into the other room, but it was empty. Shame on me to let my Alfie wander off! It was dark outside, and before I had time to adjust to the gloom Meg darted past me, calling. 'Alfie! Alfie!'

And there he was in the kitchen garden, looking up proudly, his hands and clothes grubby. He was pulling weeds, the dear heart — some of them carrot seedlings, true, but who would point that out at such a time? Even he, just turned two, had caught the girls' determination to help.

All that sad night I tossed and turned. The letter would likely have details and times for sailing. But should I stay and help Liddy on the farm now? My family farm. One part of me said yes. I loved this place and might have the strength to work it. But then what about Huw? He was not suited to the steady, relentless life of farming in these parts. And, most importantly, he was not here.

By morning I was already making plans. The letter, as I guessed, said that the *Oriental* was ready to sail and I should get myself and our meagre belongings to London. Some people, I have noticed, sink into a lethargy and a mournfulness when adversity visits. Or with the death of a loved one. They are unable to look forward. I am different. I loved Dai, my dear brother, of course I did. But this new challenge had me feverish with a new energy — almost a pleasure, I am ashamed to say. Perhaps Liddy judged me callous.

What we decided that day was simple. What other choice did Liddy have? The poorhouse. We both knew that. She could not work the farm and look after the girls. If she could find a buyer for their few acres, she would equip herself and the girls and follow us to New Zealand. Huw might have some influence with the Wakefields and find her a position as a servant or washerwoman like me.

We clung to each other, tears still close to the surface. Her good husband; my dear brother — dead. Our world changed from one day to the next. We both cursed Gareth. If they hanged him, so be it.

'Liddy, get that old skinflint Cadoc, Arial's husband, to buy the farm,' I said. 'He is always ready to add to his fortunes.' I hated to think of my childhood home in his clutches, but Liddy and the girls mattered more.

Liddy shook her head. 'But didn't you hear? Arial's run off. With her blacksmith — Bryn. Old Conti has put the law onto the two of them. His rage is all he can think of now. Oh, Martha, we'd be laughing if we were not so sad.'

So. Everything in our poor village changing. People leaving; others dead or in prison. Or condemned to hang.

I hugged Liddy. 'Gather your seeds and plants. Sell these poor acres. We will start a new life in a new land together.'

A hopeful, but surely unfounded speech. Well, we had to stay hopeful, didn't we?

Before I left I laid my hand on the hearth-stone my mother had brought here when she married. All winter it stayed warm, and so it was now. One corner had cracked over the years. Carefully I prised the shard free and stowed it at the bottom of my travelling box.

# HELL AND HIGH WATER

## MARTHA PENGELLIN

*ON BOARD* ORIENTAL, *1839–40*

Five minutes longer standing on the deck, looking down at the dockside bustle, and I swear I would have clambered down the rickety gangplank, dragging Alfie with me, back to the security of dry land. Back to Liddy and the farm, no matter what dire future might lie ahead on shore. My boy was agog with all the comings and goings, clinging to my skirts, pointing here and there — at the beasts being loaded, at the fine ladies and gentlemen waving handkerchiefs, at the sailors climbing up the rigging like monkeys. But a terrible fear grew and grew in me, sapping all my common sense, draining any last measure of appetite for adventure. What if Huw were dead or had run off on some new enterprise? What if I arrived on the other side of the world to find no husband, no friend or family, but only wild savages and a failed plan for settlement? Huw had told me of the previous fanciful and often doomed enterprises of his Colonel's older brother.

They said our voyage would last four months. Huw's ship must have only just arrived. Surely the Colonel would not have had time to find suitable land, let alone purchase it and prepare the place for all of us on the *Oriental*? The finely dressed cabin passengers on board would be annoyed if streets and houses and a welcoming committee did not greet them on arrival. Oh, it was the worst kind of folly to set out now. Perhaps Huw and the Colonel and all the trade goods were at the bottom of the sea? We had no way of knowing. Perhaps the natives had seized the goods and then killed and eaten my husband? My poor legs began to shake; I was close to throwing up. Dear sweet Jesus, I could not have left the ship so weak and faint was I.

An older lady in a shabby coat took my arm. 'Eh there, lass, you best sit down; you be whiter than snow.' She led me to a pile of rope. 'Breathe deep, sweetheart, we're all a mite a-feared. Have you no one with you?'

She clearly meant no husband, seeing as how Alfie was visible, still clinging to my skirts. Fearing I might look like a fallen woman, I shook my head and breathed deep. 'Thank you. My husband is already over there. Or I hope he is.'

'Well, then, you are the lucky one, are you not? They say we must go below and find a space. Can you manage that now, do you think?'

Dora Southey was her name, and she would become a good friend on the voyage. She, her husband and her three lads were from Cornwall, desperately poor and hoping to find a better life for their family. A brave, sensible woman, thin as a rake, her husband and boys the same, near starving I would have said, though she was too proud to complain. They all ate our wretched shipboard food with a will, as if it were the bountiful provisions of juicy, fresh-killed meat and rich milk and butter that the cabin passengers enjoyed.

Below, in the 'tween deck which was to be our home, it was all a bedlam of shouts and cries, with several big fellows trying to organise us into some kind of order in the half-dark. Single men near the stern, married families in the centre, and the few single women forward. The idea was to keep the single women and single men separated, I suppose. But, dear oh dear, what a commotion! There must have been a hundred of us, milling, chasing little ones, lugging our boxes and bundles, let alone those weeping and howling, shouting that they wanted to disembark, complaining they needed more space, that the toilet buckets were already overflowing. I picked up Alfie, who was now howling along with the general mob, all the while trying to drag my box and bundles with me.

'Come with us, dear,' said Dora into my ear. 'Let us see if we can make a nest together in the married section. My Russ can keep an eye on you.'

———

The voyage was a nightmare. Enough said. I do not like to dwell on it even now. Some babies died. The cabin passengers who were to be our employers in the new land walked the decks and fed well until the live animals (who shared our deck) were all slaughtered. We in the 'tween deck huddled in our tiny spaces. Canvas curtains were all the privacy we had; and they proved to be a curse as well as a comfort, for they prevented the air from circulating. Bunks piled two or three high, with straw mattresses, were supplied. Any covering was our own affair. In our little space the three Southey boys slept one atop the other. Alfie, who was as restless as a flea at night, slept with me above Dora and Russ. You could scarcely call it privacy.

On very rare occasions we were allowed up on deck to breathe the blessed fresh salt air, but the return below was enough to turn your stomach until we became used again to the stench. At any rate, the landed gentry complained if they saw us ragged and smelly folk on deck. Word was that we were to keep our stations in life, same as in England. Or Wales. Or Scotland. The new settlements would have landowners and workers and servants. Any mingling frowned upon. Well, I thought, we shall see when we arrive. Those of us cramped below might have other plans for the new country.

I never found out which of the passengers was Mrs Abernethy or
her husband. You would have thought she might seek me out; have
a kindly word for her washerwoman. For sure I had thought I might
be allowed atop to see to her clothes. But no. The sailors had that
all sewn up: washing was their perk, and they charged the cabin folk
for the service. But I would have done it for free just for the chance
to breathe the clean air now and then.

Food was provided. Every day our group of six, plus Alfie, who
counted as a half, were each issued with hard biscuit, salt beef
or pork, horrid preserved potato, and a pint and a half of water.
Sometimes flour. On Sundays, a handful of raisins. It was up to each
group to prepare their meal, if you could call it that. Russ Southey
grumbled that it was designed to keep us alive, nothing more. True
enough. Alfie and I fared better than the Southeys, having come on
board with a decent covering of flesh to our bones. All those summer
months eating Liddy's food had plumped me out nicely again. But
Samuel, the youngest Southey, stick-thin when he came aboard,
would not eat the potato, and his rotten teeth could not crack the
biscuit. Dora would soak the solid thing in tepid water, then spend
hours trying to coax the pap between his poor sore-encrusted lips.
By the end of three months he lay listless and close to death on his
bunk, poor mite.

'Dora, for pity's sake give him some of my hawthorn berry syrup,'
I implored, not for the first time. 'Soak the biscuit in the sweet stuff
and he might take it.'

Dora smiled her thanks and gave in. For a few days he lapped at
the sweet porridge we concocted, but nothing seemed to rouse him.
He had a fever. We all feared an epidemic of measles or whooping
cough in those close quarters, but it was none of these. Even so,
whatever was ailing him no one could cure.

'What about your employer, then? Sir William Molesworth

wouldn't want his future labourer dying. Can you not send word up top to his majesty in his fine cabin? Surely he would spare a bite of fresh food to restore your lad?'

Evidently it wasn't Sir William on board but his young brother, the Honourable Francis Molesworth. But contact was not allowed. Free-passage labourers were forbidden from begging or pestering the cabin immigrants. Sir William Molesworth had sponsored passage for several Cornish workers who were to erect buildings and clear land and be servants to their wealthy employer. The younger brother, who Russ said was only twenty-two, was to supervise all this. But he kept his distance on board. If there was a Mrs Molesworth, she might have understood, but maybe she had decided to stay in England.

Samuel died a week before we arrived. Poor Dora shed her tears silently. She had lost two daughters and a son back in the home country. And hoped for fairer times in New Zealand. So it was a sombre little group we were as land was sighted. But, sure, it did you good to be allowed on deck to see the distant hills and clouds and feel the *Oriental* leaning forward into the wind as if she also was eager to find anchor.

Would Huw be there to meet me? After such a long journey across that mighty ocean, more vast and capricious than I could ever have dreamed, it seemed folly to think that we two could arrive at the very same place. Folly, sure, I thought, and shed a tear myself. Then the ship began to buck and yaw, and we were all ordered back down below.

# LAND FOR TRADE GOODS

## HUW PENGELLIN

*PORT NICHOLSON, SEPTEMBER 1839*

So, all the discussions and translating and arguments back and forth began. Colonel was in a lather to get his hands on as much land as possible, as quickly as possible. So, Te Whaiti told me, were the missionaries from up north. Also some traders from Australia. All wanting to buy land before Queen Victoria claimed the lot. Colonel went straight into negotiations with two chiefs who boarded the ship as we sailed into the harbour. Right, I thought: two sets of trade goods. But Te Whaiti was helpful here, even though the Colonel shunned him in favour of Dicky Barrett.

'Tiki's wife is Te Āti Awa, so he favours those chiefs — Te Puni and Te Wharepōuri. They want the mana above other chiefs, so they will want to share out goods. But all six chiefs will get a share.' He smiled sadly. 'Keep six bundles, but in two heaps maybe.'

So that's what I did. If some of my counting was a tad out, I never heard any complaints.

Colonel needed signatures, and he got them — or marks on paper. But from what I heard of the discussions — usually from Te Whaiti after the event, as I was below with my boxes — neither side understood the other properly. In my opinion Colonel would have been better off listening to his own interpreter — or even bringing me into the discussion, if he had bothered to discover my skill. Then I could interpret my friend's views. But Colonel was in a hurry. This much I do know: those natives had no idea that one person could own land for themselves and forever. It was not their way.

The way Te Whaiti explained it to me, the tribe Colonel was dealing with was Te Āti Awa. But there were other tribes, Ngāti Tama and Ngāti Mutunga, living around the harbour who wanted a share of the goods. All of the tribes, he said, were from further north. They had fought, won and driven out the original tribes, so Te Whaiti said angrily, 'but my tribe and my uncle is above all these people. I have told the Colonel that he must speak with Te Rauparaha. Why does he not listen?'

'These last times,' he said, 'there has been too much fighting. Too much. Te Āti Awa want Colonel for their own Pākehā. To keep their tribe safe.' Te Puni and Te Wharepōuri wanted white people to live in the harbour with their big guns. But Te Whaiti knew that they would never, never *sell* land. Just welcome white people to come and live here alongside them.

If Te Whaiti was right, the Colonel and the New Zealand Company were heading for a big misunderstanding, if not worse.

Once when I was on deck with the first of the goods ('to give them a smell of riches,' said the Colonel), I could tell, even I with my small knowledge of the native tongue, that Dicky Barrett translated badly. Colonel had told the chiefs that one part in ten of the land sold would be kept for them and their settlements. But Dicky said, in his queer pidgin language: one part for white people, one part for the tribes. That meant, to my way of thinking, equal shares. I didn't like the fellow and thought perhaps that my mistrust meant I had got it wrong, but Te Whaiti agreed with me. 'Tiki just wants white people here, so he says what pleases the chiefs.'

Well, the Colonel got his way and the whole great harbour and much more: latitude this to latitude that — from distant hills to western coast — was signed away, and my goods distributed amid much celebration. A feast on land and a twenty-one gun salute on the *Tory* followed by a great war dance by the tribes on land.

What a sight! My red blankets arrayed on the shoulders of dancing warriors; waistcoats and petticoats and dresses flouncing around, never mind whether on man or woman. And much discharging of the newly acquired muskets. I never saw a Jew's harp being played. Nor scissors used. In the end, after all my careful shearing, the cotton duck was divided with a knife's nick and a rip. The red nightcaps were popular, though. But, dear sweet Jesus, those bits and pieces — some of them most useful, I'll admit — in exchange for all the land we could see and more besides! My trade goods, bought at a cost of five hundred pounds in total, which was equal to one year's salary for the Colonel, so Te Whaiti told me (he heard that agreement at a meeting in London), could buy all these hills and valleys, rivers and — for all I knew — the very harbour itself! Was that a fair trade?

'Wait for Te Rauparaha,' said Te Whaiti fiercely. 'I think he will be very unhappy. Heu, you must have plenty of muskets and fowling pieces for him. And liquor. Te Rauparaha is the top big chief. My uncle.' He rolled his eyes and shot out his tongue. Clearly out of sorts with the whole business.

He was right, too. But Te Rauparaha lived a distance away and the New Zealand Company was in a hurry. The message finally made its way into the Colonel's ear after all the excitement and partying: he must visit the big chief and present plenty of goods. It seemed like even the Te Āti Awa chiefs were afeared of this Te Rauparaha. Just as well I had kept a few fowling pieces and plenty of sealing wax, mirrors, two complete sets of gentlemen's clothes, a good part of a tierce of tobacco, tomahawks, iron pots, twenty bundles of Jew's harps, ten per bundle, et cetera. In my imagination I liked to think of all the natives in these parts joining together in a grand concert of twanging and pinging. Alas, I have yet to hear one single performance of a Jew's harp. What use were they put to, I wonder? Melted for bullets?

So away we sailed out of the harbour and up the west coast to where the old devil lived on an island. Rere was frightened of him. And increasingly nervous in the presence of Te Whaiti. Rere came from this area, he said, but he never talked about his family. 'I must leave the *Tory* soon,' he said. Te Whaiti will take me to shore.' Rere did not seem at all eager to be reunited with his tribe or family. 'I am not high born, not even anyone, Heu. But I am tired of the sea.' He told me that he had run away on a ship thinking that his life would be freer and more interesting. It hadn't turned out that way it seemed. 'I like the land better, Heu, even if I am of no importance.'

Te Whaiti, down in the 'tween deck with his boxes, heard Rere talking to me. 'Rere is mōkai,' he said sternly. 'He must return to his master.'

I learned later that mōkai meant slave. Rere didn't like to talk about it. He shrugged and changed the subject when I asked or suggested that slaves were now a thing of the past. 'Te Whaiti is son of a chief but he too will find anger when we reach Kapiti.' He lowered his voice. 'Te Whaiti, too, ran off to sea, and left a high-born wife. I think his uncle will not be pleased with him.'

'They will be happy to see all his treasure,' I suggested. 'Surely his mana will be great?'

Rere just shrugged.

It was true anyway that the big chief, Te Rauparaha, preferred to use his own white interpreter — a whaler, and the Colonel brought someone else too. Also white. To my mind, Colonel should have kept Te Whaiti close and had him listen and then give advice later. But thinking back now, I believe Colonel didn't want truth. He wanted land. All his and the Company's fine talk about superior civilisation and bettering the natives' lot was a cover for greed and money-making. But this was put out of mind as we approached the island, Kāpiti — Te Rauparaha's stronghold.

A fearful sight met us, there in front of our anxious eyes on the very shore as we anchored in shallow water. A scene as if laid out to frighten us. A vision from one of the old Welsh stories of battles and giants. Dead and dying bodies; blood soaking into the sand and running into the tide. No cries. Some people standing, still as rocks, staring out to sea as a boatload of our men rowed ashore. We had stumbled into a bloody battleground.

Hineroa says this story is hers to tell. So be it. It does not do to go against Hineroa. This is where I first met her, among the sand dunes, tending to dead and dying warriors.

# THE LAST BATTLE

## HINEROA

*KĀPITI AND TE WHANGANUI A TARA, SUMMER 1839/40*

By the time I first met Huw, I had been living for a number of years with a Te Āti Awa hapū on land opposite Kāpiti Island. Still a slave, although the missionaries frowned on the practice. My usual task was to scrape flax for fibre — muka we call it — which the traders on the island traded for guns or tomahawks. Making muka is very slow and repetitive work, but I had no choice.

For some weeks before Huw's ship arrived the tribes north of us became restless, demanding utu for a transgression that occured during the tangihanga for Te Rangihaeata's mother. If it had been up to the women in the village there would have been no battle of Kūititanga. I, being a slave, had no voice, but even the wives of the chiefs were against it. Those Ōtaki tribes were from Taranaki, like us. We should be at peace with each other. So the wives muttered. Some spoke openly.

'What did the missionary say?' shouted one, when we gathered to discuss the threat. 'God does not agree with fighting! We will be cursed!'

But her chief quieted her. Others — younger chiefs among them — agreed. I wished to speak also, but kept eyes and head down. At least some of our Āti Awa chiefs were inclined to peace. I should not say *our* chiefs, for they were not mine. A slave does not belong. But I was heartily sick of tending to broken bodies and fatherless children. It was all supposed to have finished with the bloody battle of Haowhenua. But Te Āti Awa and Ngāti Raukawa were always like two dogs latched onto one bone. As soon as one gained the upper hand and secured the bone the other must return to snatch it back.

'There remain insults unsettled.' So said one old chief. 'They have taken some of our people prisoner. We must fight.'

'Let us try the way of the missionaries,' countered Te Hiko. 'Why not send for our teacher Minarapa?'

Many of the young chiefs who were learning the Christian way agreed. 'Send for Minarapa!' they repeated. 'He is a powerful orator.' So Minarapa was sent for. Some of his people from Te Aro pā came also. Minarapa was a preacher to admire. Hair a little grey, mild-mannered, able to speak in the missionary tongue and to write it. Up the coast he came. Poor man looked exhausted when he was welcomed into our pā. I was ordered to care for his needs, and was glad to obey for once. My cursed reputation for strong speech sometimes makes me outspoken when ordered to a task which displeases me. I try to curb this, often not successfully. Over the years it has earned me many beatings and even worse indignities. It is not easy for the daughter of a chief who becomes a slave: one who feels her opinion is usually wiser than that of her master. I must admit that many slaves accept their status and live a more peaceful life among their captors. I am different.

So when the good teacher had recovered with some of my fine pigeon soup with potato boiled in a missionary pot, the chiefs urged him to go immediately, as news was that Ngāti Raukawa were gathering. He nodded agreement and set out, tired though he was. Three men from Te Aro walked with him for a while, but then they say he walked alone north into Ngāti Raukawa land. A brave man as well as peaceful.

We gathered — all of us, even slaves — to hear his story when he returned. Any fool could tell he had been unsuccessful, so downcast was his handsome face. Many women began their wailing even before he had uttered one word.

'Let our teacher speak,' said Te Hiko sternly. 'Who are these women who judge words before they leave this honoured guest's mouth? Whakarongo!'

So the hapū settled and listened. Minarapa has a colourful way of speaking. I found myself smiling, at one time even laughing, which earned me frowns. He told us how he had met with a friendly chief, old Ruru, who had agreed to take him to their pā. No doubt Minarapa spoke with great force and wisdom — as he did now for us when he repeated his argument. But those Raukawa chiefs would not listen.

'They will fight,' said Minarapa sadly. 'Raukawa do not listen to the new ways. Their chiefs are old. Their ears are blocked. Their eyes are blind. They do not see the unrest among the young chiefs who are the ones to die if there is battle. I have failed today and will soon return to my people.'

He spoke strongly to our Āti Awa chiefs. We all heard his words. He judged that our warriors would drive theirs back. 'But I say to you: bury their dead with suitable mana; with their weapons and taonga. Do not eat the flesh of the conquered. They are Taranaki like us, so honour the dead and send the wounded back to their own hapū. The days of taking slaves are over.'

Minarapa said this for all to hear! Slavery is something of the past. Everyone is free and loved by his Christian God. This makes no sense to me. He said slavery was over, gone, its time passed like the last storm of winter. I thought: but there will always be another winter, and another winter storm after that.

Nevertheless his words took root in my heart. If the days of taking slaves were gone, what of those who were already slaves, and had been so for many years? Myself an example. What of us? I burned to talk to this great man, but had not the courage. Would he have listened? Yes, perhaps, if I were a man and a slave. Not me, a woman. So I kept my silence. But his words began to grow, tiny leaf by tiny leaf; bud by bud. Later there would be fruit.

So it came to pass as Minarapa had foreseen. Raukawa warriors came quietly at dawn. Thirty warriors in one waka and others on land. Our men were warned secretly. Some said by Te Rauparaha himself, who watched from the safety of the sea in his own large waka. The women had heard many rumours: Te Rauparaha was angry at land being sold further south to white people. Sold by Te Āti Awa chiefs. One wife who was related to Te Rauparaha's sister whispered that the old dog was stirring up trouble to punish Āti Awa. This I could believe, having been punished myself many times by that man until I had learned to act like a conquered woman, a mōkai, and not the daughter of a chief.

For some hours, they fought among the sand dunes; first firing muskets from a distance and then rushing with taiaha and mere. Some of us women watched from the safety of a high dune, several crying out loudly when they saw a husband or brother fall.

But when it was over, and the Raukawa warriors driven back over the Waikanae river out of sight, a strange thing occurred! We had been watching the battle; Te Rauparaha and his nephew and others from Kāpiti Island also, our attention on the fighting men, while all the time a great white-sailed ship had arrived and drawn close. We had seen sailing ships before, of course; smaller ones from Port Jackson come to collect the oil from the whaling stations or flax for rope. But this one was a sight to bring awe. Many white sails; masts higher than three whare piled one above the other. It anchored some distance out.

'Auē!' cried some of the more timid women. 'It has come to punish us for the fighting!' And when a mighty roar from the ship's

cannon pierced our ears, many chiefs' wives ran back to the pā. Te
Rauparaha's canoes quickly disappearing as well, I noticed.

So it was again up to us — slaves and lowly women — to see
to the dead and wounded. Who will greet these visitors, I thought,
with the chiefs busy driving Raukawa back to their lands? And Te
Rauparaha gone, too. For we could see a boat leave the big ship and
now row towards us.

Well, there were many dead and many wounded from both tribes
lying on the sand and among the rustling pīngao. I, being strong
and tall, was ordered to carry the dead back to the pā. With heavy
heart I carried them. Young men. Fathers. Who would teach their
children now? Great was the wailing as we entered the pā. One
respected chief dead; many more wounded. A woman stood high
on her roof, ready to cast herself down, for she knew her husband
had perished.

I returned to the battleground in some fear. The white man's
rowing boat had reached the shore. But wounded were still lying
under the sun. My job was not yet done.

Listen then: that boat rowing ashore had not come to punish,
but to assist! A white doctor paying us no attention set to, stitching
up wounds. Another who had some skill set and bound a young
warrior's broken leg. A third was helping to hold a warrior still as
the doctor worked. He asked in our tongue why we were fighting.

'Out of foolishness and pride,' I said to him. What pleasure to
speak out loud the truth for once. This man would not know my
lowly status. He smiled, though; perhaps he did not understand
what I said.

'Was Te Rauparaha at the battle?' he asked. 'Is he here among the
fallen? Our chief has come to talk to him.'

I shook my head. 'Kāo. That dog paddled away when you came.
Back to the island.' I spoke too sharply; let loose my tongue. This

white man with his bright, dark eyes might report such disloyalty to
Te Rauparaha, my owner. I pointed to where the chief's waka taua
could be seen, distant now behind the unsettled waves, approaching
Kāpiti Island.

This was the first time I met Huw Pengellin, who was to become
my friend. Perhaps if I had listened more carefully to the way he
spoke our tongue, matters may have taken a different turn. A false
hope, no doubt. It was not until after he had returned to his ship
and I to the pā with the wounded man that the flavour of his speech
struck me. Some of his words were spoken more in the way we
Muaūpoko pronounce them! My old and conquered tribe! How
could that be?

# CONFRONTATION OF EQUALS

## HUW PENGELLIN

*OFF KĀPITI ISLAND, SUMMER 1839*

So. Hineroa and I met there. Same battleground. Her story and mine from different angles.

We anchored near the beach opposite Kāpiti and rowed ashore. Found there the most horrid sight. We had interrupted a battle, for the bodies were fresh killed, and several wounded and bleeding. Gore everywhere, and all lying open to the sky among the sand dunes and the grasses. The warring parties gone; afeared, perhaps, by the sight of our ship. Dr John Dorset and the ship's doctor set to, good men, to stitch and bind the wounded. Before we left the *Tory,* Dorset called sternly for bandages. Colonel would never go against Dorset, who had fought with us in Spain, so he gave the nod for me to tear some strips of our cotton goods and to bring them with the shore party.

As I set to with the doctors and Dieffenbach, I tried a word or two of comfort and was pleased to be understood. Dieffenbach, too, was surprised, for he had studied their tongue but spoke not so many words. 'Ask what the fight is about,' he whispered.

I tried rather hesitantly to attract the attention of the strange woman tending a poor bleeding fellow. Her muttered answer was full of words too difficult for me. What I understood of it was that one tribe was annoyed with Te Āti Awa for selling land to us and not sharing the goods. Or was it that the selling of land was at issue? It seemed this tribe attacked a Te Āti Awa group. Was it Te Rauparaha doing the fighting, I asked, thinking we were in for a rough negotiation, but the woman shook her head. She was tall and narrow-faced, her skin nut-brown — darker than the fellow she tended. I wondered if she had mixed blood of some sort.

Not a cry from the wounded fellow as Dorset stitched away. When I remarked on his bravery, she shrugged. Then she added something about Te Rauparaha. I think she was saying the old chief had goaded one side to attack the other. This was our first encounter with tribal war. My hands shook badly as I wrapped up the stitched wound. The natives back in Port Nicholson had seemed so friendly and gentle and welcoming. What was I bringing Martha to? Was this whole scheme another of the Wakefields' doomed enterprises — we hopeful settlers lured to a savage land?

---

Well then, I may laugh now in the telling of the next few days, true enough, but I was surely uneasy watching the two of them — Colonel and Te Rauparaha — sparring. The old chief was as wily as a fox, his eyes aglitter with menace. Clear to see why all feared him. Not a big fellow like Te Puni or his nephew. About the same height as the Colonel. Handsome tattoos covered cheeks and nose, which was sharp — a different look from some other natives. Different, too, was his shock of white hair and bushy white eyebrows. Feathers hanging from his ear. A little bent under his cloak, but despite the aged look there was a brooding anger ready, it seemed to me, to break out any moment.

I never saw him the first day or two. He wouldn't come aboard, but sent messengers to say to meet him on a little island off the big one. More of a rock, you'd say. We anchored there in the tricky, bucking waters while Colonel and another white interpreter (not Dicky Barrett) and a few of the cabin passengers landed. Colonel standing tall in the boat, puffing his cheroot. There they parleyed. This was serious stuff, quite different from the celebratory mood of the other natives back in the harbour. I think all we on board were worried about the Colonel after the terrible sight on the beach, but proud of him, too, for he showed no fear. Nevertheless, Captain Chaffers had some of his men secretly armed in case of trouble.

The next day the old chief came aboard, maybe reassured that we were not going to take affront at the dead and dying ashore. Colonel sent down for a sample of my goods to be brought up. Two seamen behind me with their firearms ready but not showing. Te Rauparaha paced forward, banging his carved stick on the deck. He examined the goods, then aimed a well-weighted kick at my mirrors, which went skittering. Another at the Jew's harps, a bundle of which slid overboard. I could scarce keep a straight face, I was that pleased!

'Guns!' he growled. I needed no interpretation to understand. 'We don't need pretty things. We are warriors and war is our business.' He took from the belt at his waist a beautiful greenstone club and flourished it in the Colonel's face, scowling ferociously.

Colonel, bless him, did not flinch, but took his cheroot from his mouth, and smiled and nodded. He gave me a sign and we brought up muskets. This was more to the old warrior chief's liking. He knew how to handle a musket, old though he may be. He held it up, examined the mechanism; handed another to a younger fellow who seemed to be his side-kick. All of the natives aboard murmured approval, stamping and banging and reaching for the goods. Those others had their eyes on the waistcoats and blankets, you could see that, never mind the old chief's sneers.

But all that stamping and carry on was nothing compared with when Colonel gave me the nod and we brought up twelve fowling pieces and laid them atop the pile. A mad scramble erupted, with the twelve double-barrels fought over amid the fiercest shouting and clamour you could imagine. One fellow who had been trying on a jacket for size ripped it off and joined the fray naked. Just as well those firearms weren't loaded or sure there would have been bloodshed.

At that point the Colonel stepped forward, took the cheroot from his lips once more, blew out smoke, and gave orders for me and two others to take all below. Well, look you, how were we to do that? More than our life was worth. I would not rip a fowling piece away from a fierce tattooed chief to save myself. Colonel laughed. Oh, he was a good man in a tight corner and was loving it all. Or if he was as afeared as me he showed no sign. Drew his sword, stepped in front of the rabble and drove them back with Captain Chaffers and Lowry either side. Then sternly ordered all to be taken below. We scuttled forward and grabbed the fowling pieces and muskets and whatever else we could carry. Stood panting in the 'tween deck to see what might happen next. Several sailors stood with us, their firearms clearly visible now, ready to shoot if the natives rushed us.

But all was quiet now up there on top. We heard the Colonel speak. Very firm he was. 'The goods will be distributed in an orderly manner or not at all.' Both translators — Te Whaiti and the other man — repeated the warning.

Miraculously, all was orderly again. The New Zealanders seem to have a great ability to change from furious to peaceful in the blink of an eye. It is hard to distinguish what is real war-fury from a sort of bluster that may be a game to them. Any rate, ship's cook brought up a crock of rum and poured a little into two mugs, one for the Colonel and the other he offered to Te Rauparaha. The old dog signalled to pour more until the mug was full, and then downed the lot! Boyo, he could drink. Held the mug out for more.

But Colonel was down to business now. Out came the paper he had prepared with some kind of rough map of the sea and the land. The chief examined it. I doubt he knew what he was looking at. Colonel wanted the names of all the land Te Rauparaha 'owned'. That is, all he was about to sell. The interpreter was useless — worse than Dicky Barrett. Te Whaiti now tried to intervene, but the chief waved him away. Seemed like no one wanted to trust my poor friend. Why would they not? Surely he would understand and warn the chief? But I reckon, thinking about it now, that Colonel Wakefield did not want the chief to understand, and nor did Te Rauparaha choose to understand. Colonel was desperate to get some kind of signature on paper, and the chief was desperate to get his hands on those guns.

So the game proceeded. Te Rauparaha pointed grandly north and south, to hills and rivers and tribal areas and named them. Colonel's nephew Jerningham wrote the names on the 'map'. Te Whaiti told me later that the naming was simply the chief showing off — pointing out all that he held sway over. 'Not giving it away, Heu. Not selling.' Surely Colonel Wakefield understood that? Some of the places named were areas that we had already bought from Te Puni and those other chiefs.

Up we staggered again with all the goods, fowling pieces last. Colonel took those himself and handed them out at a signal from old Te Rauparaha. This time they were received without a murmur.

---

Oh, it was a blessed relief to sail away at last from that place. Cook's Straits were bad enough, but around Kāpiti Island we were close to capsizing more than once. And a spar shattered in the great seas. Our fierce chief reduced to abject whimpers — perhaps he was not used to the open ocean. He was as glad as we were to part company and go our separate ways.

A parting, too, with my friends Rere and Te Whaiti. Just before we weighed anchor, a whaling boat arrived, rowing up from the south. A tall fellow wearing a fine cloak, feathers in his hair and a large pendant stood up in the boat and shouted Te Whaiti's name. 'Te Whaiti! Te Whaiti!' the rowers echoed. I understood that they were calling for him to bring his treasure. 'Ngā taonga!' Somehow it didn't feel like a happy family reunion. More like an order from above as Captain Chaffers might address a wayward deck-hand.

Te Whaiti took one look and disappeared below. I followed.

'Are they your relatives?' I asked, ready to defend his rights if not.

He took a deep breath. 'My family, yes. My wife, Te Rongo-pamamao is there. She will not be happy that I left her. I hope my gifts will soften her in my favour. Please help, Heu. Rere! Help me carry my things. We must go now.'

So we carried his boxes and bundles up, the rowers scrambling quickly aboard to lower all into the whaler, while the tall fellow saw to the stowing. Te Whaiti, dressed in his smart suit, nodded to me — a rather preoccupied farewell I thought. Down in the whaleboat, he pressed noses with the chief. The woman remained aloof. He settled, with some ceremony, on his boxes. Perhaps all would be well.

With Rere it was different. He coughed miserably, and held me in a warm embrace.

'I belong with this tribe,' was all he would say. And then: 'I will go back to Porirua. Maybe you will look for me there?'

I had no idea where or what Porirua was, but promised to find him. He smiled at last. 'I will wait for you. Ka kite.'

And down he scrambled, no word of greeting from the chief,

nor from the rowers, for that matter. On the *Tory,* everyone was preparing the ship to sail. Colonel himself was not on deck to farewell Te Whaiti, nor Chaffers his deck hand, which I thought a damn shame. I was the only one to raise a hand and shout goodbye.

---

All this time I was in a fever about my Martha. Was she aboard an immigrant ship and on the high seas? Had she even received my letter? I feared my brother Gareth might have persuaded her to stay with him. Truth was I was sick of this buying of huge land masses. These grand plans. My modest plan included a small plot, a nice ship-shape hut, my trade goods laid out for sale, and Martha and Alfie warm and safe beside me. 'Let me go now,' I said to the Colonel. 'Surely you are satisfied with all you have negotiated? Will we not return to Port Nicholson and prepare for the settlers?'

But while there remained any trade goods in the hold, Colonel would relentlessly seek more land. Success — as he saw it — made him greedy for more. We sailed south again to the other side of the Straits and started all over, with lesser chiefs — if they were even that — fighting to get their hands on what was left in return for making a mark on paper. Then back up north again to a pretty place where a river called Whanganui gave a good harbour. There the last of my goods were brought up, every last mirror and Jew's harp, a pitiful exchange for those beautiful stands of trees and rolling land.

'Now then, Pengellin,' said the Colonel when we were on our way south again, 'would you not exchange those goods of yours in the hold for a piece of a town acre in a new settlement?'

He would not give up, see? Bit between the teeth. Had his eye on a nice valley — the Wairau — in the South Island, but no trade goods to buy it with. I would not hand mine over, though, which annoyed him. So we sailed back at last to ready beautiful Port Nicholson for settlers.

Only to find the first ship had arrived and the Colonel not even there to welcome them.

# TE UPOKO O TE IKA

## HINEROA

*KĀPITI AND TE ARO, LATE 1839*

I count my new life beginning on the day I met Huw Pengellin, and also the day I found a time to talk with Minarapa. Under a sky full of storm clouds, a wind whipping the sand into our eyes, the dead bodies were laid out. Our own warriors and those of Ngāti Raukawa buried together with their weapons and their taonga. Minarapa's stern eyes watching, ensuring that no part of any body was removed or consumed.

One old chief grumbled. 'Surely it is our tradition to hold a victory feast?' And some wives of these chiefs muttered when Minarapa or the white men were not close by. 'Who are the missionaries to tell us what our customs should be? For shame!'

But the young chiefs and their wives hushed the elders politely and told them that things were different now. And Minarapa smiled at us all. He said a long prayer over our tuna and kūmara, and praised us for our modern ways. Our Christian ways.

'Christian ways can be a little dull,' said Te Hiko's third wife, sighing over her meal.

But I was glad, even though I have never taken to Christian ways.

I tell you this: if Te Rauparaha had been here there would have been feasting in the customary manner. And much liquor would have been drunk. In those days that old dog never listened to the missionaries' teaching. His ears became deaf when peace was mentioned. To forgive or turn the other cheek were signs of terrible weakness. Later, when it suited his purpose, he turned to the missionary God. I can say this now, but when I was young? I dared not even think such thoughts.

That night two white men from the big ship stayed at the pā and were made welcome. I was ordered to look after Minarapa, who was resting in the whare set aside for him. I took food and covered some fern fronds with a fine mat for his bed. He was tired and happy to lie while I rubbed his limbs and fed him a little fish. Outside the wind was rising, the thatch rattling and the smoke from the fire stinging our eyes.

'Are you of Te Āti Awa?' he asked.

He should have known. Perhaps he expected they would give the task of looking after him to a well-born woman. But then his mana had suffered from his defeat. They sent me instead.

'I belong to Te Āti Awa,' I said, 'but am not of them.'

He nodded, chewing away. 'Āe, I suspected. You do not look as if you are from the north. You are Muaūpoko?'

I was surprised he would honour me by my tribal name. A captured slave no longer belongs to her tribe. 'Āe. Muaūpoko. Many years ago.'

His feet were cracked from the long journey. I kneaded pigeon fat into them until the skin glowed a rich brown. I hoped that his groan was one of pleasure. 'Would you like me to comfort you in another way?'

He smiled. 'Thank you. But the Christian teaching is that we should have only one wife. *A man should not covet his neighbour's wife.*'

He said this in the missionary tongue. I laughed somewhat sourly. 'I have no husband and have been ordered to give you whatever pleases you.'

He rolled over to stare at me. 'You speak English?'

'Āe. It is not often useful in this place.'

'Who did you learn from?'

'From whalers. And the missionary Taylor. Te Rauparaha gave me to him for one year in return for two cooking pots and an axe. I was to clean and cook for his wife.'

Minarapa leant his chin on one fist and considered me. I knew he was Ngā Mahanga, a Taranaki tribe that had come south with Te Rauparaha. He had been a fine fighting chief for his hapū in the days before he accepted the Christian god. You could see it in his strong body and the scars to chest and leg. But now his look was not that of a warrior. He was interested in me!

'Sit!' he said. 'Tell me, have you accepted the Christian God?'

He wanted me to say yes, but with his sharp eyes on me I could not say it. 'No one has preached to me so far. I have not been persuaded . . . A slave is not so important.' In fact, I had many times heard preaching but had turned away. The words were just stories to me.

'Listen,' he said, frowning now, 'I was once mōkai like you. When I believed in Jesus and the Christian God, my life changed. For the better.'

The shock of this statement loosened my careful tongue. I stared at him. 'But you are a chief! Your words are respected here. Surely you were never a slave!'

He cleared his throat and spat. I thought he was preparing to tell me his story. But a fresh gust of wind brought a shower of insects down from the thatch and he was distracted. I brushed away the beetles. Waited for more revelations. But he was tired, perhaps, or not inclined to elaborate on his slavery.

'Did you learn to read at Reverend Taylor's mission?'

I turned my head from him. Wind from the open door played with the ferns under his mat. I had never admitted this ability. It was my secret. I did not want to talk of my time with the whalers or of Jimmy the Goat. Unhappy years. I had watched the reverend's children learn their letters, and also the young chiefs who came to learn. Having some knowledge already, I learned quickly. Secretly. No woman was ever sent to learn this precious skill. But I wanted something from Minarapa, and so I took a stick and wrote in the sand. *The Holy Bible.* And then I wrote *Te Paipera Tapu.* I quickly scattered the words and smoothed the sand so he would know that this should not be talked about.

His exclamation of surprise encouraged me to continue. 'You said earlier that the time for the taking of slaves is past. But what of those of us who are already slaves? How can I become a chief's daughter again, as you seem to have become a chief?'

I should not have said *seem.* It suggested doubt. He lay back on his ferns and stared at the ridge-pole. Took breath as if ready to berate me. I held my breath, cursing my outburst.

'Āe. That is another matter. I was perhaps lucky. My once-conquered tribe chose to throw in their fortunes with Te Rauparaha. Your tribe chose to fight him. I fear you will still be considered a slave by Te Āti Awa.'

'I was first taken by Ngāti Toa. Te Rauparaha himself.'

'Auē. Not so easy. But you are with this hapū now?'

I nodded. 'I was sent to work the gardens here. Te Rauparaha owed some favour to this tribe.'

'I am related to Te Hiko. The people here owe *me* a favour even though I failed in my attempt. I will ask that you come to work in the Mission at Te Aro. You could be useful. Teach our children perhaps. Would that please you?'

'As a slave? I will be traded again for a favour?'

A silence followed this outburst, and again I cursed my wayward tongue. Minarapa sighed. 'I also have been captured,' he said quietly, 'also enslaved. By Ngāpuhi. And now, being Christian, released to be with my tribe.'

This surprised me. So a new life could be possible. 'I can be released, too?'

He sighed again. Maybe he was considering what I said. More likely he was tired of a conversation with a lowly woman. One who possessed a temper.

Still he remained silent. 'Yes, it would please me,' I said quietly, lowering my head. I dared not look towards him.

He turned away and settled for sleep. 'We will see. But you must not expect much change — even though our pā is Christian. I and my family will still be high-born and you will still be a captured Muaūpoko. Te Rauparaha is not Christian, I think, to consider releasing his slaves.'

As I walked back to the hut that I shared with the other slaves I thought again of the white man on the beach, the one who had spoken in the accent of our tribe. The waves roared in, just visible in the moonlight: row upon row of white crests far out to sea, the black bulk of Kāpiti standing high against the rising storm. If that white man was back on board his ship he would not be comfortable.

---

The walk back to Te Aro pā with Minarapa and his small band was tiring but unusual. A woman was with us. She kept looking at me with curiosity. Perhaps my height? Perhaps her chief had not explained my presence? Whatever the reason, she did not treat me with the usual contempt but seemed ready to talk.

I fell into step with her on our way around Porirua inlet. Minarapa and two chiefs with him had been been paddled down the coast to Owhariu, where the walk over to Te Aro pā was a shorter distance.

The rest of us were to walk. 'Are you his wife?' I asked.

Her smile was mischievous. 'Not Minarapa's. That other chief with him. I was his third wife, but now the Bible says you should have only one. His senior wife is a chief's daughter and his second wife is old.'

'So he chose the chief's daughter?'

'Of course. But I am his favourite and have given him two sons, so he sometimes brings me on a trip like this for . . .' She laughed.

I laughed with her.

We talked. She perhaps knew my status but did not ask. This gave me a pleasure, so great that it is hard to describe. Perhaps after all, and despite what Minarapa had said, I might be treated differently in a Christian pā where there was a Christian mission?

'That ship we saw after the battle,' she said, ready to gossip, 'we already saw it two weeks before that in our harbour.' She was full of the story — the celebrations, the gifts the guns fired and the dancing at Pito One. Even though the sun beat down on us, she wore a fine jacket that Minarapa had given her but had come from the ship's great treasure. From the pocket of this garment she drew a little cloth pouch like the one I often saw Mrs Taylor handle. In it was a spool of thread and a paper in which fine needles were embedded.

'I will sew my son a jacket like this,' she said proudly, 'and then my chief will make him first son above the others.'

But I was suspicious. White people do not give away their things for nothing. Even missionaries like to trade. 'What do they want?'

She shrugged. 'To live among us. They are not missionaries, which is good. They don't come with rules — do this; don't do that. They just want to settle in our harbour.' She opened her eyes wide and flapped her hands in a great show of surprise. '*Everyone* wants to come and live in Whanganui a Tara! A missionary, Mr Hobbs, came some months ago with a shipload of our people from the north. Mostly slaves released by some of those northern tribes. Can you imagine? The missionaries said release your slaves, and they did! Mr Hobbs wanted to build a new Wesleyan Mission near our pā. He gave us some fish-hooks and other goods for a patch of land. Minarapa came with them, back to his people. Now we are building a Mission house for Minarapa to preach in. It will be very grand. Right beside Te Aro pā. Soon a white preacher will come, too. Minarapa is very pleased. But I prefer the Colonel and his Company. We call him Wideawake. It sounds like his name, I suppose. I don't know if he has trouble sleeping!'

'Was he — the Colonel — in that ship we saw at Kāpiti?'

That mischievous smile again. 'Āe. Probably. That is the same ship. Of course he has to talk to Te Rauparaha before he brings his people to live among us. Eh! I would like to see that meeting!'

I didn't want to admit that I would like to see this Wideawake shoot Te Rauparaha and all his hapū. Perhaps my eyes said so, for she giggled. We walked on in the heat.

---

The next day, after resting with Ngāti Toa people, we climbed up through the bush and then down a winding track beside a stream to the beautiful harbour, which I had heard of but never seen. Whanganui a Tara. Or Pōneke. Our tribe used to call it Te Upoko o te Ika — the head of the fish. I prefer this name because it is close to Muaūpoko, my once-tribe.

Perhaps it was the name; perhaps the easy time walking with Ripeka, the chief's once-third wife. Whatever the reason, I had an odd feeling that I was coming home.

# A SHARING OF SHELLFISH

## HINEROA

### THE MISSION AT TE ARO, EARLY 1840

That hot summer it seemed the whole world was changing along with my own life. Our harbour at the Head of the Fish — Te Upoko o te Ika — was so filled with coming and going (more coming by far) that we at the Mission became almost dizzy watching day by day. Minarapa told us that he, and those at Kumutoto pā on the other side of the stream, had invited the Pākehā missionaries to send a white man to teach our people the Christian ways. I thought Minarapa was a good preacher and we didn't need a Pākehā one, and told him so. I said he would lose mana if a white preacher came. He said I must learn to speak more quietly. But he said it with a smile. I was right, too.

When we arrived at Te Aro, Minarapa looked with pleasure at the progress. The Mission house was already almost finished, built by some missionaries of our race who had been left in charge.

'This is well done,' said Minarapa to the men, who were from the north. The released slaves Ripeka had spoken about. 'Now continue quickly, for the white missionary will soon be arriving.'

I was set to preparing a garden and planting food for the Mission. It was a pleasant place: Te Aro stream flowed out of the bush, down over this gently sloping land and into the sea. Birds sang with great joy morning and evening. The little green parrots — kākāriki — descended from the hills in flocks to torment us with their shrieks and their interest in any seed or fruit they spied. Minarapa held services of prayer and taught his sons and others the new language.

I waited to be invited to teach the children, and meanwhile enjoyed planting in the rich soil. No dry, sandy land to be fed here, although these tribes, like my own, knew the value of seaweed and wood ash.

I remember this as a waiting time. As if our quiet world was pausing, trembling a little perhaps, in the knowledge that something great — or fearsome — was about to happen. The sun beat down; even the winds died as if they too held breath in expectation of— Of what?

The great white ships. Magnificent at first, and then much more dangerous. The first I saw — *Cuba* its name — arrived, moving like a great winged seabird up the harbour, unchallenged, sure of itself, as if it owned the water and the land all about. One of Minarapa's men from the north — a former slave, Hone, or John, his new Christian name — called and pointed from the roof of one of our new Mission huts where he was thatching. I was burying seed potatoes beside Te Aro stream. The ship was not headed towards our side but further up past Matiu Island. This would be that wily Te Puni's doing. He had heard news and invited them. He wanted the white people over by him to protect his tribe. Minarapa said Tiki Parete's wife sent word; she is Te Āti Awa, too.

'Is that Reverend Hobbs returned?' shouted Hone.

He did not stop to think sometimes. The Reverend is not a great chief. He would possess no ship so large.

I didn't like Hone, and wished the Reverend had not left him here. Perhaps Reverend Hobbs saw good in all his converts, but I did not share this charity when it came to Hone, who was grumpy and stupid and gave our Mission a bad name. Minarapa was another matter. Always he spoke with great beauty of the Christian God. It was easy to see that even before his Christian days he had been an orator of note among his people, as well as a fighter. He was beloved among his hapū. As I was beloved and well taught by my mother in the matter of healing plants. Those days in that gentle pā, working for the Mission, I found myself remembering an earlier, happier life.

I am reluctant to describe that first ship as beautiful, but it was a sight, that first one. *Tory* I saw off Kāpiti, but from a distance and as darkness drew on. This one in full sunlight with a good wind from the south. My heart aches, now, to admit the beauty. Later, in the months that followed, as the great winged ships arrived, one after the other, each one larger it seemed, each crowded with whole tribes of white people, spilling out onto the land, measuring it, slicing it into little pieces, then I saw ugliness and greed.

Where was our Pākehā missionary to greet this ship and claim the land for his Mission? Auē. Too slow, too late! We had his Mission house ready, but Wideawake had other plans for our Mission land — and for Te Aro pā.

———

Some time later *Cuba* came over from Pito One to our side and anchored over by Pipitea. The man they called Wideawake was rowed ashore along with several other men. I watched from the beach while my toes felt in the wet sand for ruheruhe. Even from a distance you could see they were arguing amongst themselves, hands flying, and clouds of tobacco smoke rising in the still morning air. Every now and then the smoking man — Wideawake — stopped and pointed inland to the potato gardens up on the terrace or to the cleared land around the two pā. They passed Kumutoto pā, splashed past me through the stream and walked a little way towards our Mission house. Never a word of greeting to the people who stood

and stared; no response when an old kuia called a greeting from
the paepae. Rude, arrogant behaviour in my opinion. Finally, their
argument grew too fierce to allow continued walking. They stopped
on the beach. I sat quietly with my kete of shellfish, hoping to hear
what all this fuss was about.

Wideawake blew out a cloud of smoke; pointed here and there;
then turned towards the sea. 'Surely you can see,' he shouted to a
man who seemed to be the leader of the group, 'that this is a better
anchorage? And more sheltered? I want the settlement here!'

The other man, not dressed in military clothes like Wideawake,
shook his head violently. 'I have made up my mind, Colonel. Enough
of this bluster. I have the authority.'

Wideawake grew red in the face. 'I am leader of the enterprise
and leader of this settlement. My brother has given me authority.'

'And the New Zealand Company has given *me,* as chief surveyor,
authority to decide where the settlement shall be and how it shall be
laid out. My men have already—'

'Damn what someone half a world away says! *I* say build on this
side. Any fool can see—'

'You call me a fool, sir? What experience do you have in laying
out a town? None at all, I'll wager. I will decide and will draw plans
where I choose. The Pito One area has far more flat land and fewer
trees to fell. Roads are already marked on my plan . . .'

All the land and sea in these parts our people see as the head of
Great Māui's fish — Te Upoko o te Ika — with the harbour being the
fish's gaping mouth. Over where the white people were staying — at
Pito One — the coast curves gently. Behind the shore flat land slopes
away. The gullet of the fish. Our side, where Wideawake wanted to
build, jagged headlands thrust forward into deeper sea: I imagine
great teeth, and a fish-hook caught in the fish's mouth.

Minarapa, alerted by the shouting, had by now walked down

from the pā to greet these white men. He held out a hand in peace.

Wideawake completely ignored him. He had worked himself up into a fine rage by the time he noticed us watching, and strode over. 'Is this a Mission house? Who gave you permission to build on my land?'

Minarapa greeted him courteously in our language, introducing himself then explaining that the chiefs of Kumutoto and Te Aro had agreed to tapu this land for a Wesleyan mission. Wideawake fidgeted. He had no interpreter with him. Then to my surprise, the man I had met on that bloody beach at Kāpiti stepped forward. The man with a milk-white skin and eyes as black as my own. Curly dark hair falling into his eyes. Whose accent in our tongue matched mine! He was offering, I think, to translate, but the red-faced chief brushed him aside.

Minarapa then switched to English, thereby, in my opinion, shaming this bully. He explained all over again, addressing the man by his English title, Colonel Wakefield. But by then Wideawake had lost interest in any explanations. 'The New Zealand Company now owns all this land. You will have to move your Mission house if I want the land for a different purpose. Good day!' And away he walked, resuming his argument with the surveyor.

So that was the purpose of so much generosity. Wideawake thought he was now chief of all the land here! Can all the chiefs have agreed to this? If so, they do not deserve to lead their people. I said as much to Minarapa, who chided me once again for my sharp tongue. I replied that the tribes had need of a few more sharp tongues and sharper minds. In this place where strangers were disrespectful and chiefs behaved rashly, I felt free to speak what I believed.

I wanted to hear the black-eyed sailor speak again, so I followed.

'Stranger, I have fresh ruheruhe here if you care to try,' I called out to him in our own tongue.

He stopped immediately and turned, smiling. I held out a handful, gesturing that he should come closer. For a moment he hesitated, then shrugged and walked towards me.

'I am Te Hine Tāroaroa of Muaūpoko tribe.' I hoped mention of my tribe would bring forth a response.

He nodded in a friendly way, clearly not remembering me. 'I am Huw Pengellin of Wales.'

Now I switched to the white man's language. 'We met last on the beach at Kāpiti.'

His shout of surprise sent a hopeful seagull flapping away. 'Yes! The tall woman with the wounded men. And here you are again at a Wesleyan Mission. I myself am a Chapel man. A Wesleyan. How strange.'

We sat on a log. I took his knife and opened two ruheruhe, then indicated he open his mouth before sliding one in. The other I ate myself as if I were an equal.

'Reka,' he said, smiling again. 'Tino reka.'

I asked him where he learned our tongue.

'On board the *Tory*. One of your countrymen came with us to act as interpreter, another was a deck hand. They became my friends.'

I opened him another shell. 'From which tribe?'

'Te Whaiti was Ngāti Toa. He has left the ship now and gone back to his wife and family. Rere never talked about his tribe. Te Whaiti told me Rere was a slave. He took my friend ashore with him.'

Rere! Could my brother have run away to sea? I questioned Huw closely. Surely I was right about the flavour of Huw's words. But just as surely Rere would still be mōkai and not free to join me. Perhaps this man here could help negotiate a meeting?

He shook his head as if to chase away a thought. 'Please, excuse my rudeness.'

'In what way are you rude?'

'That I stare. You are very beautiful.' He put out a hand to touch my hair which hung down my back, still wet.

He told me that when he saw me in the sea I reminded him of mythical women in his home country, who live in the water — wives of Annwn — who could sometimes be lured to land by a lovesick man.

'I live on land,' I said, 'and I am real.' But I was flattered that he thought me magical and beautiful.

He laughed. 'All too real. I'm afraid I cannot get used to seeing so much . . . so much bare skin!'

His smile was cheeky. He tried to hide with a hand the bulge in his trousers. He stood. 'I should move on.' But still he stood there.

'My friend,' I said boldly, in my own tongue, 'can I offer you anything more?'

---

The day after the visit by Wideawake in the ship *Cuba*, our Pākehā missionary arrived. Reverend Buller. I did not know this man. He sailed into our Te Aro bay on a fast cutter. Too late, we told him: Wideawake has laid claim to everything.

Reverend Buller frowned. His anger can be hot like mine. 'What about our tapu? Did you not explain? How can you let this happen?'

He did not understand. Who will listen to the words of a slave, even if they are now supposed to be converted to Christianity? Te Puni and Te Wharepōuri are the two Te Āti Awa chiefs closest to Wideawake. They shared out the gifts among all the hapū and tribes who live around the harbour. Their pā are on the other side, to the north. What a surprise to some of our Mission workers to find them living here, for they are related — or were before they became slaves. Te Puni has only lived in this place a few years! Why should he have the power to grant land to Wideawake?

All the tribes have moved since guns came to our shores and into the hands of the northern tribes. Many, many warriors killed in the process. Our native missioners thought it very strange to find Te Āti Awa living in this place so far from Taranaki.

And so our world shifts. Like sand blown inland to build new hills, and waves eating away at other cliffs, our lives and lands are changing shape. But too quickly. And who will speak out to slow this tide? Where are the wise words of warning? I think of my mother saying keep your speech for an important moment. But did her dying words take root? And are there no wise chiefs left?

# A PLAGUE OF SAILS

## HINEROA

*TE WHANGANUI A TARA, JANUARY–MARCH 1840*

At first we were not concerned. All the activity seemed to be at the other side, among Te Puni's people. Huge guns were fired, but not in war. They did not come as a war party. More of a celebration, Reverend Buller said. He sailed over to one of the first ships and held a service there. We natives from the Mission were not included in that party, though I would have been most interested to see what kind of people these were to come in such numbers. Had they been driven out of their homeland as the Taranaki tribes who came here were?

So the Te Āti Awa people over that side paddled out and brought the white tribes to shore. All along the beach at Pito One tents grew like mushrooms. We could see a flagpole, and one tall whare, but the people disappeared into the scrub and the bush like rats scuttling off those ships. I said to Minarapa that it looked like the surveyor had got his way and Wideawake had lost the argument. The new white tribe would live on that side.

But another ship arrived and another, and then even another! Had Queen Victoria's tribe deserted her entirely? Or had she banished them? All day and night they were rowed ashore with a great quantity of possessions. Reverend Buller became worried. He wished for a quiet life among the natives, converting the people of Te Aro and Kumutoto. He said there were preachers aboard the ships from other churches who might compete with him for land and converts.

So we sailed across to Te Puni's side in Reverend Buller's cutter. The Reverend talking in a loud voice all the way about what he would say, how dare they ignore our prior claim; where was their respect for the missionaries who do so much good, and so on. I was included in the party as I was able to translate our language into English better than Minarapa. He does not agree with this, but it is true. Hone was left at the Mission house to commune with his sulks.

Wideawake was sitting in a very large tent, Te Puni beside him and a young white fellow who wrote everything down. Wideawake puffed on a cigar, which had a very rich and powerful scent. I think he used it to build his mana.

When Reverend Buller explained that Reverend Hobbs had already come to an agreement with the hapū over the Mission land, Wideawake interrupted. He spoke sternly. 'You have paid nothing for that land. Te Puni here says only a few fish-hooks. You have no claim.'

'It is only a matter of time, Colonel. Reverend Hobbs is at this moment gathering money and goods which he will send—'

Old Te Puni rose and spoke. He can be an imposing figure, though I am as tall. Of course, I was sitting on the ground at the time so could not display my height. In our tongue he greeted the Reverend Buller, but went on to point out the great and wonderful pile of trade goods the chiefs of our side of the harbour had accepted from Wideawake and the New Zealand Company. Their claim overturned ours, he said, and the other chiefs sitting with him all nodded and murmured in agreement.

I whispered in Reverend Buller's ear: 'Ask him does he not respect the Christian church? Is he not a Christian?'

But Reverend Buller did not hear my advice or chose not to listen to a woman. In the end we were sent away with a threat to be ready to shift our Mission house when the settlers began to build their houses on our side.

Huw Pengellin was standing at the back of the tent, listening. He smiled warmly as we passed, and spoke not to the reverend but to Minarapa and me, in our tongue. He asked if he might come back in our cutter and look at the land there.

'As a Wesleyan, I am interested in helping with your Mission. Perhaps settling on your side.'

He has the brightest black eyes and a quick way of moving, as if the sand beneath his feet was hot. His cheeks pink as clouds at sunset though his skin is pale. I smiled and Minarapa also greeted him.

Reverend Buller was not so welcoming. 'Are you a Wesleyan preacher, then? I have been sent as missioner here.'

The man laughed. 'Dear God, no sir, I am from Wales. And hope to do business here. I hear from the Colonel that the settlement will have its centre over on your side, which he calls Lambton Harbour.'

All the way across the harbour he chatted, switching from our tongue to English and back again. It was impossible not to like him.

'I wouldn't worry about your Mission house,' he said. 'It is all chaos on the beach back there. Some of the men in England who bought land did not board the ships at the last moment. Now there are too many labourers and too few landowners to order them about. The Colonel is disappointed and doesn't know what work to give the farm workers and builders and sawyers. Or who to assign the women servants to.' He laughed. 'I think the mess will be to the labourers' advantage. Certainly, I plan to benefit. Let us wait and see.'

Huw Pengellin walked into the bush, looking this way and that, sniffing like a dog, trying to guess where roads might go and which places would be suitable for a little home. He stayed for several days at the pā, cheerful as a tūī in a rātā tree. When the surveyors came to draw lines and measure lots, he talked pleasantly to them and offered them tobacco. I could see he was quick to persuade.

I enjoyed his company. When I told him how Māui's brothers

had shaped the land, he told me they had cousins back where he came from. I told him of the great bird Pouākai, and he told me a tale from his own country of giant birds that could understand humans. Their master ordered them to kill the first person on the battlefield, but when his enemy was delayed the obedient birds killed their master. We laughed together over the similarities and differences, over words and meanings. He was almost as quick to learn a language as I was.

# PARADISE

## MARTHA PENGELLIN

*PORT NICHOLSON, JANUARY–FEBRUARY 1840*

Lord bless us, even down in steerage we could feel we were arrived. After the great rolling and bucking as we sailed between the two islands of New Zealand, the ship suddenly settled, moving forward under full sail in waters as calm as a lake. At last Captain Wilson gave the order that we may come above if we wished to see our new home.

Alfie and I climbed up quickly, Dora and Russ and the boys close behind. Alfie was now as agile as a goat, no longer the toddler I had carried on board. He was looking more like his father every day, the same curly hair, though his was still fair, the same dark eyes. The same dancing feet. I would lay a penny on Huw, at the first sight of his son, likening Alfie to some elf he knew personally back home.

Early morning it was, the breeze warm and the sea sparkling. Oh, what a joy to see it all laid out before our eyes and the *Oriental* moving ahead as if she, too, was eager to reach anchor.

It did look like a lake, see, with the high mountains all enclosing us, purple-headed in the morning light like the hymn we sang in Chapel back home. To our left and right tall trees stood at the water's edge, except where small native settlements had cleared a bit of land. Two small islands sat plumb in the middle of our lake — harbour, I should say — hump-backed like a mother tortoise and her child. And there, not far away, two ships anchored — barques like ours — with many small craft moving back and forth to the distant beach. We cheered and clapped, cabin passengers and steerage alike, the little ones running to the rail and hopping with excitement until we mothers feared someone would fall overboard. But the children were used to the sea now, and knew better than the adults how to manage on a heaving deck, let alone this millpond.

Alfie must have forgotten what the world looked like beyond the hold, because he made little whoops of delight each time he noticed something different: a seagull cawing overhead, a boat paddling out to meet us, smoke from a bonfire on the beach. He fell silent, though, and held my hand at the sight of the cabin passengers dressed for shore, the women in fresh skirts and bonnets, the men top-hatted and tidy. 'Grand folk,' he said, pointing. He could see the difference.

I tried to smooth his matted hair. 'Aye, Alfie son, but we will scrub up smart enough when we find fresh water.'

I strained to see what sort of settlement might be there on shore. Too far away to make out my Huw, but still I shaded my eyes and peered. We could see a long beach and sand dunes. Canvas tents, grey-white in a row, stood among the scrub and low bush; one large thatched hut, too, but no solid houses, none at all. I heard one of the cabin passengers muttering that he expected more signs of civilisation, but I was not surprised. Oh, we were all shouting and pointing like a circus crowd, agog to be the first to discover a new sight. A flag flew on the beach. Not the British flag. Some sharp-eyed lad declared it was the New Zealand Company flag and we cheered again. What a marvel to arrive at the right harbour after four long months!

'Hats off to our captain!' shouted Russ, normally the quiet one of our little group, but not today. And the men tossed their caps and we all cheered again. Then the other two barques joined in, saluting us with their big guns — eleven rounds each. A more joyous welcome you could not imagine.

Well, soon the water became shallow and Captain would take her in no further. There we anchored, a good distance from shore. And waited.

And waited.

———

Mr William Wakefield came on board near evening. Although Huw always called him the Colonel, he was not a real colonel of the British army. In Spain he might be called one, having got his rank as a mercenary to the king of Spain, but I was not inclined to bestow the title on him. We would see if he made a good leader of all us English settlers. And Welsh. That will be a challenge, I thought, and might earn him the right to be addressed as Colonel. As my mother, who knew all the Welsh proverbs off pat, would say: to be a good leader, you have to be a bridge.

No sign of a bridge to us labourers that day. He spoke a word of welcome, smiling at the pretty dresses and top hats but hardly glancing in our direction. He said women and children would have to wait on board until tents and huts were erected by the men. That earned him a groan. I wanted to ask him about Huw, but he was busy with the landowners and the Captain, and then he was back over the side and rowed ashore. I thought of Dai and the Chartists back home trying to get votes and rights for working classes. Nothing different here, it appeared; we labourers were still the underclass.

———

Next day a strong wind ran up the harbour and we could unload neither cargo nor men. The sea too choppy for the light little boats and canoes. Next day the same. And the next. At least some friendly natives brought us fresh pork, still warm and juicy. What a heaven that was. But if the natives could come out, why did not Huw? On the day the natives came aboard, four of the crew left the ship without permission. Captain was very angry, but you could see the temptation: who would want to face a long voyage back when warm beaches, fresh food and friendly natives beckoned?

At last word came from Huw. One of the deck-hands returned, very shamefaced and hung-over. Our Captain was not one for the lash, but the tongue-lashing would have stung almost as much with all there to listen. That blessed fellow — John Horst his name — found me out later and handed me a note from my Huw. Just as well he had written it in the English tongue. Still, I was ashamed that I must ask Dora Southey to help me.

*My dearest Martha,*

*I have seen the passenger list and pray that you embarked (several did not, the Abernethys among them, so there is your washerwoman position left back on England's shore). But do not lose heart, we will think of something. The New Zealand Company has promised work for all. The Colonel's face is black as thunder when he hears a landowner has changed his mind at the last. The landowner has paid good English pounds for his town acre and country land, but who is to oversee the clearing and working of it? Truth is there are more labourers than overseers arriving with each ship, which might well work to our advantage.*

*We are under strict orders to stay ashore erecting
temporary huts and tents for you all. Nearly a
thousand souls have arrived, or are expected any day.
More in a month or two. It seems the surveyors and
planners are well behind and nothing permanent will
be decided for some time. But take heart, sweetheart,
I have the snuggest little hut set aside for us in the
lee of a sand dune (the winds can be strong here). A
Wesleyan Mission is being established on the other
side of the harbour. A very kind native missionary is
assisting me with food and advice. We can start afresh
here, be assured.*

   *Your loving husband, Huw Pengellin*

———————

Four long weeks later we were still aboard. More than once my
heart was in my mouth to see what Alfie got up to. Once I saw him
halfway up the rigging, with a sailor below egging him on. Another
time he shocked me singing a wild whaling song with words I
would not repeat. I set to immediately, teaching him some of our
wholesome Welsh folk songs. Not yet three, but quick like his father,
and with the voice of an angel.

   On the days dragged. Nothing to do but watch and pray for
quiet weather . . . When the wind died, the cargo was unloaded,
including sections of Mr Molesworth's steam engine, which Russ
said he would be employed putting together again. Mr Molesworth
shouting instructions and generally getting in the way as the heavy
pieces were lowered into the flimsy landing craft.

Next the cabin passengers left ship along with their baggage. We from the 'tween deck were greatly pleased to see them go, for now the upper deck was free all day to us. We could sit on deck in the sunshine like lords and ladies with none to say us nay. My Alfie's freckles, which had paled, along with his poor milky skin, soon darkened. Dear oh dear, the sunburn that flushed the children's skins was a nightmare those first sun-kissed days. We were not used to such clear, bright air, see, coming from cold cities and belching manufactories.

Then — was it maybe the third long waiting week? — Alfie came to me, jumping with excitement and tugging at me to follow him. By that time he spoke mostly in English, as that was all he heard on board apart from me. This time he shouted 'Come and see!' in our home tongue. And led me to the other side of the ship. Then, with a finger to his lips, he stopped behind a couple who stood at the rail, looking out to sea. The man's arm was around the woman's waist, and they spoke together. Alfie looked at me, nodding. True enough, the clever boy had spotted our Welsh tongue! All this time I had thought we were the only Welsh on board.

Alfie, forward lad, called out a greeting, and I followed. But oh, the surprise when they turned. It was Bryn and Arial! How had they managed to keep hidden all those months on board on the same crowded deck as me and Alfie? But there they were, blooming with good health; you'd have thought they were just returned from a day's picnic.

'Arial Conti, is that you?' I whispered, for true enough I was shocked.

She laid a finger to her lips. 'Nay, Martha, it is Mrs Thompson now and don't you forget it.' She smiled. 'Bryn — or John, I should say — had it all planned before we found out you were to be on the same boat. He is now John, and I am Mary. Good common names.

We kept down the other end of the married quarters. I turned my head or pulled down my bonnet any time I saw you come past. Naught you can do now.' Her eyes held a warning. 'Naught anyone can.'

No doubt she was thinking of Gareth, my brother-in-law, not to mention her own husband. She was clearly with child. Well on the way, I would have said.

Her smile was anxious. 'Are you shocked?'

Well, I was a bit, but pleased, too. To hear our own language brought tears to my eyes. 'You will live as a married couple?'

She patted her stomach and giggled. 'Isn't it clear that we already do?' She linked arms with me and squeezed. 'Oh, Martha, we can be friends here, can we not?'

We looked out at the beautiful hills.

'This is a new world. It is an adventure!'

My tears rose again. 'Oh, Arial, did you hear about the fighting at Newport?'

'We did, yes, but dared not ask details. We were in hiding up in the hills waiting for the ship to be ready. Gareth would have been involved, I imagine.'

'Ay. And arrested. They say he will hang. But Arial, Liddy's Dai — my brother Dai — was killed!' That wiped the smile from her face. I told her what details I knew, and that Liddy might come out here, too, if she could find a way. Still, speaking in the Welsh with her eased my heart somewhat. Tears were rolling down both our cheeks. It is hard to tell sometimes whether we cry out of despair or from hearing a kind word.

But I could not feel at ease until I set eyes on Huw.

Soon the labourers' bits and pieces were being rowed ashore. And the men with them. Bryn — John, I should say — was down as a blacksmith, Mary a seamstress. We all had to have trades.

'But do they have horses here? You will need horses to shoe and carts to spring,' I said.

John laughed. 'No civilisation can exist without horses, Martha. Not even wild New Zealanders. Horses have been with us since the beginning of time.'

He was wrong there, though. The first horse arrived in the harbour a few weeks after us.

—————

Finally, we women and children disembarked. That was a day to remember all my life. Huw on shore, dancing his little jig, shouting and waving, not a care who might be watching. Behind him a tall native woman, her skin as brown as a chestnut, a long cloak over one shoulder, the other bare, dark hair loose and long down her back. She smiled but stayed behind a little. Huw had not lost time making friends, then!

As we drew near, Alfie frowned at his father, sizing him up, unsure who he was, before beaming broadly and saying as clear as day: 'Taddy!'

Alfie and me into his arms, the dear, dear man. Huw feigned astonishment. 'Why, Martha, you have brought a pure wee elf from the home country to live with us?'

'No, Taddy!' shouted Alfie. 'I am Alfie!'

Huw swung him in a circle. 'Or a draig, is it? Don't fly away, little dragon!'

'I'm Alfie, see?' The boy was close to tears; it was all too much.

'Huw, sweetheart, this is Alfie, your son,' I said, a hint of warning in my words.

He heard me and hugged us both tight. 'Why, so it is! My Alfie. And my dear sweet Martha.'

All the while the tall woman stood watching. Her manner quiet, but something sharp and careful about those dark eyes.

'This is Hineroa,' said my Huw. 'She will be helping us.'

# PICNICKING IN THE SAND DUNES

## MARTHA PENGELLIN

*BRITANNIA, PITO ONE, SUMMER 1840*

Well, look you, those first weeks in that sandy and makeshift settlement were not like anything I had knowledge of, nor understanding of how to manage. But this I can say: compared with that gloomy and cold, rat-infested Newport foundry hut, this was pure heaven. A challenge, mind, but when the sun shines and the air is fresh and you see smiling, determined faces everywhere you look, the heart can't help but open, lungs too, and life seems full of promise.

There was a long beach stretching east to west between hills. To one side — the east — a large native pā, its poles pointing fiercely to the sky, though the natives were nothing but friendly. I wished Liddy had been there to see their vegetable gardens dotted here and there further back from the beach. She would have exclaimed at the rich, dark soil; the potatoes in flower and ears of wheat beginning to brown. Behind the beach amongst sand dunes, bushes, reeds and rushes grew. And behind that tall stands of trees, as magnificent as you might see in England but different somehow. Huw said the land was flat all the way up the valley, which was why the chief surveyor, a Lieutenant Mein Smith, wanted to build the new town there.

Meantime the natives helped us build little shelters from ferns and rushes alongside the river. It was like a holiday, see, washing our clothes in the river, carrying water for washing and cooking up to our shelter, and cooking over a little fire in the sand. All along the banks were people like us — farm labourers mostly, or sawyers, builders and joiners, waiting to be told what to do or where to go.

The landowners mostly had tents. They were busy with meetings and rules and would gather in Wakefield's big tent to argue. Not so many smiles from the gentry. I think they expected something a bit more civilised. Certainly they wanted to know where their town acre was and where their country acres, so they could start ordering us workers to get on with clearing and building. But we were happy enough to dally.

I never saw a kinder lot of people than those natives. They would bring us potatoes and pork and eggs and all sorts of greenery to put in the pot with the meat. Arial and Bryn (I could not get into the habit of their new names) had their whare (which is what the natives call a hut) next to ours and would share meals with us, and we would chatter away in our language all day long. The light had come back into Arial's eyes. She and Bryn had brought money with them. Was it Old Conti's, I wondered but didn't ask. Bryn was negotiating with Mr Molesworth for a patch of land further up the valley.

'Some of his country acres,' said Arial with a wink. What did that wink mean, I wondered, but again didn't ask. The valley was all dense bush, like everywhere else. They said there were native gardens here and there. I hoped Bryn knew what he was doing, planning to move away from the town areas. Not that those were in evidence either. Arial was happy to be here anyway, singing the old songs as she bashed away at Bryn's clothes in the river.

Little Alfie would be playing in the river or begging a ride in a canoe, his skin turning as brown as a New Zealander's. The way that boy opened out to the new life had my heart singing. Surely, he would do well here; already he was stringing together complicated sentences, a confusing mixture of English, Welsh and even the native tongue. He would bring little treasures from the beach or the river — coloured shells or the empty carcass of an insect or a bone. I sewed him a little sack for his treasures, which he kept tucked among the ferns of his mattress.

I missed the Southeys, who had been so kind to me on board. They were gathered together by Mr Molesworth on another part of the river bank, soon named Cornish Row, for they were all from Cornwall. Huw said Mr Molesworth was tired of waiting for his country acres and had decided for himself that he would clear land and build fences and a track right away. Dora said he was a tiger for getting things done, not like some of the gentry; all at Cornish Row admired the young fellow. Dora came into the main settlement for supplies looking happier and with a glow to her cheeks at last, dear soul. Back in Cornwall, Russ had signed that he would work for free to pay back his passage, but they were given a little allowance to buy food at the market. I wondered whether one of the gentry would employ me soon to do her washing, but meantime the natives were most helpful. Huw set up a little trestle and sold one or two of his axes at the market, but he wanted to keep most for later. For a week or two, it was the happiest time of my life, and I blessed Huw for bringing us to this new life.

Then came the storms. We could see the weather come up from the south. A great grey line of clouds advancing down the harbour. A strange sight. Back in Wales, the houses and hills blocked a person from seeing too far into the distance, but in this open place with the blue bowl of the sea in front of us, we knew hours before the storm arrived that it was coming. Well, it was no use knowing, was it? The long lines of rain were finally upon us, thunder and lightning, too, the hills on all sides echoing the boom as if the ships were firing their cannons all over again. Our little whare, which sheltered us nicely from sun and wind, proved no match for these sheets of rain.

'No, no!' I shouted to Huw, who was dancing and laughing in the rain with Alfie, the silly man. 'Help me stow the linen in our trunk, will you, and bundle up the rest in the one dry corner!' But it was useless trying, so they might as well dance. It rained all day and the next. There was no shelter, see, from the roaring wind, which drove the very beach inland until the scrub was half-buried in sand. In the end, the nice woman from the Mission, who had stayed over here with us, took me by one hand and Alfie by the other and led us away from the dunes a mile or two to where the large trees grow. Hineroa found a fallen log, and cut fern fronds and made us a dry nest.

'No point us all drowning,' she said. 'Let Huw guard your possessions while we stay dry.'

She was very sensible. There were so few women from home, I was relieved to find one from this country ready to be my friend. Her English would shame many of us Welsh, and even the Cornishmen.

I noticed when the storm struck that many of the natives had simply walked away into the forest like us and were sitting together under shelter. At first this New Zealand forest was both a marvel and rather fearful to me: in no way like our woods back home with their graceful spreading oaks and carpets of bluebells. Here, the trees tower up and up, the leaves almost out of sight above their severe, straight trunks. All manner of vines loop down from these majestic trees. Alfie was swinging upside down on one in a trice. And the ferns! Sitting there in the gloom — no shred of sunlight making its way down to us — I counted twenty-five different types of fern, from tiny ones no bigger than your thumb to great towering tree ferns. Hineroa said there were hundreds of ferns and only a few edible. She offered me a frond. It tasted nutty, like raw carrot but not so sweet.

I watched two natives up a tree trying to snare a beautiful fat pigeon.

Alfie laughed to see it. 'Apron!' he said. 'Lady bird!' True enough, the white markings on the bird's belly were exactly like a nice, neat apron. I was sorry to see it trapped by the feet and brought fluttering down.

'Do you know any stories of the wives of Annwn?' Hineroa suddenly asked me.

'How do you know about them?' I replied, surprised.

'Your husband mentioned them.'

'Huw is really the storyteller. They are fairy folk. If they come out of the water and mate with humans, things usually turn bad.' I told her about the son of one of those marriages, half-human half-water-maiden who started a long line of healers in our country.

'Not always bad, then,' said Hineroa. 'My mother was a healer. Of a long line.' She sat quietly for a while, stroking Alfie's curly hair.

I asked her if she continued the line, but she didn't answer.

When the rain finally stopped and we returned to our hut to dry out the bedding, I thought our troubles were over. But even Hineroa was not ready for what happened next. Slowly, our nice, friendly river began to rise. It crept through the sand hills and the swamp where the rushes grew, gathering pace as the afternoon wore on, even though the sun was now shining. Soon we were all gathering our belongings and running for higher ground, which was not greatly in evidence. Arial and Bryn came with us, dragging their possessions; Arial moaning with the effort as her time was close. Huw carried Alfie under one arm, a bundle in the other, for by now we were wading ankle-deep. Hineroa and I dragged the box. The other natives were nowhere to be seen. I think they knew what to expect and had hurried inland. But where could we find higher ground?

After some time of this dreadful stumbling, Hineroa called a halt. 'I think this will do. We are higher here. Let us wait and see.'

Well, the leaves were dry underfoot. Surely the river could not cover all of this wide valley? We dropped our bundles and looked around.

Arial and Bryn finally caught up. She was on her last legs, poor lass, and sank to the ground. 'Dear oh dear,' she said, happy to let Bryn stuff fern at her back and take off her wet boots. 'Am I carrying twins, do you think, Martha?' She looked around at the endless trees. 'I could kill for a cup of tea.'

We all laughed. Arial had a way of making light of disaster. She held up a fistful of dry fern-fronds. 'Huw, man, have you no match or kettle among these bundles here? We ladies demand our afternoon tea!'

The men soon had a little fire going, Arial egging them on with her saucy banter, when she suddenly stopped with a cry and clasped that enormous belly.

'Oh sweet Jesus, Martha! Oh dear! Can the babby be coming?'

Bryn dropped his kettle and ran to her. Arial looked up at me, clearly frightened. 'Not now. Oooh!'

Please spare us this, I thought. Night coming on and no one to help. I could not pretend to be an expert in childbirth, having attended only one — my own.

Bryn settled Arial on the ground and looked at me. 'Is it coming? Oh, Martha, tell me it's not!'

'Have your waters broken?' I asked Arial.

Her weak laugh was more of a whimper. 'How could I possibly tell? . . . Oooh!'

Of course, we were all soaked from wading through the rising water. But her pains sounded like labour to me. I looked for Hineroa. Perhaps she had knowledge? But she had disappeared into the darkening bush. The thing is, most of us immigrants were young, and most midwives are older women. Arial and I had discussed this, and had asked Dora Southey to help when the time came. But Dora had been doubtful. She had never watched someone else give birth. And anyway, she was nowhere near, as far as we knew.

Then, just as we were shaking out wet bedding, looking for some shred of a wrap for the baby that might be dry, Hineroa arrived with a white-haired native woman.

'This is Tiahuia, of Te Āti Awa. She will help.'

Oh, such a blessing to hear that. To tell the truth, if it were not for the natives, we would not have survived these past weeks. Food, shelter, and now childbirth! The New Zealand Company could well learn a few lessons in managing a new settlement from the New Zealanders. Even Arial paused her moaning to smile. Tiahuia knelt beside Arial, felt her belly and nodded to Hineroa, speaking quietly in their tongue and pointing away further into the bush.

'We will take her away now,' said Hineroa. 'You stay here.'

Bryn stepped forward at that and laid a hand on the old woman who was helping Arial to stand.

'Leave her alone! Don't you dare take her!'

'Where am I going?' Arial was desperate now, all her saucy quips and chatter lost. 'Bryn, come with me!' She clung to her Bryn. Huw must have understood something of what the old woman had said, for he took Bryn's other hand and told him to let the women go. Dear oh dear, we were in trouble here, with little Alfie now joining the fray, holding his arms up and howling to be carried.

Hineroa faced us all, her height rather intimidating. She spoke sternly above the ruckus. 'You must let us take Arial some distance away. It is Tiahuia's custom and mine also. We will look after her until the baby is born.' When Bryn would still not let go of his wife, Hineroa raised her voice. 'If you want this woman's help, you must let your wife go with us. You are acting most foolishly.'

A very fierce woman was Hineroa.

Huw spoke up, then, sensible for once. 'What about childbirth back in Wales, Bryn? Do they not send us menfolk away until it is all over? I say you should trust them.'

'These people are savages, though,' Bryn protested, but keeping his voice low.

Hineroa heard and glared. 'In that case we will leave you to your civilised ways.' And with no more said, she marched the old lady off into the bush. If it wasn't for Huw running after and pleading in their own tongue, we would have been in a sorry situation. I took Arial by the hand and we stumbled after them. They were waiting a small distance away, where a group of ferns screened them from our little camp. I don't believe they ever planned to leave us, bless them.

I was not welcome at the birthing. Huw said it was something about tapu, which means a kind of sacredness. He wasn't sure whether the mother-to-be was tapu or the opposite — a contamination that could bring us bad luck. He scratched his head. 'Maybe both.'

We sat waiting, shivering in the dark, huddled together for warmth beside the tiny fire. All our holiday mood and picnicking forgotten. Hearing Arial's screams brought home to me how different our lives would be now, and how little skill I had in making do without even the small comforts that we had once taken for granted. A candle; a dry blanket; in particular, a safe roof over our heads.

Then Huw, good man, began to sing a hymn — 'Llanllyfni', my favourite. His beautiful tenor voice echoed through the dark bush. 'R wy'n ofni'm nerth yn ddim.' Oh, what a warm comfort to hear music in our Welsh tongue. It was an attempt to deafen Bryn's ears to Arial's distress, no doubt. I tried to join in, 'Māe ofnau o bob rhyw', my voice wavering, but Bryn could not manage. It brought tears to my eyes to hear Hineroa join in with the English words. 'I sink in life's alarms, When by myself I stand . . .'

Perhaps all would be well. Perhaps mother and babe would survive. Perhaps for once Huw had made the right decision and we would prosper in this strange, wild land.

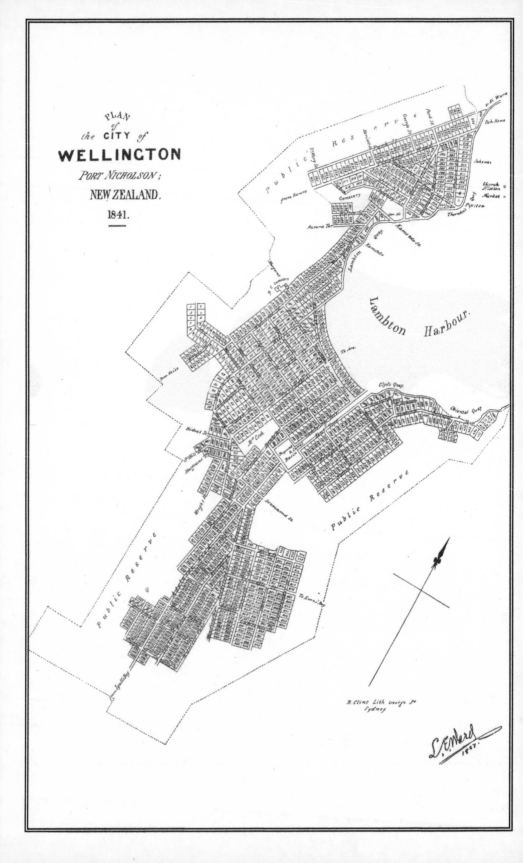

PLAN
of
the **CITY** of
**WELLINGTON**
PORT NICHOLSON;
NEW ZEALAND.
1841.

Public Reserve

Lambton Harbour

Public Reserve

Public Reserve

R. Clint Lith George St
Sydney

L.E. Ward
1847.

# PART TWO

---

# CARVING UP THE
# HEAD OF THE FISH

# BITTERSWEET NEWS

## MARTHA PENGELLIN

*BRITANNIA, AUTUMN 1840*

Those weeks and months at Britannia I seemed to spend half my life sweeping sand that drifted into our whare. Huw had shifted the doorway to face away from the sea, but still the wretched grains invaded through every crack in the rough ponga walls. There was sand in everything, even between my teeth. I was often short with poor Alfie, who wanted to play in the river. He was forever wandering off and had already had several near-escapes in the changing eddies.

'Later, Alfie,' I snapped, that day of the letter. 'For goodness' sake leave me be. Play outside where I can see you.'

'Ay Mam,' he said, and disappeared.

I was anxious, see. Huw had been away for a week, sawmilling on the other side of the harbour. It was good money, true — three pounds a day — but why did he have to go over there? We had been trying — not very successfully, I admit — to live on what I earned as a washerwoman. Huw, bless him, was desperate to make more money so we could save for our own patch, but I needed him close by.

'Plenty of felling and milling to be done this side of the harbour,' I had argued more than once. 'Here, near Britannia.' But he always had some reason to sail away from me and Alfie.

Britannia. Stupid name. No more like Britain than the moon. Tents and shacks and a dirty rowdy public house. I was fed up with all the arguments about land and who would decide where the settlement would be. Sick of all the rules. The landowners seemed to enjoy their meetings, though. They fancied themselves as a new free government; a ruling class telling the rest of us where to go, what to do. The picnic atmosphere gone now, retreating slowly as the cold weather and the storms rolled up the harbour.

To be honest I was out of sorts because of the letter in my pocket. I pulled it out again. I could make out the signature — surely that spelled 'Liddy'? The rest was all dislocated words to me. Something about Gareth. Something about the farm. Nothing about Liddy getting passage on a ship. Why did I sense a feeling of desperation?

I stumped out to the wash-house awning, took up my pole and stirred at the sheet boiling in the tub. Outside, one of the flapping sheets detached from its line and dragged a corner in the fecking sand.

'Oh, Jesus and Mary!' I shouted at poor Alfie, who was innocently building sandcastles.

But there, reaching to peg up the wayward washing, was Liddy herself! Two pale daughters trembling in the wind behind her, taller and more serious than I remembered them, but nonetheless Meg and Holly in solid flesh! Surely no mirage?

'Liddy? Oh, Liddy, tell me I'm not going mad! Is it you, then, sweetheart?'

She looked as if she might collapse. All my bad humour blown away, I ran to hold her up. Indeed, she sagged in my arms and then sank onto the little bench Huw made before he left for the other side of the harbour.

'Holly! Meg!' cried little Alfie, and they all laughed, Holly nearly knocked over by the beaming boy rushing to hug his cousins.

'He remembers us, Mam! But he could hardly speak back then: listen to him now! And look how he's grown!'

Oh, it was all laughing and crying and let us have a cup of tea and forget the blessed washing and sit down, sit down, girls, you look fit to drop. All talking at once, all questions; no answers until one of the Company men arrived with Liddy's box and information about where she could find quarters meantime, while her position was sorted.

I had to touch my friend to make sure it was her. 'Bless you, Liddy, dear heart. A miracle, sure, that you have made your way to this very hut on this damned windy beach. Is it not past belief?'

All Liddy could manage was a nod. Her eyes were closing. I could see she was exhausted. The girls, too: flopped in a heap unable to respond to Alfie's urging to come and see this, try that and shall we play by the river? On and on he chattered, until even he saw that this was not the time for play.

Soon all three newcomers were wrapped in blankets and fast asleep. All I could give them for a bed was my poor wooden platform, laced with fern fronds, which served us all. I couldn't stop watching over them. What if it was an apparition and they might suddenly disappear? They looked, all three, half-starved. What had happened? What did the letter (which perhaps arrived on the same boat) say?

Well, then. The fire under the wash-pot had died and there were still two more sheets to be boiled. What do questions and answers matter? They were here. A precious gift of family in this land of strangers.

---

Later in the day we all crammed onto the two benches, either side of the rough-sawn table in the whare. A fire in the little tin chimney kept us cosy, though every now and then a low moan had Liddy startled.

'It's the wind, never mind it,' I said, ladling a good pigeon stew into bowls. 'I cannot for the life of me find the crack. It will shriek in a storm, or sing low as now. We enjoy silence one day in three at best. You get used to it.'

We shared the bowls; there were only three. For once I was pleased that Huw was still away. I took the letter from my pocket. 'I have been trying at the reading, Liddy, but cannot make this screed out.'

Liddy nodded quietly. Easy to see she was downhearted. Surely there was more to her mood than grief over Dai's death? 'Finish your stew first, Liddy, sweetheart, and then we'll hear.'

Holly and Meg were sharing a bowl, and were surprisingly careful of each other. Nothing like the rowdy, competitive pair I remembered. But of course they were newly arrived, no doubt subdued after those endless months of poor food and crowded, dark, stinking 'tween-deck bunks.

Holly touched the letter lying on the table. 'The nice minister at the poorhouse wrote that.'

'The poorhouse! You were never in there, were you, Liddy?'

Liddy flushed. 'I was. We were, all three. If it were not for him, we would still be there.'

'Dear sweet Jesus! Would no one buy the farm, then?'

Liddy looked up from her eating. Her eyes were blazing. Anger, then, not shame burning in those flushed cheeks.

'Your Huw's brother has ruined us. Damn him to Hell.'

And there in the doorway was Huw himself, black hair full of shavings, clothes muddy, grinning as if he had only been away a few hours not the entire week. His grin quickly changed to astonishment.

'Liddy, is that you? Bless me, it is so! And Holly and Meg! You should have sent word. Martha, sweetheart, this is a blessed day, is it not?'

I was in a fervent to hear the rest of the story, but Huw must be fed, greetings and hugs bestowed, children put to bed.

'No, no, let them stay here tonight,' said Huw. 'We can sort their temporary quarters tomorrow. I'll take the floor.' He danced a few steps this way and that, brushing the shavings from his hair until all three children were laughing. 'I am too dirty anyway to grace my presence among these lovely ladies. Shall we have a story now, children?'

'Huw, for pity's sake make it short,' I said, but with little hope. Once Huw is embarked on the old tales they must be told word-for-word to the end. I smoothed Liddy's tangled hair and then plaited it to keep my fingers from drumming.

Alfie snuggled into his da as Huw began the tale of Manawyddan. Finally, he came to the end. 'So, the crops disappear from the fields for the third time and the leading marauding mouse is caught.' The children were asleep, but blessed Huw had to finish the tale anyway in a whisper. 'But it was not a mouse, it was a famous magical woman.' He kissed all three and at last came back to the table.

'I'm sorry you have to hear this, Huw,' said Liddy, 'but I cannot speak kindly of your brother.'

Huw poured a mug of porter from a crock he had brought with him. I shot him a reproving look, which he ignored. Tea was good enough for Liddy and me. We Chapel folk take the oath against drinking alcohol, but Huw says rules can be relaxed in this new country.

The candle guttered and then was blown out by a fresh buffet. When Huw went to relight it, Liddy stopped him.

'Let me tell what I have to say in darkness. It will be easier.'

I laid my hand over dear Liddy's. 'Speak your heart, dearest. Huw knows my feelings about his brother. Gareth is not welcome in our family, nor ever will be. So, was he let out of prison? Not hanged?'

'He and the other leaders are deported to Australia. Some Members of Parliament spoke up against the hanging. I would not have been so generous.'

I could hear the deep anger in her voice. Liddy, who has always been so gentle, so contented, happy to spend every day in the garden with her vegetables and fruits. What must it have been like for her, shut in the poorhouse? Huw and I leaned in to hear Liddy's quiet voice.

'When I had the house cleaned and ready to sell, and the fields and garden as good as I could make them, I approached Cadoc Conti. As we discussed, Martha, he would be the only one with money to buy. But that old skinflint told me he was already in negotiations to buy Gareth's farm and ours combined! But Gareth is in prison, I said, and anyway he has no right to approach you over Dai's family farm.

'Conti told me that Gareth had sent a legal fellow with permission to sell on his behalf. You cannot believe how rude Conti was, Martha. Did not invite me to sit down; would not look me in the eye. Pretended he had more pressing business and I was wasting his time.

'What Gareth does with his farm is his business, I said. If you are not interested in buying mine I will go elsewhere. Mind you, that was a bluff: I had no idea who else I might approach. But my anger was up, see, him being so offhand, as if I were some snail he had found on a cabbage leaf, worth nothing but to be cast aside.' Her voice trembled.

I could not imagine how her story might develop. What new dreadful outrage had Huw's brother initiated? 'Go on then, Liddy, never mind that old sour-shanks.'

'How can I not!' cried Liddy. 'Gareth has taken our family farm, and neither I nor the girls one penny richer from it! His fancy legal man wove some wicked web of lies.' She looked from me to Huw in the dark, still clinging to my hand for support. The children sleeping on the bench stirred at the sound of her raised voice.

'He said the farm could only go to a male heir. Evidently he had some paper that said Dai's grandfather had written it in a will. We only had girls. And then, so old Conti said, it seemed Gareth Pengellin was the closest male relative to Dai! Did you ever hear such nonsense? Huw, surely that is nonsense? You are not related to my Dai, are you?'

Huw cleared his throat. His fingers traced a knot in the rough wood of the table. 'Well . . .' he began, then his voice trailed off.

The two of us waited.

'Well, Liddy . . .' Again, he fell silent.

I frowned at him. Liddy needed support, not prevarication. 'I never heard any word that the Pengellins and we Jones were related,' I said, 'except through you and me, Huw. Never. In any case, would not our Alfie be closest? Dai's nephew?'

Huw rose to put a fresh log on the fire before he spoke. 'Look, Martha, Liddy: Gareth was the one to take an interest in family matters. Who married who; who was cousin to who. Plenty of families married each other in the hills around. If Gareth said so—'

'Gareth is a liar and a thief! And worse, as Martha well knows. Don't you dare support him, Huw Pengellin! His lawyer told Conti that the rule was unfortunate for me and the girls, but that Gareth would sell both farms and see that me and the girls were not left destitute. A barefaced lie. By the time I approached Conti, the deal had been made, the land sold and the money deposited in a bank in Gareth's name. Gareth deported to Australia. Me and the girls moved off the farm to make way for a manager and his family. Nowhere for us to go but the poorhouse.'

Liddy fell silent. Outside the wind had dropped. An owl hooted twice. Huw relit the candle and poured a fresh mug of porter. From the tent behind us we heard a burst of singing, and then laughter. Could this all be true? I didn't doubt Liddy's story, not for a moment, but could Gareth be so evil as to steal Dai's children's birthright? 'Perhaps he means to pay you something,' I said quietly.

'He was content for me to be sent to the poorhouse. No sign of "seeing me and the girls right". Nor any way for me to contact the wretch, for he'll be in Australia by now.'

Huw took a draught of porter. Cleared his throat again. 'So, he didn't send money for your passage? Are you sure he hasn't deposited money for you?'

Liddy sighed. She told them a happier story: of the Reverend Tapperwell, who was responsible for the poorhouse and who raised money for her and two other families to be set up with the clothing and supplies required by the New Zealand Company. Evidently rules were bent because labourers were needed in the new colony and because Reverend Tapperwell could vouch for the hardworking and upright demeanour of his protégées.

'A kind and gentle man, even though he is Anglican, not Chapel. He wrote that letter to you. Who would have thought that it came on the same boat?' Liddy managed a wan smile. 'Well, we are here at least. I am down as gardener, which is unusual for a woman, but the Company man back in England said there is a great call for people who can get English vegetables and fruit and flowers to grow over here.'

'Ay, indeed, Liddy love,' said Huw, 'you will be in great demand, I'm sure. Have you brought seeds with you, then? And did you know that Arial and Bryn are here? As good as man and wife. They have a baby daughter now. Sarah, she's called, isn't she, Martha?'

Clearly, he was eager to change the subject away from his brother. So while Huw finished his porter, I showed Liddy the ropes: how to fold her outer garments over the rack suspended from the roof and wash in the bucket outside. For a moment, we two women stood in our undergarments looking up at the stars.

Liddy breathed in deeply. 'The air! So fresh, so clean! Surely everything will grow well in this place? Oh, Martha, it is such a relief to be here.'

'It is not exactly the Garden of Eden, but it has its points. Shall we go in?'

'I fear I have been too outspoken. Is Huw hurt, do you think?'

I said nothing; put my arm around Liddy and led her inside.

Huw looked at us, his eyes alight. 'Two beautiful ladies! Goodnight, sweethearts both. I have news, too. Next Monday they are starting to auction off the sections in Thorndon, over at Port Nicholson. And your man here will be bidding for our own little patch!'

Well that was blessed news! I forgot my annoyance and gave the man a hug. A place of our own! Please, God, without sand.

But then, as I settled to sleep I thought: What about Liddy? Will she be able to make her way on her own with two young girls? I looked over at my dear friend. Liddy was smiling in her sleep. Sure, she will survive. We are survivors all.

# THE GODS ARE ANGRY

## HUW PENGELLIN

*PITO ONE, AUTUMN 1840*

So I slept on the floor that night with the ladies unhappy, to say the least, with my brother — and me by association. It was almost a relief to be woken early by gunshots. Then the ringing of the bell outside Colonel Wakefield's big tent. Out I stumbled, still fully dressed, into the wind. Native trouble, maybe? They have been restless all month over the new arrivals and the way their gardens have been overrun. But, no; over westward a great sheet of fire was rising above the scrub.

I ducked inside and grabbed Martha's spade. 'Not native trouble, Martha. It could be Cornish Row is on fire. Mr Molesworth's workers.'

They were all awake now, the children trembling. Martha, who was friendly with the Southeys, called out after me as I headed off: 'Huw, they are poor as church-mice, every one. See if you can help. And bring Dora and the boys here if they are burnt out. We can put up a bit of a tent.'

Everyone was running towards the blaze, settlers and natives alike. A couple of large dogs running in the opposite direction, tails between legs, nearly upended me. Overhead, a cloud of parrots erupted from the high trees across the river, shrieking their alarm.

But when we arrived at the blaze there was little we could do. The wind had carried embers from one whare to the next, the raupō thatch catching immediately and passing the flames on. Below the thatch, the rough bristles of the ponga logs that form the walls were equally flammable. The row had been built on a high bank of the river, against the threat of flooding, so bringing water up, bucket by bucket, was too slow, too ineffective.

All we could do was stamp out any embers that might spread to other whare lower down, and make sure all of the Cornish workers and their families were safe.

A tall native man I remembered from the days before settlers arrived deposited two children at my feet. Both were howling.

The fellow spoke in his own tongue — a Te Āti Awa man. 'Ah bad work,' he said. 'Whare are too close together. We would not build like that.'

I agreed, pleased to understand. 'True enough. Is everyone safe?'

'All safe. But I think the gods are angry. They have sent fire as a warning. Your people do not respect the mana of our people.'

He patted the two children on their heads and smiled at them. The anger of the gods clearly did not extend to children.

'Thank you. I will find their parents,' I assured him.

The fire was dying. Over as quickly as it began. One or two charred ponga logs still stood, threatening to reignite with every gust. We bashed them to the ground with pick and shovel, then doused them.

Dora was there, and Russ and the boys, standing silent in front of the ruins of their hut. I led the two children towards the group of blackened workers. Leaning down, Dora comforted the lost children, then pointed them towards their parents.

'All gone,' said Russ glumly. 'God knows we possessed little enough. Every last stitch, every last mouthful gone.'

'We shouldna come, Da,' said Russ's eldest, whose streaked face betrayed his tears. 'We were better off home. We are treated just the same here, except it is wilder. We shouldna come.'

'Ah wait, lad, wait a bit.' Russ placed an arm around his son's shoulders and pulled him close. 'Mr Molesworth will see us right, I reckon. Things will pick up.' He nodded to me and shrugged. 'Our situation could not get worse, eh? Has to improve.'

I gave them Martha's invitation to come downriver and share our whare. 'Surely the Company or Mr Molesworth will house you until new huts are built? We'll get a tent from the Company meantime.' Dora was scraping with a stick among the blackened ashes to unearth their cooking pot and what remained of Russ's axe. 'Martha will have the other labouring families organised, you can count on it. We won't see you go hungry or unclad. And even if the Company is slow to act, you have an employer who watches out for you. Not everyone is so lucky.'

---

Over the next few days, I was reminded of the Te Āti Awa man's warning. Indeed, it did seem as if the gods were angry. First, the settlement was awoken again, this time by an ominous rumbling. The very ground beneath shook. One of the poles of the whare fell onto the sleeping platform. The iron pot by the fireplace rolled onto its side, and a plate, left on the table, crashed to the ground.

'Dear sweet Jesus, they are coming!' cried Liddy. 'I can feel their feet pounding! A war party!' She gathered Holly and Meg to her and looked to Martha. 'Should we run or hide here?'

Someone in a whare close by rushed out with a musket. 'They're coming! Arm yourselves!' He fired wildly into the air, bringing down a branch.

Other guns were discharging. Women screaming. Me grinning, to Martha's annoyance. 'Well, what is so amusing when your womenfolk are terrified out of their wits?'

'Listen,' I said. 'Listen now. Do you hear war cries? Where have the pounding of native feet disappeared to? Some idiots are wasting good powder and shot.'

The gunshots died away. The eerie silence that followed was punctuated only by the crying of children.

'Would you kindly enlighten us then, Mr Know-it-all?'

'Is it a thunderstorm?' asked Holly, still shaking. 'But I saw no lightning. Did you see lightning, M—'

Suddenly the ground beneath us was shaking again, this time more gently.

I held up a hand to calm them, before telling them, proud of my expertise, that it was an earthquake. 'We felt one when we first arrived. This one was stronger, mind. You'll not see any natives running out discharging their guns. An earthquake is an everyday thing to them. Why don't we go back to our sleep?'

But for all my reassurances the women and children were still anxious. Even the rumble of waves breaking on the sand sounded ominous to them.

My plan was to catch a boat across the harbour when the land auctions over that side were held. Already the rights to town acres and part-acres had been changing hands. Houses were going up over at Lambton Harbour ahead of the unveiling of the town plan. I made sure to chat to anyone angling to buy a piece of land. Two days before, I had listened to a fellow — a watchmaker — who had tripled his one-hundred-pound investment and was already regretting it, thinking he could have done better. Dear God, I was itching to get my hands on some part of an acre before the land prices rose further.

And then, not two days later, the river flooded again. Britannia settlement at Pito One was awash. Further up the valley where the river is deeper and the current swifter, newly built homes were uprooted. A family was swept away and drowned. There was no news of Arial and Bryn and the baby, who had been squatting on unmarked land, which the natives claimed had never been sold.

It was the last straw. Even Mein Smith the chief surveyor now had to concede that the main settlement should be built at Thorndon Flat at the south end of the harbour. Good news!

I carried little Alfie to the shore and pointed to the distant hills and curving shore where white sails could be seen already gathering. The two of us singing in fine voice a little ditty of my own invention in praise of Llŷr.

I set Alfie high on my shoulders. 'See the ships?'

'I can see, Taddy!' shouted my boy.

'Would you fancy a nice wee house over there, with its own little fence and garden? All our own?'

'And Mam, too? And Meg and Holly?'

I laughed. 'Ay, the whole lot, son. Why not bring all of Wales with us? Shall we bring the elves, too, my little Alfie?'

That earned me a slap on the head from my son. 'No elves here, Taddy, no elves.'

The boy sounded so definite. It left me with an odd sense of disquiet.

# STRIKING A DEAL

## HUW PENGELLIN

*THORNDON FLAT, AUGUST 1840*

The land auction was set for August, in Dickie Barrett's unfinished 'hotel'. The whaler had bought the building from Dr Evans and had it towed across the harbour on a barge. Soon, boasted Dickie, it would have a grand portal, an enlarged upper storey and be the finest hotel in the new settlement. Barrett's Hotel.

So he said. I have never liked the strutting whaler. Former whaler, in fact, for Dickie Barrett now preferred the 'civilised' life of Port Nicholson to his ramshackle whaling station across the strait. Liquor was plentiful and he was somewhat of a celebrity.

I spent several hours scrutinising Captain Mein Smith's great map of the layout of the new town which they planned to call Wellington. At long last, after many postponements, the plan had been laid out for inspection ahead of the auction. One thousand settler acres and one hundred native ones, laid out neatly, with roads and reserves, a cemetery, a market area, a canal between Cambridge and Kent terraces leading to a lake or maybe a wharf. Large areas of public reserves surrounded the one-acre plots. It was a wonderfully neat plan, the roads and sections abruptly running out into bush wherever the land steepened. Indeed, most of the sections were still deep in bush, too. It was a marvel to see it. A clever skill, surveying. I had a notion I would be good at it, and surely in this great new land surveyors would be in demand. I had watched the lads with their chains and rods and pegs marking out those sections, all exactly the same size — one acre — even the native reserves, which seemed to be mostly on the outer reaches of the layout and nowhere near the actual positions of the three pā. Trouble ahead on that front, surely.

I had guessed right, see: Colonel got his way and the settlement would not be at Britannia on the Hutt River as Mein Smith desired, but at Thorndon (the new Britannia) or Lambton or whatever new name might be proclaimed, to the south of the harbour.

Some land was cleared along the waterfront, and of course around the pā, but most of the land now to be auctioned was covered in towering trees. The past few weeks, would-be owners, myself among them, had trampled over kūmara patches and thrashed through the ferns searching for pegs and numbers. Where, in God's name, was number 223? Where was the road grandly named Tory Street? The Wellington Terrace was obvious — its trees rose above the scatter of huts along the shore. The three pā were named on the map — out in the sea — but the one-acre plots marched inexorably through them all. The pegs marking sections close to the shore were often obvious — often right in the middle of Māori gardens and pā — but further inland was anyone's guess.

I reckoned a sharp fellow could get away with a bit of latitude if he managed to secure something in the bush. Who would know if the pegs were moved a little?

So on the day of the auction I was outside Barrett's half-finished hotel bright and early. A certain land agent, name of Lankey, in my sights. An agent for the Company, he held the rights to fifty-three town acres that had been bought by wealthy investors in London who had now decided to sell rather than emigrate themselves.

I had chosen him carefully; a flustered look on his face and a great bundle of deeds in his hand, which he kept flipping through in a distracted sort of manner. Me dressed in my Sunday suit, gold sovereigns in my pocket and my best British axe-head to add to my offer. To be realistic, a lease would be the best I might purchase, but

I was determined to try for a quarter-acre outright sale.

I took the axe from my bag; let the freshly oiled blade catch the sun. 'Ready-sharpened, sir; all set to go,' I said. 'None of your Australian rubbish. Properly tempered British steel. Now . . .' I jingled the coin in my pocket.

By this time, inside and out of the building all was bedlam. The great map lay on the large table inside; landowners and would-be owners were flourishing pieces of paper and shouting for attention; Colonel Wakefield and Dr Evans attempting to bring order. Rain threatened, and the blessed unending wind whipped up stinging dust and rattled the corners of the map.

'Here, hold this. Feel the weight,' I said, handing the axe-head to the agent, at the same time deftly taking possession of the man's sheaf of papers. Thumbed through them quickly, counting as I went. 'Good heavens, Sir! This Hon. A. G. Tollemache has bought thirty-four acre lots! Is he here?'

The agent shrugged 'No. Neither he nor his brother. Another M.P. They want to sell.'

I was pleased to notice several low numbers. See, the Company sold thousands of shares back in England before the land was even bought; each share worth, at that time, one hundred pounds. Colonel told me that a share entitled the investor to one town acre and one hundred country acres. Now, I had been talking to owners of these hundred-pound shares. Evidently a lottery back in England had allocated a number to each title deed. Low numbers get to choose a section on Mein Smith's map first. I pulled out one deed. 'This has a low number. How about one-quarter of that?'

Mr Lankey laughed. 'I will get five hundred pounds for a quarter of that acre. Maybe more.'

'I'll throw in the axe-head. A British-made six-pounder like that is as good as gold out here.'

The agent turned to look inside. The auction was about to begin. I feared I might lose him.

'There will be plenty of buyers, Mr Pengellin. An eighth I might look at, but not one with a number below twenty. My papers, please.'

'This one then, sir? Let's cut a deal,' I said with a wink. 'We both know I am taking a risk. The governor in New South Wales says all these transactions are illegal. Your shareholders in England may lose their investment.' I spread a fistful of golden sovereigns under his nose. 'At least my money is sound. One-quarter of your number 30 for thirty sovereigns and the axe? Coin safely in your pocket?'

He was tempted, plain to see. An agent whose landowner is half a world away, and might not ever know that part of one of his acres was lacking a quarter, might be persuaded to line his own pocket. And it was true that the sellers were anxious since the letter from Sir George Gipps, Governor of New South Wales, had declared that all titles of land sold by Māori to settlers must only be derived through the Crown. If the threat was upheld, the New Zealand Company and its shareholders would be ruined.

A bell rang, and Colonel Wakefield called everyone inside. The agent lowered the heavy axe into his sack and held out his hand. He wanted the coin. I merely shook the chilly hand. 'The coin will be out here when I see my name on the paper. The axe-head is a sign of goodwill. Agreed? I suggest you choose near the Wesleyan Mission for your number 30. That is good land.'

He smiled. 'You drive a hard bargain, Mr Pengellin. I imagine you will prosper out here.' And off he scurried into the gaping building where numbers were already being called.

Oh, boyo! A quarter of number 30! A bargain! I was prepared for leasehold. Lankey would have a choice of many acres when his number was called. I flipped one of my sovereigns, caught it and slapped it down on the other hand. 'Heads, we are landowners by this evening. Tails, we are persuaded to settle for lease.'

Heads it was. I must have shouted for joy, for a fellow hurrying into the crowd gave me an odd look.

Still fizzing with excitement, I picked up a stone and hurled it towards the sea. It splashed near to a cutter that had just drawn alongside the half-finished Company jetty. A smallish sailing ship, probably from Australia. For a moment my attention was caught by the ragged fellow unloading sacks of produce. Something familiar about the size and set of the shoulders reminded me of Gareth. I watched for a moment, puzzled. Then shrugged. But of course not. All Liddy's talk of him lately must have put my brother in mind.

Quickly I turned and pushed through the crowd of onlookers. Better keep an eye on that agent.

# BROTHER AND SISTER

## HINEROA

*TE ARO PĀ, LATER THAT SAME DAY*

The crowds milling around Barrett's Hotel were of little interest to me. My back ached and my mood was dark that day. Reverend Buller had suggested that he conduct a Christian marriage service between me and Hone. Minarapa had agreed.

'If you have a baby on the way,' he explained, 'then you should have a suitable husband. It is the Christian teaching.'

Of course I had argued. 'It is not *our* way, and I am not baptised Christian.'

Minarapa had then suggested marriage and baptism at the same time. He felt an unmarried mother teaching his young sons the Christian ways set a poor example.

'But Hone! How can that stupid man be a suitable husband? He is not even the father.'

'Hineroa! That sharp tongue of yours! You should be grateful that Hone is willing. And are you sure he is not the father?'

I did not deign to answer, but continued to press my point. Surely, I should be free to choose a husband? Is that not the Christian way? Reverend Buller had weighed in to explain that even in Pākehā custom an unmarried mother could not always choose.

I would not give in. 'Did you not say that slavery was condemned by Queen Victoria and the British Government? Am I not a free woman and no longer a slave? Are you telling me now that some of these women arriving day after day from your country, Reverend, are still slaves?'

The reverend had sighed and explained slowly, as if I was an idiot, that none of the women arriving here were unmarried mothers; all were of good character and most married.

A rage came upon me. My mother would have advised caution, but I could not let the dispute lie. The Reverend surely knew, I said, that it was the custom of my people to offer a woman's comfort to important visitors — no doubt to the Reverend himself when he visited kāinga when he first arrived. (That had him blushing!) So how was it a matter of shame if a child was the result? Did he not himself have children of Māori descent by now?

Minarapa had tried to look stern, but could not hide his amusement. Even so, he persisted with the plan for me and Hone to marry. No longer slaves, but both low-class: suitable.

If I had to leave the Mission, so be it. I could never agree. At least in Port Nicholson, where the whole world seemed to have gone mad, surely I would be free to come and go? Who would notice?

Huw Pengellin was standing outside Barrett's where all the activity was. In all probability the father of this child who weighed so heavily. The sight of him brought another thought to feed my worry: my brother, Rere. I had been close to finding him! But now if I travelled over to Porirua — Ngāti Toa territory — I could be forced back into the life of a mōkai: ownership. Neither Te Rauparaha nor Te Rangihaeata followed the Christian ways as far as I had heard.

A survey peg was planted right in middle of the Mission garden. Another outrage. I pulled it out and tossed it into the scrub. The baby, disturbed by my bending, kicked. Rest easy, little one. No one will dictate to us. I reached a hand inside the wrapping of my warm blanket to cradle my stomach. This one would not be taken.

Later that week, still at Te Aro pā — but for how long? — Huw appeared with news of Rere.

'I sent him a letter a while back, and someone from up at Taupō pā has replied that Te Whaiti wants to visit the Colonel. He is coming soon and will bring Rere with him.'

I could have hugged this Welshman, but he was too short and I too cumbersome. 'Rere is coming here? To the Mission?'

'Well, to Thorndon. I think his master — is Te Whaiti his master, do you think? — wants to ask a favour of the Colonel. They say that Te Whaiti is ill. He may need Rere to help with the translation.'

'It will be his tribe wants to ask a favour and are using them to interpret. Are settlers arriving in his area?' My bones ached. 'Can we sit down?'

We found a log sheltered from the cold breeze. Behind us someone was felling a tree, the axe-blows sending the scrub around us shivering with each thud. Somewhere else there were shouts and the rasp of a cross-cut saw.

'I think Porirua area is less settled by Pākehā,' Huw said, speaking in my language; a pleasure to hear the Muaūpoko flavour, though it was fading now. 'I think that part is laid out as country acres for those who have bought town acres.'

'What! The Company has bought land up that way? My old land? Sold by Ngāti Toa?'

Huw nodded. 'Āe. When we first met — on the beach off Kāpiti — that's what the Colonel was up to. Buying land.'

Te Rauparaha is a cruel man and my enemy, but I was surprised he would sell what he had so recently occupied. Te Rangihaeata, too. They were forever conquering new territories. I watched the tree-feller attacking the tōtara with such force. 'Greedy people are often stupid. That tree has been there for many generations. The land needs it.' I tapped Huw's knee. 'You, too, Huw. You are quick to cut down a tree if there is money in it. Will you buy some of this once beautiful land, too?'

He looked away. So that was his plan. In the silence I felt another kick. 'This baby! So active. I think you must be the father.'

Huw looked so alarmed I had to laugh. 'Are you not pleased? Martha has only one.'

'Oh, Hineroa. Martha would not be pleased. Not at all. You haven't spoken to her, have you?'

I took his hand; opened my blanket. 'Feel. Feel how strong.'

His hand wandered over my belly; stroked my warm skin with a cold hand. He touched my swollen breasts gently. And then a little roughly. That made me jump. They were too tender.

'Ah, Hineroa, look at me,' he said, his head hanging. 'I am a no-good boyo. Sorry, sorry, sweetheart.' He folded the blanket back and tucked it in tenderly. 'But I tell you this: if it is mine, then I *am* pleased. It would have to be a secret, mind.' He sighed. 'You are a splendid woman, Te Hine Tāroaroa, and a clever one. Never lose sight of that.'

It was good to hear a compliment; so rare at that time. 'Well then, no-good boyo, make sure you bring my brother to me if you hear he has arrived.'

———

Some time later, Huw was as good as his word. And just in time. I was packing a small kete and preparing to leave the Mission. Where to, I was not quite sure, but maybe Kumutoto pā across the stream might have fewer Christian rules and would welcome a strong woman with maybe a male child on the way.

The man making his way across the little bridge with Huw did not look familiar. But then Rere had only been a boy . . . Could it be him? He looked too old; used a stick. I held my breath as he stumbled, then ran to meet him.

'Rere? Can you be my brother?' He straightened; yes of course it was him: that wide grin, the way his hair grew back from his forehead. It was him.

Tears streamed down my face. For a long moment we stood close, noses pressed, hands and elbows grasped. Rere wept, too, a high keening that spoke of sorrow and loss.

At last we pulled apart, stepped back to regard each other. Huw had slipped away. Rere was dressed in settler clothes, rough trousers and a ragged jacket; a cap over his unruly curls. His feet were bare. He coughed.

I smiled at him through my tears. 'Tungāne! How I have longed to say that . . . My brother.'

He nodded, then coughed again. 'Tuahine! We must bless my friend Huw who has brought us together.' He looked around, but Huw was by now almost out of sight down by the shore, heading towards the growing settlement of Thorndon.

We moved arm in arm into the Mission house. On an empty bench, just inside the door, we sat, out of the wind. Perhaps no one would notice: I was no longer welcome there. 'You are not well? That cough!'

'Ah, don't worry. Not too bad. Many of our tribe are coughing these days. It's a bad winter.'

'I know just the herbs to help with that. We will soon have you well again.'

We fell silent. So many questions to be asked; hard to know where to start. Huw had told me about my brother's escape on a whaling ship and his return with the Colonel on the *Tory*.

'Was the tribe annoyed that you ran away?'

'Āe. At first they were very angry. In the end they left me this jacket and trousers. And gave me a wife.'

'They should be proud. That was a brave thing to do; join a whaling ship. And also you now surely have knowledge of the ways of these Pākehā who are settling here like flies.'

'Āe. You speak truly. I have some uses. Te Rangihaeata himself has brought me here today because he is angry with Wideawake and wants me to help Te Whaiti with translation.' Rere cleared his throat. Spat. 'Te Whaiti also is very unwell.'

'Do they still see you as a slave?'

'Āe. That is how it is. But surely you are the same?'

'They say the days of slaves are over. Are you free now, my brother? Free to come and go? To jump on another ship?'

Rere looked down at the sand that had drifted into the church. He picked at a loose thread on his jacket. 'Free? To go where? No. Ngāti Toa are my family now. My wife and child are at Porirua.'

'Oh, Rere! A boy? A girl?'

'A boy. Just new-born.' He smiled. 'I will always be of no importance. I must respond and obey when asked to do even women's work. But I am used to it, tuahine. They are the only friends I have. Where, Hineroa, are our Muaūpoko people now? Where? And would they welcome us? I am safe enough with Ngāti Toa. They are kind to me.'

I thought of my mother. What wise words would she say? My brother's spirit seemed broken. He was clearly sick, but broken in another way, too. Huw said he was treated as an ignorant savage on board the *Tory*. How could I heal his spirit as well as his cough?

As we made our slow way back to Colonel Wakefield's makeshift office, Rere said, 'Heu tells me you speak English, too, and even write it. You were always the clever one.'

I laughed. 'I would hate to think what Te Rangihaeata or Wideawake would say if I stood up and spoke the translation. What is the argument about?'

'About who sold what piece of land. What else! Our chiefs say that our Porirua area, the kāinga and pā and Mana Island, were never part of any agreement. The Colonel says it is down on paper, written and signed. The Pākehā put such trust in marks written on paper! Te Rangihaeata says the paper has no use except to wipe—' He grinned. 'I can't say that in English now, can I?'

'I see your difficulty.'

'But, tuahine, if you are living here among so many white people you must take care. Our tribes are growing angry.'

'Here, too. Minarapa says the chiefs this side of the harbour were not included in the negotiations. I believe it was all that show-off Wharepōuri's doing. He liked to be seen handing out the white-man gifts. It's true enough that there are many cooking pots and blankets and axes to be seen here.' I touched the wool of my brother's jacket. 'So tempting, eh? All these wonderful things. A woollen blanket. An iron cooking pot. I should not be so hard on the chiefs, I suppose.'

Interesting to hear that unrest was spreading. I assured him that I would take care. Also that I would come and visit him with herbs to cure that chest of his. 'Is it safe, do you think, for me to come and go? I do not accept that I am a slave or even bonded in any way.'

He put an arm around me — as much for support as in brotherly love, I thought. 'Let us ask Heu. I think if Heu brought you, you would be safe. He has invited us to eat with his family; he wants our blessing for his new whare and piece of land.'

'New whare? So he *has* bought land?'

'He has. Not far from here.'

'He'd better hammer his pegs in deeply,' I said.

# HURRAH FOR THE MOTHERLAND!

## HUW PENGELLIN

*THORNDON FLAT, LATE 1840*

I failed Martha's expectations — and my own — twice, see. Once coming back without a fortune from the Spanish war, and then the misery of the foundry. So this little hut on our own piece of land was like finding the pot of gold at the end of a rainbow. Bryn helped me build it, and we had it up in a week. Two small rooms, a brick fireplace, an iron roof (no less!), a wooden door that swung on British hinges, which was a rarity. Some of the walls slab; the rest ponga logs which would be replaced when Bryn brought his next load of timber across the harbour. Best of all, the light in my Martha's eyes when she looked on me.

My quarter-acre had a frontage onto Hill Street; not near to the Wesleyan Mission, but never mind, it was a desirable area. For a full week now I had walked out of a morning, out of *my own door*, felt the land under my feet and marvelled. Who would ever have dreamed? A second son and a wife with no dowry now landowners on Hill Street! 'Street' was a rather grand name for the dirt track that rose up from another track named after Mr Molesworth's brother the Earl, who had remained in England. I had to explain to Martha, who wanted a view, that when more sections were cleared, sure we'd be able to see the entire harbour and all the excitement of ships coming and going. Liddy's unpleasant employers up the hill lived in a house whose glazed windows and fancy doors came out from England and whose walls were made of Australian brick. Just you wait, I told Martha — maybe more than once, I was that excited

— and we will match their house in a year or two. Who's to stop us?

She told me to calm myself and stay clear of her washing lines with all my dancing and prancing!

The day Hineroa and Rere paid us a visit was the same day the new Commissioner arrived. What a sight! What a performance; you could make a fine drama out of it. Martha had missed it. Liddy, too. So I was in the middle of recounting the drama with full impersonations when my friends arrived. The hut was crowded. Liddy helping Martha fold sheets; the three children chewing their bread and bacon at the great slab of rough-sawn wood which served as table. A nice cosy fire burning in the brick fireplace.

'Haere mai!' I shouted. You cannot imagine the pleasure it was to welcome still more guests to my own residence. Then switched to English for introductions. This was the first time Liddy had met Hineroa. Rere was new to them all.

Thank goodness Hineroa was wrapped in a blanket. Her swollen belly not obvious, though you could count on Martha's sharp eyes to notice. My dear wife shooed the children from the table and urged the visitors to come inside. 'Sit down, sit down. Huw is telling us about the military. Did you see them arrive?'

She poured tea, almost as proud as me to have guests, while I continued the story.

'In comes the ship. Not more settlers this time, you'll be glad to hear, Hine, but Lieutenant Shortland and thirty soldiers sent by Governor Hobson. Straight over to Pito One; rowed ashore, every infantryman smart in their red and white. Down come the flags quick-smart. They tear down the Company flags, the Māori flags, even the grog-shop flags that signify nothing much, you'd have to say.'

Martha interrupted my lively flow. 'Huw Pengellin, you are making all this up. You have been over this side all day. How do you know what shenanigans were happening across the harbour?'

Well, it was all over Thorndon, I told her. 'Soon as Shortland set sail for this side, every available craft followed to watch the fireworks. Molesworth came in his cutter. And Evans. Te Puni and Wharepōuri came with them. So, they landed down near Pipitea pā. Soldiers first. Then Lieutenant Shortland in full uniform. He lined up his contingent and marched up, trying hopelessly to keep them in some sort of formation over the rough ground. Oh, it was a sight!'

Hineroa frowned. 'It is not a joke, Huw. I saw them come. They took over two whare built by some other person. Now they are housing themselves in the barracks that Wideawake is building on top of native gardens. And why have they come? Do you know that, since you seem to have all the answers?'

'Aye, well, I suppose you are in the right there. But the confrontation was what we all wanted to see. Between Shortland and Wakefield. The Colonel hastily bedecked in his full military uniform that the Spanish government awarded him. The newly arrived contingent smartly to attention. Down comes Wakefield's Company flag. Up goes the Union Jack. Smart salutes from the soldiers.

'Well, you could tell the Colonel was seething. He is used to being top dog, see, and all paying him due respect. Shortland gives him a nod. "Mr Wakefield," he says — the emphasis on the "Mr" — "I am ordered to read this proclamation by Lieutenant Governor Hobson."

'Which he reads. See, word has reached Hobson up in the north that the Colonel and the Company are running their own republic down here in Port Nicholson and have no desire to answer to the British government.' I looked around at them all and spread my hands to make the point. 'Which is more or less true. The Company makes the rules we live by. The Company punishes wrong-doers and puts them in prison. The Company decides where roads and public buildings will go.'

'And what native land', said Hineroa, 'will now be used for white people's houses.'

I was not going to let Hineroa's lecturing spoil my tale. 'So it seems this Shortland — a fussy little fellow, if you ask me — is to be Colonial Secretary, whatever that means. All prisoners in the jail at Pito One to be handed over. He will make the rules. Someone is coming to investigate the land transactions.'

Rere, who had sat quietly sipping his tea, broke in. 'So did Wideawake fight back?'

'Well, look you, Colonel was not pleased. Not at all. Anyone who knows him could see. Maybe in his haste to dress up fine he forgot his cheroot. For once, he had no smoke to blow out. Nothing he could do, though. Just smile through gritted teeth. Shook hands with Shortland. Said, stony-faced, that all the settlers were loyal to the Crown and that the Colonial Secretary was welcome. But some of the landowners, crowding in to hear what was being said, were annoyed. Didn't take to Shortland. One shouted out from the back that we were doing just fine without any government laying down law. That we had survived these months with no trouble, so the soldiers could all go back north and leave us to get on with ruling our own settlement.'

Hineroa managed a tight smile. 'Our chiefs quarrel, too,' she said. 'Te Aro and Kumutoto are unhappy with Te Puni. Ngāti Toa unhappy with everyone. I see trouble ahead. For all of us.'

Rere coughed. Martha put a plate of stew in front of him. 'Huw, love, pay some attention to your guests. Hineroa, would your brother tell us how *his* meeting with *Mr* Wakefield went?'

Rere smiled his thanks and ate, but stayed silent. Hineroa watched him in that careful, quiet way of hers. The hand that she laid on his shoulder was tender. Then she answered for him. 'I slipped in and watched along with a crowd from Pipitea. Wideawake did not hold back at *that* meeting. Nor did Te Rangihaeata. The chief shouted and danced and raised his stick on high. He pointed out that settlers were moving onto native gardens at Porirua. That the land was never sold. That it is Ngāti Toa's right, alone, to sell food to the white men. That he will block any white farmers bringing goods to Thorndon for sale. Or to Pito One.'

'True,' said Rere, taking heart from his sister's lively account, 'Te Whaiti spoke all this to Wideawake. Wideawake blew smoke like always. His eyes very angry. Wideawake said my chief signed at Kāpiti. And got many blankets and guns for the land. He said the land belongs to the Company.' He shook his head. 'We were afraid to say these words to Te Rangihaeata. No use those two talking. But Wideawake should be careful. Shortland, too. Te Rangihaeata is a very proud man. He will not be beaten.'

———

Later, when Liddy and the girls had gone back to the immigrants' barracks and Rere and Hineroa had left, too, I sat beside my Martha. Tucked a few curls back into her bun; played with her ear in a way she always enjoyed. A happy time to end the day. She looked tired. The washing business was surely exhausting, but she never complained. I took her hand, wondering how to introduce the subject. She raised an eyebrow and told me to say what was on my mind. She knew me too well. I cleared my throat. 'It seems Hineroa has to leave the Mission because of her condition. Would she be useful helping you with the washing? Or Liddy with the Hardings' garden?'

Martha removed her hand. 'Hineroa is a very outspoken woman. She might not fit in. Or want such work.'

I judged it best to leave the matter. 'Think about it, then. Tomorrow I will accompany her and Rere back to Porirua. She is worried about her brother's health. And her own safety.'

Martha eyed me very sharply. 'You have your own family to worry about, Huw. You are away too much as it is.'

# THE GUNRUNNER

## HUW PENGELLIN

*PORT NICHOLSON, LATE 1840*

I found Hineroa, rolled in her blanket, outside Te Rangihaeata's pā at Ngāūranga, sheltering under a group of tall tree ferns. She was shivering a little, but greeted me warmly enough.

'Would the chief's wife not welcome you inside?' I asked her.

'I do not wish to accept hospitality from a man who killed my parents,' she said.

'But Rere is happy to?'

'Rere is bonded to him.' She sighed. 'He accepts our customs. Sometimes I wish I were more like my brother. I do not always agree that our ways are good. But today I feel as if I do not belong anywhere. I do not have a tribe. And the Mission will only accept me if I marry stupid Hone.'

She moved a little deeper among the sheltering ponga. 'You go inside, Huw. Te Rangihaeata will welcome you. He fights against Wideawake, but he is friendly to any white man who might do business with him. Already I have seen a white man go inside. No doubt a trader. I will wait here for you.'

I had left, to Martha's displeasure, and walked from Thorndon Flat around the foreshore to reach Ngāūranga, where the Ngāti Toa chief kept a small establishment for trading purposes. The bridle track up the hill and over towards Porirua met the shore there. Te Rangihaeata had built a comfortable whare close to the water and palisaded it. That gave him access to the ships which arrived in the harbour. I took time to admire the carvings on the posts that stood either side of the entrance. I knew the chief was a fine carver, and wanted to please him with a few compliments.

Despite Hineroa's reassurances, I felt nervous. The chief's savagery was legendary. I waited at the entrance until one of the wives called me in. When I replied in her language, her smile broadened.

'Haere mai! Te Rangihaeata is with another man of your race, but he will welcome you. Perhaps you will be of some use.'

The whare was large. Sleeping mats lined the floor on both sides of the room. At the far end I recognised the chief from that time on board the *Tory*: a fine, decorated mat draped around his shoulders and the white-tipped black feathers in his hair. He was seated on the floor with an array of guns laid out before him. Someone — not Rere — seemed to be translating. A white man squatted awkwardly beside the guns.

At first I didn't recognise the trader. The only light in the room was from the open doorway and a small square opening in the wall beside it.

Te Rangihaeata motioned me to come forward. He seemed friendly enough and greeted me politely. I replied in what I hoped was a suitably formal and humble fashion, and was rewarded by a curt nod of approval. Not a full nose-to-nose greeting, but reassuring nevertheless.

'This man is offering to sell me these guns,' said the chief. 'Do you understand weapons? Are these of good quality?'

Clearly, he didn't recognise me from the *Tory*. Just as well, perhaps. 'I can tell good from bad,' I said, and approached carefully. The gun-runner rose and turned to face me.

It was Gareth. A thinner, gaunter, more ragged Gareth, but undeniably my brother. For a moment we stared at each other. Then Gareth raised a finger towards his mouth. The movement of his hand was slight but clearly meant to silence me.

A wave of anger left me breathless. How dare Gareth be trying to make some kind of profit when he had stolen Liddy and Martha's farm? How could he be here instead of imprisoned over in Australia?

Gareth proffered a hand, which I ignored. Te Rangihaeata watched closely.

'So, then,' said Gareth, his eyes now flashing anger, 'tell this native that I am offering top quality.'

I answered in English, which I hoped the chief's translator would repeat. 'This "native" is a powerful chief who is quite capable of killing you right here on the spot if he understands that you have insulted him. Or cheated him.' I picked up a musket. Turned to Te Rangihaeata and spoke directly to him in te reo. 'This is poor quality. It is from the past. Also I can see that it is not new. Someone has polished the metal to make it seem so. If you want to buy, I suggest a low price.'

The chief's quick glance over to Gareth was chilly. 'Āe. I had thought so myself. Good advice.'

It gave me great pleasure to think that my big bullying brother did not understand.

'On another matter, chief: would you release your bonded man Rere to guide us up to Porirua? His sister is here and would like to bring certain healing herbs and cures to your people. She has skill in this area. She has heard that there is illness among your people.'

Te Rangihaeata inclined his head, muttered something to his wife, who was sitting at some distance, and turned back to Gareth. An imperious wave of his hand dismissed me.

Outside, still fuming, I waited with Hineroa. 'I cannot come with you,' I said, 'but Te Rangihaeata has given you permission to go with Rere. I think you will be free to come and go.'

Gareth was still inside when Rere came out carrying a small bundle and a stick. I embraced him, and then Hineroa. But my attention was on the rowing boat drawn up on the sand where a young man was fidgeting, glancing up at the imposing palisade, clearly ready to run for it if there was trouble.

I wished brother and sister safe travelling. 'I will try to come and see you. But now I have family business to see to.'

Hineroa came close to me. 'If you come,' she murmured 'you will see your child. I think it will be born soon.'

They disappeared up the track and were swallowed by the bush. Hineroa carried both bundles, but Rere walked steadily enough. Perhaps she would be able to cure him.

———

Gareth finally stomped out of the whare and down to the shore, his face thunderous. When he saw me leaning against the boat, he checked his stride. Had he forgotten that he had just met his brother in this strange land? And in circumstances that required a great deal of explanation?

'What do you want, then?' Gareth's words were harsh, but I could see shame and — was it hope? — behind his brusque manner.

'Gareth.' I couldn't find the words. My brother often made me feel like this — torn between love and anger.

'*Never* use that name again! I am Hamish. Hamish Scott.' Gareth's hands were shaking. Was it anger or fear?

'I thought you were . . .'

'Transported? Yes. Imprisoned? Not anymore. That's all you need to know.'

Two women came down from the pā carrying bulging sacks. They dumped them at Gareth's feet. 'And the rest!' growled Gareth.

Four more sacks were carried down and deposited. Gareth called to the young man by the boat to help load the sacks.

Clearly Gareth would like to be left alone, but I waited. When the boat was loaded and the two men about to shove off, I walked down and jumped aboard.

Gareth glared. 'What did you say to that native? You ruined my deal, you idiot.'

'I told him the truth. Those were old guns. Shoddy. The chief knows all about firearms. He knew for himself.'

Gareth pulled on his oar. He was panting. He didn't look well. 'Now,' he muttered, 'I have to sell these potatoes if I am to make any profit. I need cash.'

'Te Rangihaeata uses barter. All the natives do. They are good traders.'

'And anyway,' raged Gareth, 'why should you take the side of a native? Surely it is in your interest if the natives are poorly armed? If their guns are defective? I was doing you settlers a favour.'

I stood up in the little boat; began to rock it by shifting my weight from side to side. I knew Gareth couldn't swim. 'Look you, Gareth Pengellin, I am ashamed to be your brother. We know what you have done. You sold Dai's farm and took the profit yourself, didn't you? You had no right. None that I can make out. We were never related to Dai and Martha. Now here you are trying to make a profit while Liddy is forced to work all hours of the day in some other person's garden.'

The other fellow tried to keep the boat steady. 'Hey, settle down, you fool, you'll tip us all in!'

But by now I was in a fine rage. I shifted my weight again and the laden little boat took on a slop of water. On dry land Gareth would have struck me down; here, he turned pale. Finally, I sat down. 'So now what we will do with these pitiful sacks is take them home to

Martha and Liddy. And we will discuss how else you can pay back what you owe.'

'Liddy is here?' A strange mixture of fear and hope in his voice. 'With you?'

For a while the two men rowed in silence. Something else occurred to me. 'You may not have noticed, but we are now under British rule. Union Jacks everywhere. Answerable to the Governor of New South Wales. I suppose you are an escaped convict?'

Gareth rested on his oar and the boat began to turn in a circle. His head drooped. 'Oh, Jesus, Huw, leave me alone. You have no idea . . .' Suddenly he vomited over the side. The handle of the oar flew upward. Now the boat was rocking of its own accord.

'God Almighty!' roared the other fellow, grabbing the second oar. 'Leave it till you get on shore, will you? You'll have us all drowned!' He rowed mightily and the boat straightened up, heading for the beach, then he ran the boat hard up onto the sand. He ordered us out, unloaded three of the sacks, and told Gareth that he was on his own. 'Don't need any convict trash from Australia on my cutter.' And he pushed off.

We faced each other over the potatoes. Gareth looked about nervously. A large native on a barge nearby was unloading timber slabs onto the sand. Several women from Pipitea pā were ankle-deep in the water, feeling with burrowing toes for shellfish. Further up, a soldier leaned against a tree smoking his pipe.

'Can we go somewhere more private?' said Gareth, trembling. 'Just for now? I can explain it all. I didn't mean to cheat Liddy and the girls.'

We carried the sacks up to a patch of bush. Here, we were out of sight of the soldier. Gareth sank down on his sack, head in his hands. 'I can't go back. For pity's sake, brother, don't give me away. It is brutal over there. You can't imagine.'

I looked down at him. Never, ever, had I seen my brother like this. Gareth had always been the bully, the accuser, the righteous one. The guards in New South Wales must be a tough breed to have put such fear into Gareth.

'So explain, then. If you didn't mean to cheat Liddy, what?'

Gareth told a rambling, broken story. The lawyer he sent was right: the farm had to go to a male heir. Gareth knew of no close male heir, so he thought it might as well go to him. 'I thought if I kept the money for her we could marry, see, and then she could stay on the land. Until I got back.'

But then everything went wrong. The lawyer who had falsified the relationship took a big chunk of the sale price; Gareth was transported with a bank promissory note hidden in his sock. 'But I couldn't take it, Huw — being in chains, hard labour, beatings. I got known as a troublemaker. They were going to send me to Norfolk Island. The worst prison on Earth.'

So, Gareth had used most of his money to bribe a guard to let him escape onto a trading schooner bound for New Zealand.

Gareth drew his ragged shirt closer around his shoulders. The sun offered little heat and the breeze was keen. 'You say Liddy made it over here?'

'No thanks to you.'

'She knows I bought the farm?'

'She does. She had to go to the poorhouse with the girls.'

'Ah, Jesus. She would not favour me, then?'

'Good God! Is that all you can think of? Of course not!'

Gareth stared out to sea. He picked a potato from the open mouth of the sack and looked at it. 'Well, shall we take this good food up to her? Maybe if I find work and do well she might change her mind?' He staggered to his feet. 'Could we at least try, Huw? We are family, are we not?'

I suppose I was moved by his desperation. How else could I imagine that his reception would be other than one of righteous fury? Martha, especially, would blame me if I brought Gareth to the house.

'Don't expect these poor potatoes to soften your welcome,' I told him. 'And if Martha or Liddy decides to betray you to the authorities, that's up to them.'

# TOKOTOKO RANGI — SPEAR FROM HEAVEN

## HINEROA

*PORIRUA, LATE 1840*

That track up from Ngāuranga was a challenge: me heavy with child, and my brother wheezing with every breath. Also the track itself was so different from last summer, when I had walked down with Minarapa's party. Then, the pathway was narrow, winding through dense bush, rocks carefully placed in stream beds to assist crossings. A pleasure to place one foot after another. Now the track ran straighter and was often wider, but muddy, rutted where the stream had decided to divert down or across it. Twice, as we toiled up, we came across gangs of workers, Pākehā and native, felling trees, benching the track, digging out roots.

Poor Rere kept stumbling where rainwater had gouged out deep hollows. What was the point of this wide track? It only made travel slow. What stupid Pākehā leader had ordered such work? I grumbled to Rere that Wideawake's decisions were even more difficult to understand than those of some of our own leaders.

Rere stopped, his wheezing gasps a real concern. Clearly, he could go no further, so I searched for a fallen log or a mossy bank where he might rest, but all I could see was mud and devastation. 'Can you continue, brother?' His face was pale and his cough more pronounced.

He nodded. 'They will bring horse and cart up this track,' he said when his panting slowed. 'I saw it in England. Everything is moved by horse and cart.'

I had seen the first horse arrive in Pito One. Seen Wideawake ride it, much to everyone's astonishment. Now there were several. The Mission had a wheelbarrow, which I thought a clever invention. And Reverend Buller owned a small cart but no horse. Still, it was hard to imagine that a horse could pull a loaded cart up this steep track. Surely not? Even if they managed to improve it. But Rere assured me that horses could do many surprising things.

'Shall we go on?' he said.

The next work gang we met were arguing. Two were native, two Pākehā. We waited at a distance, fearing to be caught up in a fight.

'This work is for settlers,' one man was shouting. 'The Company pays *us* to do this work. Go back to your pā!'

The native he addressed shrugged and continued to work. Perhaps he didn't understand, but neither Rere nor I felt inclined to translate. The settler tried to grab the fellow's shovel from him, but was not strong enough. When the second settler joined the fray, the second native stepped in, too. After a bit of shoving and shouting, the native workers moved up the track a bit and continued digging.

We eased our way past the settlers. Rere paused to talk to one of our countrymen. 'Does Wideawake pay you for this mahi?'

'Āe, friend. The Pākehā are not as strong as us, nor as quick. He pays us real money.'

'And is this good mahi that you do? Is it good for our people?'

The fellow shrugged, looked at the ruined track. 'Maybe good for Ngāti Toa. They can then bring food from their gardens at Porirua down to the settlers. Get rich.'

The other worker joined in. 'But now Pākehā are settling in Porirua. Soon *they* will bring their food down to sell. Te Rangihaeata will not be pleased.'

Rere smiled. 'He is already not pleased.'

The first man picked up his shovel. 'We are Ngāti Mutunga, from Te Aro Pā. What Te Rangihaeata thinks is no concern to us. We buy

Pākehā things with our pay. Cloth. Axes. Cooking pots.'

'Rum. Tobacco,' said the other, grinning. 'Very good.'

Further up the hill, the going became easier. Widening hadn't reached there. Even so, I was glad when we breasted the hill and looked into the bush-clad valley ahead.

'Sit a while,' I urged Rere. 'We are not in any hurry. Eat.' The journey to his kāinga near Taupō pā would take three days, maybe more, depending on Rere's health. We chewed on the roasted kūmara and the little pigeon meat I had cooked and then stuffed into a gourd, pouring the fat over the flesh to keep flies away.

My brother assured me that the kāinga ahead would give us a place to sleep. 'Ngāti Toa will know me,' he said, a little sadly. 'They do not admire me, but they know who I am and will not turn me away.'

But I was nervous about staying overnight at these unknown kāinga. So we sheltered that night under a large tōtara, hidden from the track. I settled Rere on a fallen log, gathered fern fronds, and laid them together with handfuls of moss in a hollow. All the time a great warmth filled me. To care for my brother eased my many worries. I unpacked my precious gift from the Mission: a small metal box, stuffed with dried moss, wrapped in green leaves. In the centre of this bundle a feebly glowing tōtara ember had survived the day. As Rere dozed, I crushed a dried fern frond and sprinkled the pieces on the ember and blew. Little flames appeared. Soon we had a fine little fire surrounded by a circle of stones. The branches of the tōtara bent low overhead as we warmed our hands and hearts.

Rere's face looked healthier — perhaps even happier. I roasted more kūmara on the hot stones, and we ate a little more of the pigeon.

I kneaded my brother's feet. 'Was it a happy time, when you ran away to sea?'

He tilted his head to one side and then the other, considering. 'Āe. Mostly good. Not all.'

I thought of him when he was young. The way he preferred making up stories and playing jokes to learning a warrior's skills. 'Was it hard mahi on the ship?'

'Hard, yes. I liked it better in England.'

He told me of a wide river and huge buildings either side. Every day ships large and small arrived along the river and tied up. He worked there, loading and unloading the boats.

'You cannot begin to imagine, sister. Not even in your dreams. Tall buildings built entirely from stone! They stretched away from the river, row after row after row all filled with people. I carried sacks of fruit and vegetables, and many other things I knew no name for. Or what purpose they might serve. Carts drawn by horses carried these goods away then returned with yet more sacks and bundles and crates for loading back on the boats.'

Rere's eyes widened as he spoke, remembering such sights. Sometimes his words came with a smile — like his first taste of a fruit called an orange; others a frown of distaste: 'There was much dirt — underfoot, in the great river's water and in the very air we breathed. I was disgusted to see men throw all kinds of rubbish in that river.'

After no more than one Matariki, he said, he longed for clean air, the trees and rivers of our country; to hear our tongue spoken again, even though he knew his return would bring some kind of punishment. He had no permission from Ngāti Toa to leave. When he heard that the ship *Tory* was taking on hands for a voyage back home he joined the crew.

'I am glad you came home, brother.'

He settled back against the trunk of the tōtara. 'Āe, sister; it was like a game to me. Fun to begin with.'

We tucked into each other, cloaks pulled tight, and settled for sleep. Rere whispered to me: 'Do you think my illness is tokotoko rangi? Are the gods angry that I — a mōkai — ran away?

I pulled him closer. 'No, brother. Your illness is mate tangata; I am sure it comes from the Pākehā, not a punishment from the gods. I have seen such an illness in white people. They call it consumption. Perhaps you caught it breathing that dirty air over there. The tohunga will not be able to cure you, I fear.'

———

Our welcome, two days later, at Rere's kāinga was disappointing. No welcome call greeted us. Wailing rather. Rere's wife was ill, their baby feverish. Many others in the kāinga lay listless or coughing. Three children had recently died. It was the spotted fever disease brought by the Pākehā. I had seen measles in Pākehā children: a dangerous and easily spread disease, but only occasionally fatal. At this kāinga it seemed that none of the little ones survived.

Down at the stream the tohunga was immersing a feverish child to cool him. His chant entreated the gods to free the child of the curse. The boy moaned and thrashed and then lay still.

I should not have spoken out. It helped neither the child nor my brother, but the words were out before I knew it and I could not take them back. 'I have seen our people die of that treatment. The cold sinks into the chest and brings on a more deadly disease.'

The tohunga glanced once in my direction without pausing his chanting.

'It is a disease of the white people, not tokotoko rangi,' I said. 'Can't you see that they are worse off, not better? They start to cough! He will catch a disease of the chest!' Hasty words. My cursed sharp tongue. The tohunga turned, pointed a finger at me and glared.

The mother of the sick child grabbed my arm and dragged me away. 'Who are you, you stranger, to insult our tohunga? Go away! Go out of this kāinga! If my son dies, the curse will rest on you and your unborn child.'

The tohunga continued his chanting. The baby died that day.

Heavy-hearted, I collected kawakawa and mānuka leaves and others that I remembered my mother using. I laid them on hot stones, covered them with wet fern fronds and invited Rere's wife to sit beside the pungent steam with the baby. 'Breathe, breathe!' The wife's cough was eased, but the baby could not take in the steam. Alas, he was past help. My little nephew.

Rere wept as his son was taken away from the kāinga to die. 'Auē. I am surely cursed. I have offended the gods.' He would not look at me; would not allow me to comfort him. The wife, also, now a little better, vented her anguish on me. 'Leave us in peace. The tohunga is our healer. How can you know what is best when you don't belong here?'

A bitter moment. This was not at all how I hoped it would go. I had imagined myself healing the sick as my mother used to; being praised for my skill and welcomed at Rere's kāinga. I had hoped my healing skills might earn my brother a higher status. But in fact the opposite was true. I had no standing there.

The word soon passed around that I was Muaūpoko — a tribe never to be trusted by Ngāti Toa. It seemed that over time the kāinga had perhaps forgotten — or learned to accept — Rere's tribal origins. Now he was tainted all over again.

# WAEWAE

---

## HINEROA

*PORIRUA, A WEEK LATER*

For a few days I stayed on, hoping that the tensions between Rere, his wife and me might ease. They did not. One day, feeling desperate at this rejection — at my inability to care for Rere — I walked down to the sea.

The flat-topped island Te Mana o Kupe, Te Rangihaeata's stronghold, was catching the last of the sun's rays, the sea calm. As I watched, the clouds flared: crimson and gold near the horizon, deep purple above. The white-hot sun drowned — half a sphere, a quarter and then gone. My hopes drowned, too. I sat on. Further north along this same coast I had met Minarapa and Huw Pengellin. At a time when I had felt a better life might be possible. Now I felt that the circle had closed.

The earth still held the sun's heat. I caressed a warm stone. Crying is a weakness, but it was a bitter blow that Rere should turn away from me. He was sick and needed me, but the sickness had also crushed his fighting spirit. I would not be able to heal him without his acceptance.

The baby kicked. I eased my back against the rock to give the baby more room. A warm trickle ran down my leg. I groaned. Not now, surely not now? But I realised, as the first weak spasm tugged at my back, that it was indeed now. I stood carefully. My last baby, born many years ago, came quickly, not like the first who struggled for hours to emerge. Slowly I walked back up towards the kāinga. There was an old white-haired kuia who had smiled to see me steaming herbs for Rere's wife. Perhaps she would help? A contraction gripped. Auē! This baby would come quickly.

Up above, on the brow of the hill, someone was watching. Not the white-haired woman I remembered, but another, holding a kete. The woman beckoned. I staggered up the last steep slope.

The woman smiled. 'Āe, I thought so. I would recognise that tall woman anywhere. We were slave women together at Raumati last year.'

'Mere! This is my lucky day after all. Oooh!' Another contraction arrived. 'Is there somewhere we can go?'

The older woman nodded, took my arm and led me into the bush. 'I have been sent here to help with burials, so it is a pleasure to help with a birth. I saw you arrive and thought there can hardly be two women so tall. There is a birthing place in here — belonging to the kāinga where you stay. No one will bother us today, I think. Here.'

What a relief to see the small clearing, sheltered by trees; two posts set in the ground, close together. I squatted and gripped the posts, straining at them until the contraction passed.

Mere had been collecting flax for bindings. There were several dead whose legs must be bound into a sitting position for burial. With her fingernail she separated a long strip of flax and laid it on the ground. 'I will come back,' she said, 'but if the baby comes soon, you can tie the cord with this.'

I was too distracted to reply.

Alas, it was not a quick birth after all. The contractions came fast, but the baby would not emerge. Oh, where was Mere? Surely it was the right moment to push? Something must be wrong. In all my years of bondage I had never felt so alone. I had a sudden memory of the stink and boiling black smoke of the whaling station; of the kindness of Jimmy the Goat, who taught me to read; of my mother's bravery, standing up to Te Rangihaeata in the certainty that she was about to die. Why was I remembering all this? Was I, too, about to die; this precious baby with me?

Cautiously I let go of the pole with one hand and reached down. Surely this was the baby's head? But why was it stuck? I felt again and realised it was not the head my fingers were touching but the baby's bottom! Oh, this would need help. I tried to stifle my screams as I felt my body splitting. Somehow I needed to free the little legs. Surely if only one leg could be coaxed out, the rest would follow. 'Help me, little one,' I whispered. 'Come on, you must work, too.' And reached down again, feeling for a foot or knee.

As if the baby heard me, one leg, then the other, struggled to come through, and then in a rush the whole lovely child emerged, feet-first — whakawae — but alive, with cord tangled around one foot and bloodied from my split skin, but alive and bawling and my own. No one was there to pronounce whether the baby should be left out to die or adopted by a chief and raised to be a fighting warrior. My own.

The whenua passed out of my body. I tied the cord with the flax and used my teeth to cut it. The baby's cries were softening now. I cradled her. 'Hello, little one. Nothing wrong with your lungs. Maybe you will be as sharp-tongued and wilful as your mother. And grandmother. Oh bless you.'

Mere arrived with a kete for the whenua. She clucked in concern at the blood. 'This was not your first, surely?'

'No, no, but she was born feet-first. Is the tearing bad?'

Mere gathered a handful of rain-damp moss and inspected the split, before stuffing the moss firmly in place. 'You will heal. So she was whānau whakawae? The gods are smiling on you, girl. Feet-first into the world means a smart child who will walk with confidence.' She looked up as a fresh bout of wailing came from the distant kāinga. 'The gods know we need some strong ones these days.' She pulled back my cloak to inspect the now-sleeping baby. 'Welcome, little Waewae. Ah. I see. The father a whaler?'

I didn't elaborate.

Mere smiled. 'You were always a mystery, girl. Who could ever tell what you were thinking?' She got ready to leave me then — another death to be managed. 'Stay here and rest anyway. There is no one in the hapū about to give birth. Change that dressing in the early morning when the new moss is fresh with dew.'

I thanked her. My exhaustion now overlaid with the deepest happiness. 'Bless you, Mere.'

'Where will you bury the whenua? This is not really your place.'

'I have somewhere in mind. Will you help my brother while you are visiting this place?'

'I will. But I fear for him. Come back soon.'

My eyes were closing. The baby suckled. I slept.

# HINEROA'S TŌTARA

## HINEROA

*KĀPITI COAST, A FEW DAYS LATER*

The view as I trudged up over the hill filled me with a sudden dread. There, out over a wild sea, lay Kāpiti Island, its seven peaks cloud-capped, the bush-clad slopes dark against a gloomy sky. I braced myself against the buffeting wind, one arm cradling the baby, the other holding my cloak tight. On my back the whenua, wrapped in pukapuka leaves and tied with flax, was packed safely in the kete. My fear — perhaps unfounded, but real all the same — was that I might be reclaimed by Te Rauparaha or one of his chiefs; that I could be returned to slavery, either on the mainland or — worse — on the island. My legs threatened to give way.

I told myself that things were different now. As I had walked around the inlet and up towards this point where the sea stretches far into the distance, I had noticed white people cutting trees, ploughing land, burning dry brush. Only a year since I came this way with Minarapa, but now there were many open clearings. I walked gingerly past several sheep and a cow. A whole plot was covered in some golden, waist-high kind of grass. Surely these were signs that the old ways no longer ruled? That tribes no longer fought each other? Perhaps I would be safe returning to the place where I grew up.

I breathed deeply, steadied myself and the baby and began the descent. Down below, where the waves crash, I knew of rocks bristling with shellfish. My mouth watered. This was the right thing to do; the right place to bury the whenua.

Late in the afternoon, strengthened by a meal of the plentiful mussels and the new shoots of mouku, I arrived at Paekākāriki. It worried me to find no sign of new Pākehā settlers. A few remaining whalers would be here, no doubt, drinking at Scotch Jock's. Best keep clear of them. They would all be affiliated to one chief or another. Quietly I circled around a kāinga where children played and cooking fires smoked. It looked peaceful, but they would not likely welcome a Muaūpoko traveller.

I entered the deep bush at the foot of the towering, sea-facing cliffs. Oh! The stream where my mother and I had collected herbs! And there the tōtara tree — much taller now — where my mother had buried my own whenua. I sat with my back against the trunk and fed the baby. I spoke to my mother. 'What name should she have, this little one? Your granddaughter. Is Waewae suitable, since she came feet-first?' I had no tohunga to suggest a name, nor any experience of naming.

Nearby, closer to the stream, a second, younger tōtara was struggling up through the dense bush. Perhaps its roots joined beneath the soil with those of my own tree. I started to dig. What was the proper way? I possessed no experience of burying whenua either. How deep? Should the kete be buried, too, and the wrapping of leaves, or just the bloody afterbirth? I decided on the leaves without the kete. It was peaceful, digging in the sandy soil, my hands enjoying the dampness. The sweet smell of the young tree mingled with the sharp, salty tang of the wind off the sea. When it was finished, I stood and sang what I remembered of a song my mother sang. The baby slept.

A child, half-hidden behind a kawakawa bush, was watching me. I could see tangled hair and dark, solemn eyes. And then the bush shook and the face disappeared. My first thought was to move away quickly, but then I decided, no: this was *my* place, and is now my daughter's place. I picked up the baby and stood tall, waiting. Someone would come.

Soon a woman of about my own age emerged from among the trees, baby on hip, led by the solemn-eyed child. We looked at each other for a long moment, the newcomer frowning. I tried a smile and a word of welcome, signifying that I was welcoming the other to *my* place. It was perhaps too bold a move. The other's frown deepened.

But then the woman stepped forward; accepted the welcome. 'I know who you are. You are the tall one — Hineroa. You served at the battle of Kūititanga where my husband was killed.'

So she would be Te Āti Awa. 'I was there.'

'You were the slave who brought my husband's body back to the pā, when others were fearful of the Pākehā ship and the white men on the beach.'

'I am no longer a slave,' I said, trying to sound stern. 'My whenua is buried here, and now my daughter's also.'

The woman laughed. 'You are a bold one! Some would say once a slave, always one.'

'I would not say that.'

'And some — of my hapū — would say that this is Te Āti Awa land and you have no right to come here. Or bury whenua here.'

I eyed her fiercely. 'Do *you* say that?'

The woman put down her squirming toddler, who dashed off towards the stream. 'I say, thank you for bringing my dead husband back from that battle. A battle which should never have taken place.'

'You speak truly,' I said. 'They say it was the last battle. It was a stupid decision — one which robbed you of your husband. So where is *your* whenua buried?'

The woman ran to rescue the toddler, who screamed at being deprived of the shining water. 'Auē. I was born during our migration from Taranaki. My whenua is buried in a strange place and my mother died before she could tell me where.'

We sat together, two mothers, under the tōtara and talked — of children and families and food — simple, ordinary things. After a while the other woman rose and apologised for her lack of an invitation to the kāinga. 'You are very noticeable. Some in our hapū will remember who you were bonded to and will expect you to return. Also . . .' She hesitated. 'Are you and the baby well?'

'We are.'

'There is a great deal of sickness among hapū on the coast. But we, here in our kāinga, are well. Our tohunga says white people have brought the sickness and your baby . . .'

'Is half-white, yes. You have a wise tohunga. I think these diseases are spread by Pākehā. But Pākehā children don't seem to die of it. Strange, eh?'

'Āe. Strange. I will send my boy here with a kete of food in thanks for bringing my husband home.'

'Thank you. And you are welcome to sit here in my place and think of your own whenua, wherever that might be, and hope for better times.'

I sat on as the light faded, listening to birdsong. The boy brought food, laid it at a distance and disappeared again. Tomorrow I would go back to Rere. Perhaps there was some way I could help. If I could learn to curb my tongue.

# STARVING SETTLERS

## MARTHA PENGELLIN

*PORT NICHOLSON, AUTUMN 1841*

H uw was right. By autumn the trees in front of us were felled and a fine view of the harbour had emerged. Also more sun for my washing lines. Less pleasurable was the sight of Gareth drilling the volunteers down on the beach. 'Volunteers' was hardly an accurate term, as all the settlers had no choice but to give up their time at least once a week for this marching in line up and down the beach, muskets or some imitation gun over their shoulders. All very well, but who was to pay them for work-time lost? Wakefield and his cronies had made the rule originally, and now Lieutenant Shortland continued the practice. We all knew the natives were becoming restless at the loss of land. But Huw said that the sight of our disorderly men trying to march in line only made the natives giggle. He was not keen on the drill.

Goodness knows how Gareth wormed his way into the Colonel's good books; persuaded him that he was experienced at moulding a rabble of settlers into an army. When Huw had brought him up to the house some months ago, Gareth had been ragged, nervous, half-starved. Now he was back to his loudmouthed, bullying ways, working on the Porirua Road and earning enough money to build a little hut on land which I was sure he did not own.

Once, when Huw was away, he had come up behind me as I was bringing in the washing. The sheets shielded us from prying eyes, I suppose. The wretch wrapped his arms around me, pressing tightly into my back. The stench of liquor on his breath.

'Gareth Pengellin!' I had shouted for all the world to witness. And when he cringed away, I turned on him. Back in Wales — in that other life — I would have run.

'You will never touch me again, Gareth Pengellin, or the authorities will hear your name and know who you are.'

'Have a heart, Martha dear. Your brother-in-law . . . a harmless embrace . . .'

But he was uneasy, I could see, so I pressed on. 'And Liddy. I've seen you look at her in that way of yours. She doesn't want your attention. Now off you go; I have work to do.'

I turned my back on him. Left him standing among the sheets. It pleased me then to think how I had changed; how much bolder I had become. Having my own business was part of it. I was almost as strong as a man from all the pounding and wringing and hanging out. My arms and face freckled from the sun. My hair bleached, too — more gold than brown — and the curls more unruly than ever.

Liddy chided me. 'Wear a bonnet, Martha, you'll ruin your looks.'

But I won't. I love the sun. And, anyway, Huw likes me this way. I am his wild fairy woman, come out of the wilderness to tempt him.

As I folded the sheets and sorted them into piles for delivery to the three homes I serviced, the children, mud-spattered and barefoot, came whooping up from the stream.

Alfie held up a battered tin. 'Look, Mam, what we caught!' He tripped and fell with a crash, sending a shower of creek-water and a little crayfish into the air.

I shouted at them to stay away from my washing. 'Holly, you imp, you're filthy. Meg, wash your sister off this moment!'

All three stopped with exaggerated gestures of care, and tiptoed, giggling, over to the rain-barrel.

'Dip some out,' said I, but it was hard to keep a straight face with them all three so happy. 'We don't want the whole barrel filthy, do we?'

They knew the drill, but could forget. I tried to have them clean and quiet for when Liddy came to pick them up. Poor Liddy. The temporary 'barracks' where her shipload of immigrants had been housed was simply a large rat-infested barn, scarcely better than the quarters on the ship. The immigrant ships had arrived so thick and fast that no other quarters were available. And there, months later, Liddy and the girls still lived. Shame on the Company. Only canvas partitions between families; drunkenness and violence rife. Not a happy place for two young girls, but Liddy insisted on keeping them with her — partly a protection for herself, no doubt. She had a new employer up on the Tinakori track: three days a week for a landowning family who treated her unkindly, and refused to have the girls mingling with their own two children.

Over the hill she came now, weary but pleased to see her girls running to meet her.

'Mam, Mam!' they squealed. 'Look what we found!' And it's hugs and kisses all round and careful inspection of the crayfish.

'It's a kēkēwai. We should cook it,' said Holly, who was almost as quick as Alfie with native words.

I could see a fresh bruise on Liddy's arm, but said nothing. Liddy had her pride. Her employer was rough and demanding, and Liddy was not one to stand up for her rights. Truth was, she had no rights. She must stick it out until she had worked off her passage. Three more months, and then Liddy could come and work with me.

Liddy sat on the bench with the children gathered around her. 'Look,' she said to them, 'down on the beach there. Isn't that Bryn's cutter? What's he up to?'

Her eyes were sharp. I would never have spotted Bryn's boat among the crowd. The harbour was always full of boats, from the large immigrant ships to smaller barques and cutters from Australia or further north or simply across from Pito One. Every day new goods unloaded — windows and doors, hardware of all description, sheep and cattle and horses, seed and farm implements — and offered for sale, either at the market down at Pipitea or in the general stores springing up next to Clyde Quay or Lambton Quay. Huw was a great one for picking up bargains: the old try pots for my wash tubs a fine example.

Alfie squinted down at the activity. 'Yes, it's Bryn. Shall we run down and invite him up?'

And he and the girls were away off before I could say nay.

Bryn and Arial had done well for themselves. Not only had they paid for their own passage, they had had money left over to buy the materials for a little boat. So Bryn was cutting timber over in the Hutt Valley, sawing it into planks and bringing the timber over to Port Nicholson, where it was sorely needed. A tidy business. This time, though, his cutter was loaded with people.

Bryn waved as he and the little group came up towards the settlement. 'Martha! Liddy! Come and join us! We are off up to the Colonel to complain. Would you not swell our crowd?'

His 'crowd' consisted of four men and three women, one with a child on her hip. Their clothes hung limp on skinny bodies that had clearly once filled the rags more amply. Bryn, his face sunburned, jacket straining over broad shoulders, looked too healthy in comparison. The group waited a little distance away while Bryn walked up.

'I could not fit more in my boat,' he said, 'but there are many, many like these up in the valley in sore need. The Company is treating them outrageously. Come along, would you?'

'Well done, Bryn,' I said. I'd heard something of this latest action. I brought a fresh loaf from the house and broke it into chunks for the waiting group. Passed around mugs of fresh rainwater. They would need strengthening for the walk along to Barrett's Hotel. Wakefield was bound to be there at this hour of the day.

So we joined in, Liddy and me, the children skipping along with the group, curious to know what was afoot. 'Watch and listen,' I told them. They were old enough to understand.

I was curious myself, never having been inside the Colonel's exclusive club. He and other leaders in the New Zealand Company had formed a lodge, which met upstairs in Barrett's Hotel. Membership strictly controlled. Invitation only. None of the likes of us welcome, unless our purpose was to serve their dinners. Liddy's employer belonged, and two of the families I washed for. Most evenings they drank there, gambled, so they say, and talked about life back in England. On a warm evening, laughter from the open windows would spill out over the beach, together with the rich smell of roast meat. I felt uneasy approaching the place, and was ready to turn back if I saw my employers.

Bryn was fearless, though. He marched his group into the downstairs saloon and led us up the stairs and into the club room before anyone had the wit to stop us.

Colonel Wakefield, his face flushed, cut-glass brandy balloon raised in his hand, looked up in surprise. And then annoyance.

Bryn, good man, was diplomatic. 'Sorry to interrupt, Colonel, but this is an emergency which requires your urgent attention. May we have one minute of your . . .' He looked around at the well-heeled members, 'your precious time?'

The Colonel leaned back in his chair. 'No, you may not. If there is an issue, make an appointment with the Company Secretary, Dr Evans. Please leave at once. This is a private club.'

One of the men in Bryn's little group growled. Another cleared his throat loudly. The baby started to cry.

But Bryn forged on. 'I see Dr Evans is here, Colonel. I am pleased that he can record our conversation. This group here is from the

Hutt. They represent a much larger group of immigrant labourers. They cannot wait for an audience tomorrow. They are starving. You have cut off their wages without warning. The Company promised' — Bryn's voice rose — '*promised in writing* to find them work until their passage was paid off. This situation is not right. It is not fair.'

The Colonel rose. He was clearly very angry. I edged towards the door. One or two of the club looked at their leader in surprise. They hadn't heard of this, it would seem. I held onto Alfie's hand, ready to run if there was violence. But the Hutt group remained stubbornly in the doorway, blocking our exit.

The Colonel spoke to the members, not Bryn. 'I have released these labourers from their obligation to pay off their passage. A generous action, wouldn't you think? They are free to work their little patch in the bush. To make their own way.'

Bryn raised his fine, deep voice over the murmurings from the diners. 'Their patch in the bush will not supply food until next year. What are they to live on meantime? You promised wages!'

Again, the Colonel ignored Bryn and addressed the club. He would not even look at the pitiful group. 'Too many landowners have stayed in England. It was assumed that landowners would employ the labourer settlers. The Company simply doesn't have the funds—'

One of Bryn's group raised a fist. 'Look at you all. You have plenty of funds for fine food and drink!'

'We can't feed our children!' shouted the woman with the baby.

Bryn tried to calm them, but the group moved forward. One snatched a hunk of roast pork from the buffet. Another pocketed two apples.

'Landlord!' roared Colonel Wakefield. 'Evict this rabble!'

Bryn pleaded with him. 'At least resume paid work for a month or two. They are desperate.'

'They have had a week's notice. No more wages. Now get out. Out!' Wakefield's face was purple. I thought he might take a fit, but didn't wait to see.

A group of rough sailors from below manhandled us down the stairs.

Outside, the Hutt people gathered around Bryn. Clearly they looked to him as a leader. 'What now?' asked one.

A woman from Barrett's kitchen came out with a tray of food. 'It's only scraps, but you're welcome to them.'

Plain to see those poor folk really were starving. Having eaten my bread, they carefully shared out the food, wrapped it and tucked it into pockets. They would take these scraps home to their families.

Bryn talked to them. 'Maybe I was wrong to confront him there, but it's good that the other club members know what's going on. He won't help. That's clear. We will have to help each other best we can back in the Hutt.'

As they walked back down to the cutter, I asked after Arial. 'How is she doing, Bryn? Not lonely up there in the bush? Do you have friends?' I couldn't imagine fun-loving Arial enjoying an isolated life.

'She is in need of company, true. Little Sarah is a handful. Last week she toddled off and we spent hours searching for her. Arial was out of her mind. Finally, we found her asleep deep in the bush, none the worse for her adventure. I would have brought the two of them today, but the starving settlers make a stronger point. Arial is bonny and well at least.' He was clearly proud of his wife.

'Bring her over next time you come. We can gossip in the old language and have a laugh. She was always one to raise everyone's spirits. Your Sarah should get to know our young ones, too.'

I waved the little contingent goodbye. Arial alone in dense bush: surely that was hard for her? But perhaps she, too, had changed and loved this new life?

Later Huw came home looking sheepish, as well he might. He had been drilling with the soldiers, and Gareth followed him up.

I stood square in the doorway, blocking entrance. Huw was too soft on his brother.

Huw frowned. 'He just wants a word. He has proper employment now. Just a word.'

Liddy stayed inside. I folded my arms. Said nothing.

'And maybe a bite?'

'If he comes in, Liddy and the girls will leave. You know that, Huw Pengellin.'

'She has a place to stay. He's lonely.'

'He will only plead with Liddy; try to explain; offer marriage.'

'He's my brother. He's changed his ways. Liddy could do worse.'

Liddy touched my shoulder softly. Then she pushed past, girls in tow, and walked away up to her quarters.

'Liddy!' shouted Gareth. 'Listen! I can help you!'

But she wouldn't turn or acknowledge him in any way.

Well, I was caught between Huw and Liddy, and furious with my husband. 'You should know better than to bring him here.'

'It's my home, too, sweetheart, and Gareth is my brother.' At an angry growl from Gareth, he corrected himself. 'Hamish, I should say. And Liddy needs a place of her own.' He beckoned to Gareth, who came into the house, a smug little smile tipped in my direction.

I could not be civil to that man. The pot over the fire held my attention while I held my tongue. Surely Huw could understand that Gareth would make a terrible husband for Liddy? Now that he felt safe from deportation, he was just as rude, just as opinionated, as before. Worse, possibly.

Gareth sat at the table as if he owned the place. 'Hey, Alfie boy! Didn't see you down watching the military drill with the other boys. Watch and learn, boyo, watch and learn.'

Alfie came to the table for his food, but was wary of his uncle. Caught the tension between the families, no doubt, and would always side with his cousins. He adored Holly and Meg.

'They are our friends,' he mumbled. Already he had picked up native words and scattered them among Welsh and English. Hard to make sense of his chatter some days. Children from the nearby pā also played on the beach or in the bush behind, and Alfie was happy to mingle with them. Many landowners did not allow their children such freedom. Now the boy bolted his food and then, at a nod from me, escaped outside.

My black-eyed boy was growing up wild. In a couple of years, he'd be old enough for school, but there was no school. Or none for labourer families. The Wesleyan Mission might take him, but, being around at Te Aro, a long walk for a little lad. And I had no schooling to teach him.

When I brought a kettle of tea to the table, Gareth was ranting on about the natives. A queer, excited glint to his eye. 'There's trouble, Huw, big trouble. Our militias will be needed soon enough, sure. The Company gangs up on the Porirua track are full of it. Did you hear?'

I plonked a mug of tea in front of him. 'So you say, Gareth, but Huw says the natives have cause for grievance, don't you, Huw?' It gave me a guilty stab of pleasure to see Gareth's look of alarm as I mentioned his old name.

Huw always had the latest news and enjoyed imparting it. 'They do, Martha, but this is a different matter. Te Rangihaeata has blocked the track. Up at the Porirua end he has brought down trees. Mounted a guard at his pā up there.'

Gareth laughed. 'That chief who cheated me out of my guns, we'll show him now! He chopped down a bridge that our fellows had just built. He won't get away with it.'

I waited for Huw to take the side of the natives. I don't always agree with him, but that day anything that put Gareth in his place was music to my ears.

But Huw disappointed me. He scratched sawdust out of his hair. 'I reckon he's gone too far this time. Thing is, he wants all the Porirua trade for himself and his tribe. Several settlers have cleared their country acres up his way and are growing good crops. The chief's fighting men only allow their own tribe through the blockade with their trading goods. Settlers can't bring food to Port Nicholson.'

Well, he had a point. I knew a settler family — all six of them — who would be down in the dark searching around the beach for shellfish. Soon, they would be at my door or those of other homes, begging for leftovers. A food blockade was a cruel idea with so many settlers desperate. Still, I wouldn't agree with Gareth. 'It's not only the Porirua trade that's the trouble,' I said. 'Why doesn't the Colonel do something about those poor families in the bush in the Hutt Valley? The Company promised them work, but now they are left with nothing. The Company releases you, he says, as if he is giving them a precious gift. Grow your own food, he says. Work hard, he says. He has no idea!'

'True enough,' said Huw. 'The Company is in trouble, is the thick end of it. Running out of money. Bryn and Arial say families are starving up there.'

Gareth's mug of tea slammed down on the table. 'Bryn and Arial? Would that be the Arial who is married to Cadoc Conti? I thought I saw someone who looked like Bryn the other day. Don't tell me—'

I interrupted him. 'They are here and happy with a child. Which Cadoc never managed to give her. Best forget the past, *Gareth Pengellin*.'

Perhaps he heard the threat in my voice. For a moment he sat there, lips pursed. 'I am Hamish Scott, and you know it. Will you quit goading me, woman?' But he couldn't let the argument go. 'Martha, Martha, surely you know it is wrong? She is married to Cadoc. She took his money when they ran away. What would they say in Chapel? What does the Bible say? "Thou shalt not covet thy neighbour's wife." Eh, then?' He spread his hands as if making a point from the pulpit. 'We must denounce them. Cast them out.' He looked from me to his brother. 'Huw?'

Huw shifted uncomfortably. 'It's different here. They are our friends.'

'Oh, dear me. How different? We are under British rule, are we not? They offend against God and the rule of law.'

It is hard to find the right words when the Bible teaching is quoted. Yes, I had been shocked when I first encountered Bryn and Arial on the ship. I knew what the Bible said. But they are good people, and a good family, and Welsh to boot. The fact that Arial left her husband, even took money, seemed less of a crime out here. The lines between right and wrong, the Bible teachings, felt somehow a little blurred. It was more important to survive. And survival needed a certain freedom. 'Leave it, Gareth,' I muttered. 'Nothing to be done now.'

'Nothing to be done? Do they come to Chapel?'

'No, they do not. And you will do well to keep your big, loud mouth shut. British law, you say? Are you not an escaped criminal? Should I denounce you, then? Is that my duty?'

That shut him up. After a while, he said quietly, 'I should never have been locked up. It was a peaceful demonstration.'

'Peaceful, my eye!' I shouted. 'People were killed. One rule for you, Gareth Pengellin, and another for those who offend you, eh? Well, Bryn and Arial are our friends. If you can't accept them, please don't come again to this house!' I pushed around the table and stormed out to find Alfie.

# THE PĀKEHĀ DISEASES

## HINEROA

*PORIRUA, AUTUMN 1841*

Fat blowflies droned around Rere's head. I batted at them with a switch of kawakawa leaves, but they cunningly changed direction and attacked from the other side. Rere's eyes opened as I swore.

'You have learned new curses,' he whispered. 'Do you remember our mother saying to keep curses for important matters?'

The first time he had spoken for hours. Two days ago Mere had helped me carry my brother out to this open space, a distance from the kāinga. He was dying, but the heart continued to struggle on, the breaths coming in laboured, creaking bursts.

I wiped a trickle of blood from his mouth. 'Āe, I remember. I'm surprised that you do.'

His eyes closed again. Breath bubbled in his throat. When the breathing eased, he spoke again, very faintly. I leaned in to hear. 'Those were happy times. They . . . come back to me. I thought they were . . . forgotten.'

The baby hidden under my cloak pummelled my breast and I let her suckle again. A hungry little one. These two days had been peaceful; in a strange way almost happy. Now that Rere was dying and removed from the kāinga I was free to tend him. His wife did not come. This was work for bonded people. Further away, four babies, their little skins blazing with the rash from measles, lay on the bare ground crying weakly. They would die in hours. I was fearful for little Waewae. The measles disease was spreading like wildfire through kāinga all up the coast. Children died every day.

Rere coughed, choked. Blood poured from his mouth. I held my own breath as his ceased. Then released it as he breathed again — a long, shuddering groan.

I fought the flies for ownership of his blood. 'Your memories of England? Are they happy, too?'

His eyes opened — searched for mine — closed again. 'I have seen . . . many things. Even a chief would not. No other . . . slave.'

Later, when I thought he might be sleeping, he added, 'I am glad for those memories. Carriages . . . strange sounds . . . music. They are . . . taonga for me.'

Someone was standing behind me. A touch on my shoulder. Huw Pengellin, with tears in his eyes. He kneeled beside me. 'Have I come too late?'

'Not quite. He will be pleased.'

Huw was holding his own bunch of kawakawa. That was impressive. But he had always been quick to learn new ways, as I have been with Pākehā customs. He swatted at the flies and leaned in close. 'Rere, taku hoa, my friend. This is Huw.'

Rere's eyes flew open. His cracked lips split wide in that old cheeky grin. 'You came!'

Huw laid a hand on Rere's head; let it slide to cup his wasted cheek and left it there — a tender, loving gesture. That surprised me. Even a dying slave is tapu and not to be touched. Especially the head. Another slave may, but then a slave doesn't matter. I have always thought the custom was intended to prevent anyone catching the dying person's bad luck. It seemed Huw had not learned this yet.

Huw continued to stroke his friend's cheek. 'Sorry I was not sooner. The track is blocked by bloody Te Rangihaeata's men.' He snorted. 'A dying friend was no argument. I had to talk trade. Trade with Ngāti Toa. That did the trick.'

I wanted to argue with him. Wanted, for once, to side with the

Ngāti Toa chief. 'You are changing, my friend. Now that you are a landowner you side with the Pākehā.'

'No . . . Not really.' But his eyes were on Rere.

My brother's gaze rested sometimes on Huw, sometimes me. There was an exhausted pleasure in his final minutes. Then his lips began to turn blue as if they were tattooed. He tried to speak, but all that emerged was a stream of frothy blood. As we watched, Rere's eyes, still open, turned opaque, his face paled, the rattling breath silenced.

I waited to be sure. Then I wailed, fingernails dragging down my cheeks. Across the clearing Mere, tending the dying babies, joined in. We gave him a chiefly farewell, our lament rising and falling, sobbing fading to moans, and then rising again higher and higher to set the birds joining in with their own alarm. There would be no lengthy tangihanga for a bonded person, so this would be his farewell.

When our voices died away, I noticed Huw was staring at something else. My cloak had fallen open. My beautiful baby with dark hair and eyes and skin the colour of milky tea was joining in the lament. He offered the baby a finger, which was grasped firmly.

'She is mine,' I said, with full force behind the words.

'Yes. Yours.'

But his tears, I thought, were now for more than his dead friend.

# THE RACES

## MARTHA PENGELLIN

*PITO ONE, OCTOBER 1842 (A YEAR LATER)*

For once the weather obeyed my orders. A fair breeze from the north and a lovely, warm sun dried my sheets and shirts almost as soon as I had them on the line. I'd be through by midday and able to sit quietly for an hour. Huw, in high spirits, arrived just as I was folding the last load. He was leading his mule, which he'd bought from an Australian trader a month ago. The mule was pulling a little dog-cart.

I asked, with some misgivings, where the cart came from. 'Don't tell me you were throwing dice with the whalers again?'

He grinned. 'Not quite. I have sold some flax fibre to our new rope-maker down on Lambton Quay. With part of the profit I bought, for a few shillings, two wheels that got damaged on the trip out. Then Bryn mended them for me in return for . . .' He winked. 'Shall I go on?'

I had to laugh. 'Spare me the details. As long as you don't end up in our new gaol. Flax fibre, though? That's a new enterprise, is it?'

He tied up the mule, loosened the traces. 'It is, Martha, and a lucrative one. Hineroa has a group of women down at Kumutoto working for her. They sell it to me. The demand for rope is huge. This could make our fortune.'

I folded the last sheet. 'Hineroa. She can make fibre? She works for you?'

Huw wouldn't look at me. He fussed around with the mule, which he called Muka. 'Well,' he said, 'make sure you finish your washing today. Tomorrow we are going to the races. How about that!'

He was trying to divert me. Mention of Hineroa made me uneasy. The way he watched her. And that beautiful child. When Hineroa called in to our cottage, which was quite often these days, she didn't show much interest in Huw, but even so . . . To be honest I felt rather intimidated by her. She was friendly, yes, but distant. You never felt she was paying attention. Or was it the other way around: the attention was fierce, but lacking in what I would call ordinary warmth? And the way Huw would talk to her in her own tongue excluded me.

A few days ago I had come back from delivering washing to find Hineroa sitting on our bench outside, reading our newspaper.

'Listen to this,' she said. 'They're going to race horses on the beach at Pito One. Have you ever heard of such a thing?'

I explained that horse racing was common back in England. I suppose my reply had been offhand, maybe even rude. She had that effect on me.

Hineroa had looked at me with those dark, careful eyes. 'I never saw a horse until I came here to Whanganui a Tara. They are still a little frightening to me.' She held up the newspaper. 'I think you never learned to read? Would you like to learn? Does Huw not teach you?'

It had been a simple question, asked out of curiosity, I suppose, but I felt belittled and ashamed. Of course I would give anything to be able to read, but Huw had never suggested teaching me and I was afraid that I might not succeed. And here was a native woman who had learned somehow in this wild, untamed country.

Unwanted tears stood in my eyes. 'One day. When I have time, I'll learn.'

Now, all over again I was ashamed to ask Huw details of the races. Everyone else seemed to know. 'Should we take Liddy's girls?

I don't think the Harrisons will give her leave. They are so awful to her.'

Huw was in a good mood. Any improvement in our fortunes — even the ownership of a little dog-cart — sent his mood soaring. He came behind the bench and wrapped his arms around me. Pulled me tightly back against him. 'Holly and Meg and Alfie can ride in style, maybe even you, too, love. I will walk with the mule.' He laughed and hugged me tighter. 'Sweetheart, I have such a need on me, and we are alone for once.'

'At least come inside then, you bad boy. Mrs Titch is watching.' I said, pretending alarm. But my heart was singing. Huw had not been so attentive for many months.

---

It was a long journey around the harbour to Pito One, but crowds were walking or riding along with us. Some labourers — those who had earned their passage or else had been given leave — set out early, even before dawn, like us. Alfie threatened to fall out of the cart with all his waving and shouting, determined to show off to his walking friends how grand he was.

I was being left behind. 'Alfie, enough of that,' I shouted. My ankles, swollen from standing all day, every day, over a tub, stumbled on the rough stones. Four-year-old Alfie was becoming a handful, as were many of the new settler children. With their parents so busy, they ran free with no one to discipline them.

Muka pulled the children over the bumpy track, his dainty legs finding purchase where some of the grander horses stumbled. What a sight — this great procession straggling along the coast, chatting and laughing. A spring cart full of ladies in fancy dresses and hats passed us. Another cart rumbled by, bedecked with flags and laden with chairs, no doubt destined for the backsides of the landowners' wives. I smiled to myself, thinking that the Pengellins would be sitting atop our own wee cart viewing the races in comfort, too.

By mid-morning a whole flotilla of boats of all shape and size was on the water, heading across. One of the immigrant ships, flying a motley collection of flags, especially several Company ones, brought Colonel Wakefield and his inner circle; a less impressive cutter carried Shortland, the Colonial Secretary, and government officials. Huw rattled off the details of who was who and what their rank. These days he seemed to know all the comings and goings of the settlement. He pointed out Te Rangihaeata's impressive whare as we passed Ngāūranga, and then, a little later, insisted that the children jump down, so he and I could ride. A grand moment. Off ran the children, eager to beat the wheeled carts and bullock wagons. And bless me, wasn't I smiling and waving just like Alfie! It was such a pleasure, that day. Huw, chatting at my side, clucking the mule along. All my worries and doubts dissolved under the bright sun by the sparkling sea.

'Who would have thought,' he said, winking at me, 'back there at the foundry, that we'd end up with our own business, our own cart and mule?'

'Businesses! We have two. Don't you forget your wife has a profitable business.'

'Aye. We have been blessed. Some of these folk walking today, not so fortunate.'

'Liddy for one.'

'Liddy, yes. We must find her a husband.' He held up a hand to stay my words. 'If she won't have Gareth, then another. God knows there are plenty of single men . . .'

We bumped and rattled along, chatting. I couldn't think when I had been so happy.

The scene was utter pandemonium when we arrived at the beach and tethered the sweating mule under a bush. Several groups of natives were lounging on the sand, enjoying the sights. They didn't seem to realise that they were in mortal danger from pounding hooves. A group of carousing whalers on shore-leave had dragged their boat up onto the beach. Right in the middle of the race track.

Huw pointed out a gesticulating figure decked out in a pink jacket. 'That's Jerningham Wakefield, the show-off. He's Clerk of the Course. He can't organise a tea party, let alone a day of races. Can you wait here, Martha, while I lend a hand?'

I was proud to see him speak to the lounging natives; laugh with them, then chase off a wandering pig. The natives, in no hurry, moved higher up the beach, roping a couple of other pigs and a dog as they went. A man with a handcart rolled along the beach, messing up the newly smoothed sand, calling out 'Ginger pop! Ginger pop! Ha'penny a drink. Bring up your mugs!'

My mouth filled with saliva. I handed the children two mugs and a penny. 'One for you, one for your da and me. Walk careful now; no spilling.'

And there were Bryn and Arial strolling along the beach for their mug of ginger pop!

'Arial! Come up here with us!' I called. What a delight to see them. Bryn carrying their newborn in a basket, Arial and Sarah walking hand-in-hand beside him.

They had long ago given up their assumed shipboard names. 'So many immigrants!' Arial had scoffed months ago. 'Who will be checking? There'll be plenty more like us, who've run away from an unpleasant situation.'

'Will you look at the toffs in their own cart!' she laughed now.

'Bryn, sweetheart, where is *my* cart, then?'

Bryn promptly pointed out that they owned a boat and we did not.

'Cart next!' Arial demanded. 'Oh Martha, isn't this a grand day? Both our men have done so well and here we are at the races. Is it not a strange turnaround for us? Did you place a bet?'

I still counted my pennies and was shocked to think that with two young ones Arial would fritter money away on a chance. But I held my peace. Arial looked so happy and well. Her baby couldn't be more than a month or two, but there Arial was, slim and neat, resplendent in a green beribboned dress and bonnet. I tried to tuck my wretched frizzy hair away under my dowdy bonnet and bent down to admire the new son.

Huw returned full of the news. 'There's Mr Molesworth on his Calmuc Tartar.'

And talk of Molesworth! Here were the Southeys, waving and shouting, Dora in a new coat, the two boys broad-shouldered like their dad — young men now — and strutting in front of the ladies.

'Dora Southey, look at you!' cried Arial, who clearly knew the family. 'Where did that new coat come from, then? You never sewed such a fine garment?'

But she had. I felt dumpy in my old Sunday best, beside this new finery. But then I had my own business, and we lived in our own house with an iron roof and drove a cart.

Huw described the rest of the race line-up. 'Your Mr Molesworth, Russ, I like his style. A very determined man — he'll want to win. Dr Dorset is riding Mr Hunter's Temperance. Dorset was in the Lancers with us in Spain. He can ride alright. But Colonel's horse, Beau, is the favourite. Mr Watts will ride it. Don't know why the Colonel don't ride himself. He was a fine horseman in the Lancers. Anyway, I have put a pound on him for the one-mile sweepstake.'

I gaped. 'A pound! Huw! What if he loses?'

Huw grinned. 'This is my lucky day. He'll win. Or maybe they'll let him win.'

'Oho! Who's the daring one, then?' laughed Arial. 'Bryn, why not put a pound on, too? I have a feeling Huw knows something.'

Finally, all the bustling came to an end and the race began.

Down they came, seven horses pounding over the damp sand, riders in jockey's colours, with whips and boots, as if this was in England, not a wild, savage country half a world away. There must have been six or seven hundred people watching and cheering. Huw, fearful that his cobbled-together cart might collapse, had to quieten Alfie and the girls, who were jumping and whooping for the Colonel's Beau. And sure enough, Beau won; Huw trebled his pound, as did Bryn.

The Southeys lost on their man's Calmuc Tartar. 'But only a shilling,' laughed Dora. 'Not like you spendthrift toffs!'

Huw and Bryn splashed out on a handful of confits. I smiled to see Alfie, who had never tasted candied fruits before, nibble cautiously at first, then gobble them down with delight. I was pleased to note that he stuffed the last two in his pocket for later enjoyment. Good boy!

No sign of the hungry petitioners who had come out of the bush to plead with Wakefield. It is not so different here after all, I thought. Wakefield's famous plan to bring out England's class system and plant it here intact is working for some. The landowners don't care about the poor here, any more than they did back in Britain. Well, some do. Mr Molesworth is good to his labourers. And not all of us are trapped; not all. Some are escaping the net, for all that the Wakefields and their like want to keep us beholden to them.

I smiled to think that soon some of the landowners might have to learn to wash their own linen.

# MUKA

## HINEROA

Preparing muka calls for a steady rhythm and a tireless hand. I am something of an expert, having spent many years scraping flax on the Kāpiti coast. So that day I had no problem keeping my attention on Mr Halswell while my knife never broke rhythm. The Commissioner for Native Reserves didn't imagine for a moment that I or any of the other toiling women understood either the issue being discussed, or his language. I could follow his words; we all understood the issue. He was arguing with some of the elders at Kumutoto pā. His words were an odd mix of English and a sort of pidgin Māori that I found belittling.

'He wants the whole kāinga to move,' I said to my companion.

Pīpī, scraping in a rhythm that matched mine, nodded. 'Āe, I heard. They say this part is sold to the white men.'

'The chiefs say they didn't sell. But did they not join in the gifting?' I raised my sharp knife. 'Did this good tool not come from that wily dog Wideawake and his ship full of treasure?'

Pīpī, who had been a slave for longer than me and was more accepting of her status, smiled and went on scraping. After a while, she said, 'It was a treaty, that's how I understand it. To allow them to live among us. They have no right to uproot Kumutoto pā.'

I dipped my hand in the bright stream that rushed down from the hill behind us and onto the beach. The years had taken their toll: my fingers were cramping.

In front of us long lines of muka fanned out in the stream.

The scraped fibre would soon be ready to dry. The argument was becoming heated. Mr Halswell explained that this area was now laid out in sections; that the track beside the stream was now called Woodward Street and the track along the beach Lambton; that settlers had already paid for these sections and the whole kāinga would have to move to the native reserves, which, as he pointed out on his map, were clearly marked.

The chiefs looked out to sea, declining to look at the map. They thanked Mr Halswell politely for the information and walked away. Pīpī laughed. 'They won't move. How can anyone shift us? We lived here first.'

Waewae had toddled too close to the stream. I called her back. All the time my hands scraped steadily at the green flesh of the flax leaf. I had my own prized flat stone, which was raised to just the height of my hands when I sat beside it. The work was pleasant enough in fine weather and with someone to talk to. That day was cloudy and the sandflies bothersome. I would prefer to be at the Mission, teaching children to read, but the demand that I marry Hone had put an end to that possibility.

As if the thought of Hone had conjured him up, there he was, on the beach looking this way and that, perhaps searching for something. He was smartly dressed in white man's clothes and walked with a swagger, swinging a stick. As if he were a chief. Oh, dear, it seemed that he was looking for me. I ducked my head, but was too late.

'Hineroa! Hine!' His wave of greeting was exaggerated. 'Here you are. Minarapa sent me to find you.'

'Here I am.' I bent to my scraping, indicating that I had urgent business that could not be interrupted, which was true in a way. Huw expected a full day's work, but at least he paid in coin, not food or trinkets as other traders did.

Hone stood in front of me, frowning. I kept up my scraping.

'Now, Hine,' he said, 'what is this nonsense?'

I laid the cleaned muka aside and picked up a fresh flax spear. Waited uneasily for more. Hone looked too pleased with himself.

'Minarapa says you are bonded to him to work for the Mission. He has heard that you are working for a white man. For money, which you keep. He says that is not the agreement he made with Te Āti Awa.'

Pīpī giggled. A good bit of gossip. It would be all over Kumutoto soon.

My words were quiet, but they carried force. 'My agreement with Minarapa and the Mission ended when he would not allow me to stay unless I married you. I am no longer a bonded person. And I am sorry, but I do not choose you as a husband.'

Pīpī gasped and then chuckled. This was clearly even better gossip.

Hone swore. He rolled his eyes and stamped his smartly shod foot.

I spoke calmly. 'Find another wife, Hone, in your white man's clothes. I would only make you very unhappy.' And I bent back to my scraping.

Hone, goaded and shamed in front of the watching women, charged forward, grabbing me by the arm. He was large and strong and dragged me to my feet. But he was also foolish: he left my knife-hand free. I brought the blade up to press against his cheek.

'Hine, Hine!' whispered Pīpī. She understood how dangerous my actions were. Indeed, the arm with the knife began to shake. This was not how I would like matters to progress. If Minarapa was supporting Hone, it would be unwise to set up any sort of situation that called for revenge. Even though Hone was also of lowly status, he was a man.

I lowered the knife. 'I have work to do here, and my child to care for. Tell Minarapa I will come at the end of the day to discuss this matter.' I knew I was making matters worse, but could not give in.

Wise Pīpī intervened. 'Eh, Hineroa, go with him and talk to the chief. I will watch the child. Best not stir this angry fellow further. He reminds me of the bull that came off the boat last week: so maddened by the sea voyage it tore to pieces one of the fine racing horses. Listen to my good sense, woman. Your choices are not as plentiful as flax leaves.'

Hone glowered at us. Others were watching now and enjoying the spectacle. Truly, Hone had a look of that bull. He was almost pawing the ground and snorting at my disobedience. Perhaps I would be wise to swallow my pride and go with him to see Minarapa now.

---

Hone strutted as he led me up to the wharenui at Te Aro pā. He pushed me down onto the paepae. 'Wait here. I will explain your bad behaviour to the chief. I think he will not want to speak to you.'

The grounds were well swept; the palisades in good repair. The Mission house close by was neatly thatched; children inside were chanting. Perhaps the new Reverend had found another teacher? How much bigger and more imposing Te Aro was than Kumutoto. Yet Kumutoto, with its rushing stream, its access to flax swamps and its jetty, was the centre for muka trading. Every week or so, a cutter arrived from Australia to load up fibre for rope and to unload whatever had been ordered by the settlement. I preferred the smaller Kumutoto. But of course I belonged to neither — nor to Pipitea. It was a feeling that both challenged and frightened me. Even a slave should belong somewhere.

I waited. The sun, now clear of the clouds that had obscured it all day, emerged to warm me. But in a few minutes it would sink behind the ravaged slopes of Ahumairangi. Waewae would be hungry. Where had that wretched Hone gone?

At last Minarapa came to the opening and invited me inside. With him was the new missioner. Minarapa greeted me gravely and introduced the Reverend John Aldred. He indicated that I should sit beside them on the mats. I pulled my cloak tight. I heard my mother's voice: guard your tongue, girl; keep the sharp words for moments of importance.

Minarapa cleared his throat. 'Hone tells me you are disobedient to him and unwilling to become his wife, either in the Christian way or traditionally.'

I nodded.

'Also I have heard that you are working for payment for a Pākehā man over at Kumutoto.'

I inclined my head again.

'The arrangement I made with Te Āti Awa at Kāpiti was that you would work for me here at the Mission.'

I spoke to the reverend. 'I would happily come back.' Then repeated my words in English in case he had not understood.

Reverend Aldred opened his Bible. He pointed to a passage. 'Would you please read this?' He was young, clean-shaven with curling brown hair, his face stern but his voice gentle.

I read, 'Matthew five verse eight. "Blessed are the pure in heart, for they shall see God. Blessed—"'

'That will do. Now, can you translate that for me into your tongue?'

I waited until I had it clearly in my head. 'Ka koa te hunga . . .' I looked at Minarapa, not sure if I had it right. His nod of approval encouraged me. '. . . hunga ngākau mā: e kite hoki ratoa i te Atua.'

The reverend looked surprised. 'Where did you learn this?'

'I was . . . given . . . to a group of whalers for a while, to help with domestic things. A young whaler had a Bible.' I risked a quick glance up at him. 'He . . . befriended me. And taught me. Another time I was given to Reverend Taylor and I watched him teach the young chiefs.'

'Impressive.' Aldred turned to Minarapa. 'She would be very useful at the Mission with the children. And to assist me. Is there some way . . . ?'

Minarapa sighed. We waited in silence. A flock of kākāriki flew chattering overhead, heading for home on the hill. Finally, he spoke. 'It is true that perhaps Hone is not a good match for you. Even though you have both grown up slaves.'

I could have pointed out that the English had abolished slavery, but held my peace. After all, they knew this.

Minarapa continued in his quiet, measured way. 'Perhaps, Reverend, you might send Hone to another Mission, a little distant from here? To save his pride? Maybe closer to his ancestors. And perhaps this woman could be permitted to teach at the Mission if she married another. Or she might give her child to be cared for elsewhere?'

Aldred nodded. 'Good, good. Wise words.'

Wise! His words were unjust. I had promised both Waewae and myself that I would never, *never* let this child be taken away from me. What arguments could I muster? Surely Minarapa understood my predicament? I tried to speak quietly, knowing that my resentment would anger the chief. 'As you rightly say, I was of the bonded class. Also, as you know, I do not belong to any of the tribes in this place. I have no right to offer her as whāngai to any family. I believe no Te Aro or Kumutoto or Pipitea whānau would welcome a child of mine.'

Aldred frowned. 'Perhaps a childless settler family?'

'Also . . .' I sensed my voice rising, but was powerless to keep calm. 'Also, everyone at the Mission knows I have a child. Knows I am without a husband. It will be no different whether I bring the child with me or not. Surely it is not our way to bring shame on a "bonded woman", if she has children out of wedlock?'

Minarapa rose. 'I made it clear to you some time ago that a Christian mother is a married one. Everyone in Te Aro understands that. We are making an allowance for you because of your usefulness in reading. Do not expect another allowance, Hineroa.'

With that he motioned Aldred to come with him and walked out of the wharenui and across to the Mission house, leaving me alone with my fury.

As I walked back along the beach, fuming and plotting, a bell rang out somewhere behind me, the sound of its tolling shredded by a cold wind that had risen suddenly from the south. Out on the water several ships and smaller trading vessels tossed at anchor. Another bell joined the first. Something clearly amiss. I looked back to the motley row of houses along the waterfront. There, behind Te Aro pā, smoke was billowing from a larger building close to the pā. As I watched, flames rose and the smoke streamed towards me. A third bell sounded. People at the pā were running and shouting. The smoke caught in my throat. The fire was coming towards me. I ran towards Kumutoto where Waewae might be in danger.

# DIRTY HABITS

## MARTHA PENGELLIN

*THORNDON FLAT, NOVEMBER 1842*

At first I was pleased with the fresh breeze: it brought the sulky fire under the copper back to life. Finding dry kindling and wood was ever a chore. Felled branches lay everywhere, but they took months to cure. The children were willing scavengers, beginning to know what I needed, but sometimes they made mistakes. Today's woodpile was too green. I heard the bells, but paid no attention — the sound was distant, and hauling hot sheets out with the wooden dolly took all my strength and concentration. I beat the heavy load on the wash-board to squeeze as much water as possible back into the hot tub, then tilted the board so it slid down into the rinsing water.

'And don't get me started on water,' I muttered to no one in particular. Clean water was hard to come by, so I would twist the rinsed linen over a bucket so what I collected could go back into the hot, soapy tub. Pipitea Stream had become polluted, and our own rain barrel couldn't provide enough clean water for all the washing. Often Huw would plod home weighed down by a couple of cans of clean water from Kumutoto Stream. But mostly I had no choice: find a side stream which ran more quickly, or wait until rain cleared Pipitea Stream.

There were the bells again. Was a storm on the way? That would be a blessing. A good rain would clear Pipitea Stream for a few days.

The linen flapped wildly in the rising wind. What with my aching arms and the difficulty pegging out, I was ready to give up my good

business and go inside for a cup of tea. Then I looked down the
shore and saw it. From our position up on Thorndon Flat we could
usually see most of the harbour. But now that view was hidden by
billowing smoke and great leaping flames. Dear God, how had that
happened so quickly? And where, oh where, were the children?

'Holly! Meg! Alfie!' They could be anywhere. Surely they would
be playing over by the stream, not down on the beach? I called again
for Meg, hoping that the sensible girl would bring the young ones
home when she noticed the smoke.

No time for folding linen. I whipped the lot — wet and dry —
from the lines and bundled it all inside. The smoke was thick by
now; hard to see where the flames might be. Oh, I was in a frenzy of
worry for the little ones. Everything was wood and thatch, see, and
built close. Thank goodness our own little cottage had an iron roof.
When the smoke veered away, swirling in the fickle wind, I could
see flames jumping from thatch to thatch. The Bank of England —
surely the only thatched one in the world — was already ablaze.
People running everywhere. The natives down at Pipitea pā were
quickly dragging their smaller whare to the ground, tearing off the
thatch and flattening the walls. Another group from the pā were on
the roof of Mr Evans's large warehouse, detaching the raupō thatch,
which had started to burn. They ran with it down to the sea — the
whole blessed roof! — and cast it adrift. What a sight! It moved
across the bay, the flames reflected in the water. Slowly it sank, the
bright flare drowned. Another roof followed. You had to marvel at
their quick, efficient movements. Oh, but where were the children?

Suddenly, out of the smoke, Hineroa came running, holding Alfie
with one hand, Holly and Meg close behind. Thank God!

They were more excited than frightened, the scallywags, jabbering
away.

'Did you see that roof floating out to sea?'

'A flaming roof!' shouted Alfie. 'Like a pirate ship!'

'Lloyd's Bakehouse started it!'

'The butcher's house has burned down!'

Hineroa released the children and turned back to peer through the smoke. 'Browns' Hotel has gone. Evans's trading post and Willis's. Oh! The fire has reached Kumutoto.'

I gathered the children to me. What now? Should we run? Or take shelter in the cottage?

Suddenly Hineroa's naked toddler was thrust into my arms.

'You will be safe here,' she said. So certain! How could she be sure? 'The men know what to do. Will you mind Waewae while I help?' And off she ran before I had a chance to thank her. It still felt dangerous. The Titches' whare next door was thatched in raupō. Reg Titch was a tanner who stored his hides under a canvas awning. They could catch. And even the Harrisons' big house up behind had three thatched outhouses.

Liddy came running down, grimy from her work on a property up on Tinakori Track. She threw me a grateful smile and hugged the girls to her. Together we watched for signs of fire on the Titch roof, but now it looked as if the wind had changed direction and was heading north.

Liddy pointed down at the pā. 'Look at that! They've flattened almost all the whare. How can they bear to?'

Inside the palisades, only the wharenui was still standing, and even that had had most of its roof removed. I suppose they were used to dealing with outbreaks of fire. Their own fires burned on the ground and sometimes in the middle of the hut; it would be easy for fire to spread.

Holly, who had several native friends and had quickly learned the language, piped up. 'I bet those whare will be back up in a few days. You watch. I bet!'

Alfie was coughing. I shifted little Waewae to the other hip and cuddled the boy. He had been rather listless these past few days. Not eating well, and pale. I should take more care of Alfie; something was not right. And where, oh where, was Huw?

———

Later, when Hineroa returned for Waewae, I thanked her for bringing back the children. 'Where were they?'

'Down on the beach digging for shellfish with some of the children from the pā.' She came inside, took from her kete a piece of cooked potato and sat to feed the toddler. She picked up the *Gazette* and read while she offered morsels of the cold stuff to Waewae's eager hands. Well, she had brought the children home and I was grateful, but still her familiarity with our home was unnerving.

The kete of shellfish which Holly had dumped at the door was welcome, though. I filled the pot with water and hooked it up over the fire. The flames, catching on the twigs Meg had brought in, were unnerving, too. This wild country! A brick fireplace and an iron stove would not go amiss.

Hineroa looked up from her reading. 'Do you think Alfie is well? He seemed tired and lacking in spirit to me.'

The suggestion was a further irritant. I wished she would leave, and yet in fact I *was* worried about the boy. Perhaps he had worms? He had been eating poorly and his bowels were loose. If he didn't get any better I might ask the doctor to look at him.

Waewae seemed to have gone to sleep on Hineroa's lap under her cloak. The mother nodded, smiled, opened her mouth to speak and then closed it again. Finally, she came out with it.

'Martha, there is some writing in this paper that makes me angry. The native pā are called dirty; we are described as ignorant of clean, civilised behaviour. But I believe that the unclean behaviour of the settlers, not the natives, is what is making Alfie sick.'

'Unclean?' I said, in the mood to argue.

'Your people pour the contents of their chamber pots and other unclean rubbish into the stream here. When there is no rain, the river becomes dirty. We would never do such a thing.'

She was right, I had to admit. I had never seen the natives use the stream in that way.

'We build our whare iti,' said Hineroa, 'away from the pā and away from the river or sea. The land cleans what we deposit there. I tell you, Martha, your people want to get rid of our pā and so they describe us as dirty.' Hineroa's voice was rising, but at a little wail from Waewae she lowered her voice again. 'I think you should keep Alfie from the stream. Why do people not dig holes for their waste?'

Huw and I had dug a little netty. Several neighbours the same. But I had seen those at the barracks and the temporary accommodation further up the hill dumping goodness knows what into the river. 'I don't like to use the water from the stream, but what choice do we have?' I said, dropping the shellfish into the boiling water and watching them open.

Hineroa rose. 'I will show Liddy and the children. There is a — I don't know your word for it — wai puna not far from here. Our people use it. The water comes out from under the rocks at the foot of the hill.' She smiled. 'It is the most beautiful clear, cold water. But it is our secret because we do not admire the dirty ways of the settlers.'

Dirty ways! I scooped out the opened shellfish. Threw watercress and potato into the boiling water, peeled an onion and added salt. A good, warming soup for Alfie.

Liddy and the girls, carrying water tins, ran off after Hineroa, who had left at a smart pace, child nowhere to be seen under the cloak. Alfie drooped on the bench outside, watching them go. I sat beside him, coaxing steaming shellfish into him, but after a few mouthfuls he threw up violently.

I led the poor boy inside. 'Come on then, sweetheart, let's put you to bed.' He was flushed now and complaining of stomachache.

By the time Huw arrived back from his flax business, I was really worried.

Huw was out of sorts and covered in soot. He scooped water from the rain barrel to wash himself, but all he did was smear the soot more widely over his body. 'Damn and blast!' he cursed. 'That blessed baker and his wretched open fire. Half the waterfront is burned down. Our store by Kumutoto has gone, with all the muka inside. And now the natives will be back at the pā rebuilding their whare while the flax remains unscraped. This is a blow, Martha.'

I poured a cupful of water over his head and scrubbed him down. The rain barrel was low, and now I dared not go to the stream for more water.

Huw brightened to hear about Hineroa's secret source of water and her help. 'Hineroa is a blessing. It's uncanny how quickly she picks up information. She hasn't lived here any longer than us, but she knows everything.' He went inside to check on Alfie. 'How's my little elf, then? How's my five-year-old?'

Alfie was crying. 'It hurts, Da. And I'm not five yet.'

'Well, soon enough, though, and we'll have a party. Hineroa will help you get well.'

And would I not help with my good soup and my mothering? I didn't care to hear any more about wonderful Hineroa. Besides, Alfie had been sick again.

'He doesn't even want me to tell him about dragons,' Huw said. 'It's serious, do you think?'

I cleaned the moaning boy. 'Oh, dragons, dragons. Can you not find me some dry wood, then?'

When the little party arrived back with cans brimming, they were full of the news.

'How could we have missed this?' said Liddy, beaming. 'The spring pours out steady and pure into a little rock pool that the natives have built. It is delicious, Martha, just taste!' She held out a cupful.

'The bushes hide it, see,' said Holly. 'And Hine tells us we should keep the secret unless the people at Pipitea invite others to use it. It is tapu. We should thank the gods when we take some, she says.'

Meg looked up at Hineroa. 'I said ngā mihi; is that alright?'

'That will do very well,' said Hineroa gravely. She was holding a bunch of nearly circular green leaves. Crossing over to the fireplace she inspected the kettle, which was always on the hob, close to the fire. 'Not water from the stream? Is this rainwater?'

It was of course. She poured some into a bowl and added several leaves. 'This is kawakawa; it should help Alfie, if it is not too late.'

Too late! We all looked at Hineroa in dismay. I had a sudden picture of the little Titch baby who had died a week ago after a short illness that included loose bowels and vomiting. Hineroa steeped the leaves in the boiling water then took them out, squeezing the last drops from the limp foliage.

I was doubtful. 'Are you sure? He has just been sick again.'

'I am sure it won't harm him. And I am sure it may help. But I am *not* sure it will be a cure. This is not a disease I understand. But let us try, Martha.' She handed me the bowl of greenish liquid.

I hesitated. It smelled peculiar.

'Try it, love,' said Huw, rocking Waewae in his arms. 'Hine's mother taught her useful cures. At least try.'

The two of us went into the room where Alfie lay, flushed and moaning. 'My tummy is sore.'

I sat beside him. Held the bowl to his lips. 'Drink a little, sweetheart.'

Alfie wouldn't touch it; he turned to face the wall, his lips pressed firmly together.

'Just a little.' I cradled his poor hot head. 'Hine has brought you some good medicine.'

Alfie's questioning look at Hineroa was full of doubt.

'He rongoā pai,' she said. 'Ka inu ai!'

The words were stern. I would never speak to a child so forcefully. But Alfie, his eyes on Hineroa, obediently opened his mouth and took a sip.

'Wait!' Hineroa took the bowl from my hand as the boy went to take another mouthful. 'Let us see if he can hold that down.'

I stroked his sweat-streaked hair. Sang to him. 'Huna blentyn, ar fy mynwes.'

Hineroa brought the bowl again to his lips. 'Ka inu ai.'

Alfie drank. His eyes began to close.

'Clyd a chynnes yd yw hon . . .' I stroked and sang.

We watched him together, my unease with Hineroa forgotten. Alfie seemed more peaceful.

'That is a beautiful song,' said Hineroa, 'but I don't understand the words.'

I thought that perhaps I had never seen her smile before. 'It's a Welsh lullaby. My mother language.'

'Ah. You have two languages like me. A home language and English. So my little Waewae will need to have three languages.'

I didn't think about the significance of those words at the time, but the meaning must have taken root, waiting for other signs.

Hineroa put down the empty bowl. 'I will bring fresh leaves tomorrow.'

# PRESSURES

## HUW PENGELLIN

*THORNDON FLAT, LATE 1842*

Dear God I was itching to pick up my axe, walk out and fell a tree. Or strike a lucrative deal with a trader. Best of all head off into the bush. More and more, this strange brooding country drew me. I wanted to explore. There was a darkness — a mystery — in its tall mountains, and rushing rivers, its wild, changeable weather and impenetrable forests. The gods dwelled here, sure, be they mine or Hineroa's; the giants and mythical creatures. I could feel them there, watching — threatening sometimes.

But at this particular moment I was stuck inside, Gareth glaring at me from across the table. Martha was the one to solve domestic problems, but she would say nothing. For days now she had been withdrawn.

'Are you not man of this household?' growled Gareth. 'You have a dead man's children eating your bread and spending all hours of the day cared for by your wife. I am willing and able to look after Liddy and her brood. It's time she moved out of that rat-infested accommodation and into my perfectly suitable hut.'

Liddy was in fact in the other room, no doubt hearing every word, while she put her girls down in the big bunk bed beside Alfie. The lad was still poorly. I tried a wink to Martha — you deal with this — but she would not. Something was eating away at her. Perhaps I could guess; but bringing up the matter was quite beyond me.

Early evening it was, the hut already dark. This wild country could turn summer to winter overnight. For three days rain and hail had rattled on the iron roof and found every available crack to enter our little room. The flame inside the lantern flattened, rose and flattened with every gust. Shadows advanced and retreated, deepening the mood that seemed to brood between us. I stuffed another rag in the gap above the door.

Gareth pushed away his empty plate. 'Huw, in the name of God, are you listening to me? You are my brother. You should take my side in this. Martha is sheltering a family that should be with me!'

'I cannot force her, Gareth.'

'Hamish!'

'Hamish. Why are you so nervous? No one is listening. If Liddy will not, she will not. Find another woman.'

'But don't you see?' There was a sort of desperation in his argument, a weakness that I had not noticed before. 'Can't you bloody understand, you idiot? I am obliged. It is my moral duty.'

Martha spoke at last. 'It is your moral duty to pay her back for the money you got for her farm, Gareth. That need not include marriage.'

'She's right, Gareth, a valid point.'

But Martha would not smile back at me.

'I am off on patrol duty in the morning. You, too, Huw. Let's settle this now.'

I disliked patrol duty. Gareth enjoyed it. He was all for punishing the tribes up in the Hutt Valley for their mischievous marauding, but you could see their point. When survey pegs are planted in the middle of native kūmara and potato gardens I might well be inclined to pull them out, too. Or when settler gardens are producing food on what Ngāti Tama consider native land, why shouldn't they help themselves to some of the produce?

'Call her in. Let me talk to her at least.' The whine in my brother's voice annoyed me. Since his time as a prisoner in New South Wales, some of Gareth's belligerence had been replaced by self-pity. As if he was owed something for his time spent there.

'Give it away, brother, leave it rest. There's nothing to be done if she doesn't like you.'

Martha cleared the table noisily. 'Go on off home, Gareth. She won't come out while you are here. We have said she can sleep here till the storm passes.'

'My cottage is dryer that yours!' shouted Gareth. 'And empty. She would come if you didn't pamper her.'

Liddy was standing in the doorway, half-hidden in the dark. 'No, I would not, Gareth. God forgive me, but I cannot forget what you did. And I cannot like you either. I will make my own way somehow in this terrible land.' She looked to me. 'Thank you for the shelter tonight, Huw. Are you sure?'

Martha answered. 'Of course he is. Rest easy.'

Gareth took his coat from the nail. Slapped at my head. 'So women *do* rule the roost at this household, *little* brother.' And out he stumped, taking no care with the door, leaving it gaping.

Well, I shut out the storm. Came back to the table. Martha had poured me a mug of tea, without any word. I began to dread what would be said next. But Liddy was back in the room, cradling her tea. 'Alfie is still restless,' she said. 'The fever is down, though. I must ask your Hineroa more about her herbs.'

I was about to protest that Hineroa was not *mine*, nor Martha's for that matter, when a tap at the door saved this dangerous conversation. Surely Gareth hadn't returned? But no, it was Bryn Evans, a rain-soaked apparition in the doorway, red eyed and holding his howling daughter.

Bryn opened his mouth to speak, but no words emerged. He was shaking all over. I removed his coat while Liddy took Sarah, quickly removing her wet clothes and wrapping her in a piece of blanket.

She towelled the wet hair and cuddled her by the fire until the crying subsided. Whatever had brought this about?

Martha poured more tea and added a splash of rum to Bryn's mug.

I tried to lighten the mood. 'Eh, Martha, soon we will have to add a room or two. We have become a hotel, is it?' Not a bad idea come to think of it.

But Martha was not laughing. 'Whatever is it, Bryn? Where is Arial? And the baby? Tell us, friend.'

Bryn took a gulp from his mug. He tried to talk, but a great sob engulfed the words. I never thought to see Bryn in such a state.

Martha put an arm around him. 'Drink your tea, man, you're safe here.'

In the silence, Liddy sang quietly to Sarah, who was settling to sleep.

Bryn took a shuddering breath and then another. 'Oh, it is good to hear our Welsh spoken. I have longed for it these last two days. Bless you, Liddy. God bless you, Martha and Huw.'

Then he told us his dreadful story slowly, tears running down his cheeks all the while. 'That damned river rose, see. I thought I had built the house far enough away. But in the upper valley of the Hutt where we are . . . were . . . the river rises quickly. Arial took the baby over to neighbours, you know how she loves a chat. That was the first day of the storm. The Averys were heading downriver and said we should go, too, in case the river rose. Arial came back laughing at their timid ways. "You have built us a home to last," she said. "We'll be safe."'

Bryn shook his head. 'She said those very words. I was proud and agreed. More fool me. Oh!' He turned the mug in his hands, looking into it as if he saw the events unfolding in the dregs.

I added rum for him and then poured myself a tot, too. This was clearly not going to end well. 'Take your time, man, we are with you.'

'Arial and the baby were fine, both of them. You saw the wee boy at the races. But another neighbour who had birthed our son was in trouble the next morning. Her family had built too close to the river. She came running, crying for help. Four children, she had, and the father away trying to find work. Their little hut awash. I helped carry a few of their pitiful sticks of furniture to higher land and made sure the children were all out safely. Oh, I spent too much time! If only . . .'

We waited, knowing worse was to come. 'I saw their little hut float away, but never thought mine — Sweet Jesus! I came back to our solid house, built by my own hands. There was my Arial, shrieking on the roof with the baby in her arms, and Sarah, too, and the raging river all around. *All around it.* Huw, you never saw such a sight. Logs and huts and animals tossing in that brown, furious water. Bodies, too. And as I ran . . . As I waded into that torrent, my house with Arial and the baby and Sarah just . . .' He covered his eyes. 'The whole house came adrift, see, and rolled into that river as if it were twigs, not solid timber slabs. Rolled into the river and swept away like a ship riding a storm.'

He looked around at us all. 'I can't swim, see; my dear love Arial neither. But who could survive in that torrent, be she even champion of the world? It were a wild, evil beast that I never would like to set eyes on again.' Bryn's voice broke into sobs again.

He could not go on. We sat silent. Surely there was more, for here was little Sarah.

'I ran along the bank, stumbling over whatever was in my way, her shrieks in my ears as the house turned and twisted. I prayed to God in all his mercy to send a shingle bank or a quiet stretch or a log — anything that would slow that fearsome, rolling ship that was once my house. Arial scrabbling and clinging as it rolled. But she couldn't, see . . . She couldn't hold both the children and stay on board. Sarah slipped into the water.' He looked over at his little daughter, sleeping now. 'I suppose not understanding, she didn't fight — or maybe . . . Whatever reason, she floated and a current brought her near enough that I could use a branch and bring her in. But by that time . . . By that time . . .'

'Sweet Jesus,' whispered Martha.

'Oh, Bryn,' said Liddy, rocking little Sarah.

What word of comfort could I offer to my friend? Lost in the horror of it all as I was. I had learned to swim over at Britannia, but I have never been fond of water. 'Did they find her, Bryn?'

'All the way downriver. Near the sea. Washed up. The baby still in her arms. Both dead.' He shook his head as if to banish the memory. 'Those dreadful shrieks: I can't get them out of my head. We came all this way to free her from old Cadoc, and now she's dead.'

A fresh flurry of wind-driven rain rocked the whare. I laid a hand on Bryn's soaked shoulder. 'The natives say that after three days a storm like this from the south will break and bright sun follow. Perhaps tomorrow we might. . .' But I could think of no cheerful action we might take. 'Will she be having a funeral?'

'I have brought her body to the church. Others are drowned, too. My neighbours.'

Liddy left off her singing. 'Arial was so lively. And so happy here with you, Bryn.'

'Aye. You people are my only family here. Can you help?'

'Of course we will,' I said. 'Of course, friend. Will you go back there? To the Hutt Valley?'

He hung his head, clearly desperately tired. 'I don't know . . . can't even think. My business is there and my land, but I can't do it on my own. Rebuild the house . . . And Sarah . . .'

Martha, finally emerging from her sour thoughts, fetched a blanket. 'No more talk till morning. We can only offer the floor for you, Bryn. Little Sarah can maybe tuck in with Liddy? If you are right, Huw, the sun will be out tomorrow and we will see then. Bryn, sweetheart, you need to sleep now.'

So, I was off the hook for tonight. I felt ashamed of my relief.

# AN EXPERIMENT

## HINEROA

*KARORI TRACK, SUMMER 1842–43*

On the first day of the arrangement, I swept out Gareth's hut, lit the fire and prepared a stew of potato and bacon bone — all I could find. Waewae was asleep on the mat we both shared. By the time Gareth returned, I was sitting comfortably on the floor reading his Bible.

Gareth stood in the doorway looking at me. I decided not to stand up. I was no longer a slave; better not begin this in the manner of a slave.

I greeted him politely enough. 'I have made a stew and cleaned your hut. Please help yourself.'

Gareth remained standing. 'No welcome for a tired man returning?'

'Welcome,' I said, still reading. 'Do you approve of the cleaning?'

Gareth stacked his pickaxe in the corner, hung his coat on the nail and sat at the table. He waited. 'I am ready for my supper,' he said. 'Do I have to explain to you that a woman serves supper?'

Clearly he was irritated. Perhaps best to serve him. I needed this to work. I closed the Bible, served him his stew and sat down to eat it with him. The way his eyes rested on my body as he chewed warned me that this arrangement might not be as simple as I had hoped. 'How would I say "welcome" in Welsh?' I asked with a smile, hoping to divert him.

He told me and I tried it out.

'And how would I say "go to sleep"?'

His snort of laughter was followed by something that I suspected was not what I had in mind.

'I mean — would I say that to a child?'

He frowned. 'What is all this about? Our language has nothing to do with you.'

'I am interested in language and like to learn. If you don't want that, never mind. I can learn from Martha or Huw. Is there anything else you want me to do before I attend to the child?' I picked up the plates, took them to the basin and washed them out. Stacked them to dry, and put what was left of the stew in a lidded tin away from the rats. He was standing behind me; too close. I could feel the heat of him.

'You can come to bed with me now,' he said. His voice was tentative, his eyes not meeting mine when I turned.

Was this part of the arrangement that Huw had made? Was I expected to comfort him before he slept? Huw had said nothing about this, nor did I believe it was part of Pākehā custom. I told him I didn't want to comfort him. Maybe later, I said, when we know each other better. Not now. Do you agree?

He moved closer. I placed a hand on his chest — gently, I hoped — and pushed him away.

He seized my hand and held it in both of his. 'No, I don't agree,' he said. 'I expect this.' He moved my hand down his body and held it against himself. 'I am going away tomorrow. A show of force against your people and I — I need — some comfort.' After a moment he added in a quiet voice, 'Please.'

So be it, I thought, no harm done, if he behaves. Huw had warned me that his brother could be rough. I unlaced his trousers and spoke firmly. 'But not in the bed, Gareth, I do not want another baby.'

He took breath as if to argue, but at my touch nodded. I thought his smile betrayed — could it be gentleness?

Afterwards, when he was snoring in bed and I sat by the embers, watching Waewae finish off her kūmara, I thought that perhaps this might work. Gareth had not been rough. Rude, perhaps. But he had accepted when I spoke sternly. Perhaps he needed a strong woman. And if he was willing to put a roof over my head and provide food for me and the baby, I would be happy to cook and clean for him . . . and give him pleasure from time to time. A strange man, Gareth. A man with two names. Something not right in his head. But for the moment I was pleased to be warm and fed. And respectable in the eyes of the Mission. I watched the flames as they faded into glowing embers. Perhaps in time I could make an acceptable life for Waewae. As a Muaūpoko I would need to be careful in order to earn respect from the tribes in this harbour.

But in a white man's world? I settled beside my daughter on the mat.

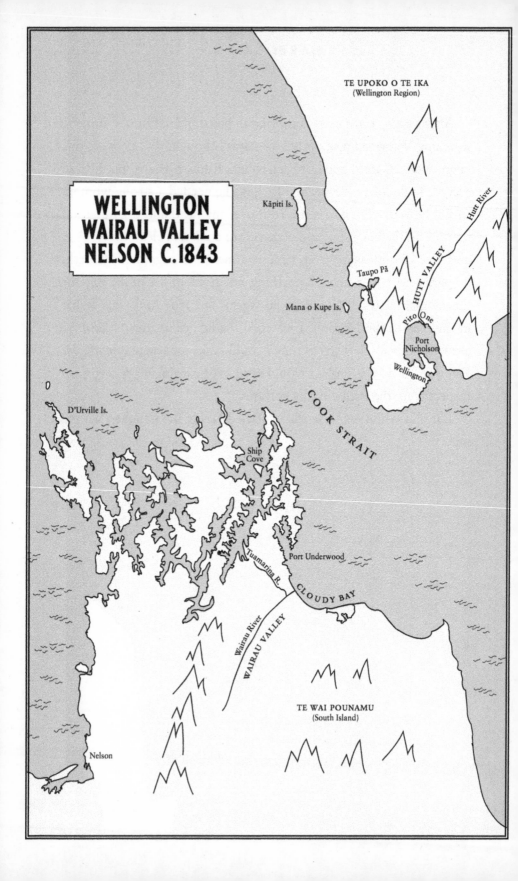

# PART THREE

—

# FIGHTING OVER THE SCRAPS

# A SORRY AFFAIR

## HUW PENGELLIN

*PORT NICHOLSON, WAIRAU AND NELSON, 1843*

That old plodder, Land Commissioner Spain, was to blame in my book. Could never make up his mind; would hum and haw over the easiest of cases. What was his problem? we would argue over our pints down at the grogshop. Was he afeared of the natives? Or of the Colonel? Or of Lieutenant Governor Short? Caught between a rock and a hard place, I would suggest, he's trying to please all three, and in the end satisfying none.

A new problem to add to his worries when we came back from an expedition up the Porirua road where Te Rangihaeata was up to his usual tricks, stealing settler property, breaking down bridges. Me and Gareth in the militia along with some of the regulars from the barracks. The chief's Taupō pā up that way had grown huge. Enough to put the wind up us, I can tell you. Even Gareth, who would rant on against the natives (if none were around), was in awe.

'What's he planning? You could quarter an army inside those palisades. We need to warn Short,' he'd said. But I noticed he was as reluctant as the rest of us to arrest Te Rangihaeata. We came back empty-handed.

Land Commissioner of the same opinion. 'It is not clear,' he droned, 'that the natives are subject to English law.' And so on and so on. The chief was to be left alone. Which encouraged the fellow and his Ngāti Toa to carry on with his raids.

Well, look you, I was torn both ways. Te Rangihaeata could see what was happening: see the settlers spreading out his way, farming what he considered his domain; making money from land he maintained had not been sold to the white man. Probably he saw more clearly the future, because by the time of the awful Wairau battle there were more of us settlers than Māori on both sides of the strait.

In a settlement as small as ours, everyone knew the gossip and the rumours. The Colonel's older brother Arthur, over in the new Company settlement in Nelson, was in trouble. Well, most of we labouring classes, as the Company likes to call us, could see with our own eyes that all the Wakefield settlements were in trouble. I said to Martha that she and I together could do a better job of running Port Nicholson than either the Company or the governor over in New South Wales.

Arthur Wakefield kept sending messages across to the Colonel from Nelson. 'We have no country acres. Where can our landowners find the country acres promised them? The land all around Nelson Bay is mountains.' And so on and so forth, week after week.

We heard it all from the agents who were selling on behalf of the absentee owners back in England. The stories they had been fed by the Wakefields, who promised endless spreading fields of arable land waiting to be cultivated, huge profits to be made by buying cheap and selling dear. All lies — or, at best, misguided.

Early 1843 it was. I was earning good money as a chainman to the Company surveyors at that time. When my flax business burned down, I decided to have a go at the surveying, which suited me fine but displeased poor Martha. She would like me to be at home day after day, but — well — see, I am an adventurer. I love my dear Martha and poor Alfie, but I am not cut out to stay in one place for long.

'You are a family man now,' says Martha, 'and the only family I have for thousands of miles. I need you close.'

But this great wild unknown country puts a kind of thrill into me.

What is over the next hill or through this great stand of trees? Where does this river come from? Oh, I am happy out with the gang in the bush with my chains and my rods. A bedroll and a bag of provisions. One day, I said to Martha, I will be a surveyor myself and teach Alfie the trade. Pengellin and Son, surveyors, I said. Sounds grand! But she burst into tears, which is not usual for Martha, and she begged me to stay at least on this side of the strait.

She was upset on account I was asked to work under Chief Surveyor Tuckett in Nelson — just for a few weeks, I promised her. I was one of the few who spoke the language and could bring back news to the Colonel. (As it turned out, I would be gone for months, not weeks, and accordingly would pay a price with my unhappy wife.)

A whole great valley had been found down there, which would serve very well for the Nelson landowners' country acres. The Wairau Valley near Cloudy Bay. But the survey was being slowed down by the natives, who would pull out the pegs and rods as soon as they were planted. Ngāti Toa land. So Te Raup and Te Rangi (as we called them for short) would be behind the unrest for sure.

I thought back to that time on board the *Tory* when the Colonel had begged me to give him my own trade goods so he could purchase that very area. As far as I knew, he never did buy any of that land, so what was the use of surveying it? But when I tried to put this point to Wideawake he wouldn't even see me. They said he was angry most of the time and would hear no word against his precious Company. What we simple settlers knew was the Company was going down. Riddled in debt and we labourers left to fend for ourselves.

So the cutter left us at Port Underwood, where we met up with Tuckett and his men. I liked Tuckett and Cotterell, the other surveyor. Both Quakers and honourable men. A Quaker will not fight, which is helpful when there are arguments flying.

'Now, men,' said Tuckett to his new recruits, 'we have our work cut out here. The chief is Ngāti Toa and an older brother to Te Rauparaha himself. The land is definitely not empty, as I was informed by Arthur Wakefield. And they insist this valley has never been sold.'

He cautioned us to go about our work in a quiet and peaceful manner. 'The word is that Land Commissioner Spain will arrive shortly and pronounce on the matter. Meanwhile, if the natives pull up our pegs, collect them the next day and replant.' He sighed. 'It seems wasted effort until ownership is settled, but the leaders in Nelson have given the order that we proceed.'

So proceed we did, and wasted effort it surely was. I looked at that beautiful valley with its high, forbidding mountains to the west, and easy, rolling land beside the river. Patches of tall bush, but also scrubby, stony land where the braided river meandered down towards the bay. A peaceful place. The natives — or Māori, as they are mostly called these days — were peaceful in their operations and very effective. They would come at night; creep in behind us as we moved out wide or upriver with our theodolites and poles and chains and rods. Behind us, the next day most of our work undone.

One evening Tuckett asked me and another chainman to sit with him and interpret. The Ngāti Toa chief Nohorua's three sons had walked into our camp. Tall, handsome fellows, all three. They were Christian, they said, all baptised, and sat politely with us on the banks of the river as the sun set behind those craggy mountains. Christian they may have been, but their English was not good.

The oldest son warned us that Te Rauparaha and Te Rangihaeata were on their way. Those great chiefs were angered by Commissioner Spain's delay and were coming with a large party to settle the matter themselves. Tuckett sighed when he heard this. 'Tell them we will not fight. We are peaceful men.'

We shared what food we had, which was not much. And thanked the young chiefs.

'Well,' said Tuckett, looking around at our little camp — simple raupō huts, a fireplace of river stones, and our piles of survey posts cut from the plentiful mānuka trees that lined the banks. 'I think we should stay here until they come. I don't want you out on your own. Day off work tomorrow. Shall we catch fish, eh?' Said with a smile. I think he was fed up with pressing on in such a futile way.

And indeed there I was in the river with a makeshift rod when Te Rauparaha's party arrived. A frightening sight for some in our group as the chiefs raised their taiaha and presented their muskets. But I had plenty of experience of their habit of posturing. I laid down my rod, and approached with my hands free. Te Rangihaeata danced up and down, grimacing and shouting.

Te Rauparaha spoke. Tuckett gave me the nod. A proud moment for me to do the interpreting. 'They order us to leave,' I reported back, after conversing with the chiefs, 'but they will not harm us if we go peacefully. We are to remove all of the equipment that we brought with us and place it by the shore. They will only destroy what we have taken from their land.'

So back we marched to the bay, carrying our equipment. Warriors with feathers in their hair prancing beside us to keep us in a tight group. As we left the camp, they set fire to the whare and the mānuka survey rods.

I had to admire their sense of justice: sure enough, they destroyed only what we had taken or built from the land. I decided not to share that view, mind. Some of the men were itching to lash out, but Tuckett was firm. 'Stay calm; just walk away.'

On the shore, we were met by Cotterell's party, also rounded up and carrying all their equipment. A tidy campaign: old Te Rauparaha knew his business alright. A pile made of all the survey tools. Two young surveyors left to guard the pile. The rest of us escorted to Port Underwood for evacuation.

Te Rauparaha spoke to Tuckett before we left. His words were stern. He explained that this land was Ngāti Toa land; his brother Nohorua was chief; that a large band of his tribe had just arrived to prepare gardens and plant potatoes — a sacred process which signified ownership and should not be interrupted. 'We do not want war,' he said firmly, 'but we will defend this land until Commissioner Spain arrives.'

I was glad to leave when a cutter finally came to fetch us. The chief was right, I was pretty sure of it. The Wairau was never mentioned in those original gifting arrangements so far as I remembered. What was the Colonel up to? He knew he had not been gifted the land. He should have warned his brother Arthur. All the killing that was to come could have been avoided. Should have been.

––––––––––

So I missed the battle, if that is what it could be called. Lucky to have missed the sorry affair; otherwise I would not be here to tell the tale. On our way back to Nelson, our cutter came up with the *Victoria*, the government brig from Nelson. Aboard a group of angry Nelson worthies who thought to deliver a lesson to the Ngāti Toa.

'Come aboard!' shouted some loudmouth. 'Come aboard, Tuckett, and all your men! We'll show them what-ho!'

I heard later it was Thompson, the Nelson magistrate. A hothead clearly, out for a lark.

Tuckett shouted back that he was a Quaker and a pacifist and would not fight.

'I order you to come aboard!' shouted Thompson. 'And all your men. We need to make a show of strength. You need not fight. They will soon cave in.'

Do they realise who they are dealing with? I wondered. Those two chiefs are seasoned and skilful warriors who have taken over a large part of these islands with their muskets and their cunning in warfare.

'Don't go,' I whispered to Tuckett. 'They won't win against Te Rangihaeata.'

I shouted out that I was not a Nelson man but under orders to bring back news to Colonel Wakefield in Port Nicholson. Which was true enough, though some would say cowardly. Most of the survey party, including Tuckett, went on board, though. Cotterell, too; the other Quaker.

A woeful, sorry tale. Many settlers back in Nelson and in Port Nicholson were outraged that Commissioner Spain finally, weeks later, came down on the side of the Ngāti Toa. But he was right for once. If only he had made his decision a week or two earlier. If only that loudmouth Thompson had kept his temper in check. So many lives butchered needlessly — including the Colonel's brother Arthur. And an unfortunate boost to Te Rangihaeata's hatred of settler land-grabbing.

Colonel made no public announcement about the settler deaths. Tuckett told me he was angry and upset, as he would be, his brother being among the dead, and his friend Cotterell dead also. But Tuckett's story was a different one from what we read in the *Gazette*. The newspaper said that Arthur Wakefield and the others had died bravely in battle. Tuckett was there, though; one of the several — labourers and survey-party men mainly — who had no cause to fight. They ran away into the scrub when Magistrate Thompson started raging and whipping up aggression among those poor deluded landowners who remained.

'Te Rauparaha didn't want to fight,' said Tuckett. 'Nor even Rangihaeata, for all his threatening poses. They said to wait for Comissioner Spain's judgment. They said to go away. Mind you,' he added, 'they'd positioned themselves in a very advantageous place — we had surveyed it a week before, remember? Where the Tuamarina River meets the Wairau.'

I nodded. A pretty place. A steep bank on the west side and then scrub-covered flats on the east. Ideal for pasturage, we had thought. Tuamarina River is not large — least not when we were there. But just too deep to wade, too wide to jump. About half a chain wide, I would have said, maybe less. Tuckett said the Ngāti Toa party was on the flat, eastern side, hidden among the scrub. They had a canoe wedged side-to-side across the river as a bridge, which meant the settlers would have to scramble across one by one, along the canoe, or swim over using the canoe as an aid. Either way, hopeless for combat.

Tuckett told me all this back in Nelson while I was waiting for a boat back to Port Nic. We sat on a stone wall down by the waterfront. Nelson is as sweet a place as you could imagine, the big, wide bay with an island giving shelter from wind for anchorage. Mountains in the distance. It seemed strange to be talking about those bloody deaths in this peaceful spot.

Tuckett himself was not a man of peace that day, though. His voice trembled with anger. Or was there also a bit of shame mixed in? 'Cotterell should have walked away with me,' he said. 'The argument had nothing to do with us. Arthur Wakefield should have walked, too. He should have quietened Thompson. But they say Thompson was the senior man on the day. Being government, not Company.'

'There's the problem,' I ventured to say. 'Lines of command not clear.'

'We are not an army, Huw, but you are right in a way. Settlers look to Wakefield, but it's the Governor in New South Wales and the Lieutenant Governor up in Auckland who are supposed to be in charge these days.'

He told me how Thompson kept waving an arrest warrant for Te Rauparaha and his nephew for destroying government property. Tuckett snorted. 'That is, the poor raupō huts we surveyors had built. Trumped-up charge if ever I heard.'

I had to agree. They didn't touch all of our equipment, only what we had used from their land. As they had promised.

'He was playing with fire, Huw. A first-class idiot, Thompson. A bully, to boot. Ordered his men to put handcuffs on the two chiefs! Can you imagine!'

Dear God. Setting a flaming torch to a tricky situation instead of trying to calm it! Tuckett said Thompson was red in the face, a raging bull.

Tuckett wiped a hand over his face. I reckon he was weeping, poor fellow. 'I am a man of peace, Huw; my God tells me fighting is wrong, that no good will come of war. So when gunshots and war cries were exchanged, I shouted to my gang to follow me away from the scene. One had fallen already, shot dead. Most came with me, thank the Lord, for all who stayed were killed. My friend Cotterell among them.'

I looked away so as not to embarrass his tears. I have been in war with the Colonel in Spain. We were drilled and armed and uniformed. But what stupidity to take simple, untrained labourers, and even the leaders of the settlement, and set them against battle-hardened warriors. I heard from the preacher who buried them that those who remained — the Colonel's brother among them — had surrendered, laid down their arms, and, when that had no effect, lain themselves face-down on the stony soil we had pegged out just weeks before. But, because they had killed Te Rangihaeata's wife, the chief demanded utu. That was their custom. The wife was high-born. Te Rauparaha gave him the nod. His nephew clubbed them to death, one by one, with his famous greenstone mere. An awful, painful, senseless death.

We sat in silence, looking out to a milky sea. A brig was trying to reach anchor in the light breeze. Hard to make sense of it all, the right and wrong of it. I wanted to be back out in the silence of the bush looking for new pathways, new rivers.

Later that day, I was helping a Ngāti Toa man unload vegetables down on the jetty. We fell to chatting. When he heard that I had arrived aboard the *Tory* he told me a surprising thing. Te Rangihaeata's wife, the one who was shot in the conflict, was Te Rongopamamao! Te Whaiti's wife! When my friend, the interpreter on the *Tory*, died, evidently Te Rangihaeata, who was his cousin, took Te Rongo as wife. This was customary, he said. Well, true enough, said I, it is often the case with us. When a man dies in warfare, say, or of disease, the brother or cousin may take the widow. But what a strange connection! What would Te Whaiti have thought, I wondered. I had not suspected that he was so high-born. And if Te Whaiti had lived and Te Rongo were still married to him, would the conflict have ended differently? No sense thinking on that I suppose; nevertheless it shook me.

But worse was to come. A letter came, delivered by hand from one of the Port Nicholson surveyors. Hineroa wrote that my Alfie was at death's door. I should come home quickly.

# WELSH CORNER

## MARTHA PENGELLIN

*THORNDON FLAT, AUTUMN 1843*

All very well Huw saying he was needed across the strait, but what about me? Did I not need him? Run off my feet, me, with Liddy and the girls, and now Bryn and his Sarah hanging about. Not to mention the washing. Well, I should not say Bryn was hanging about. A tiger he was, working all hours of the day and some nights, too. His way of dealing with the grief, Liddy said. She had been the same when Dai died — couldn't sit still, had to be up and doing.

But suddenly our little quarter of an acre was sprouting buildings. A new whare — just a raupō hut with thatch for Bryn and Sarah — and another room to our cottage for Liddy. All put up by Bryn with some instructions from Hineroa on the best thatching and weaving. 'Little Wales' Liddy called our place, roses in her cheeks again, now that she was free from the dreaded Harrisons. When her passage was worked out, they had kept her on for a pittance and offered her and the girls a rough shack on the back of their acre. For a while she had stayed there, more for the sake of the garden than the pay, but in the end she found work elsewhere. When they heard she was leaving, they offered to pay her more, and a better accommodation, to tend the beautiful garden she had laid out but she wouldn't take the offer. Her pride was worth more.

I went with her when she gave them the word. The two of us standing at the front door in our Sunday best. Mrs Harrison frowning to see Liddy so bold and not at the back door as usual. Liddy handed her a bunch of sweet peas cut from the Harrisons' own garden. 'I am no longer your gardener, Mrs Harrison,' she said, as bold as brass. 'I found you unkind to me and my girls, and your husband made unwelcome advances. I will not work for you in the future. I hope you will learn to love and care for the plants yourself.'

She had practised it all up in front of me and Bryn. Even Bryn had managed a giggle.

Oh, it was a tonic to see Mrs Harrison's mouth, usually so tightly pursed, drop open. One day soon, I hoped, I would say the same to those I washed for. I had in mind a little guest house away from the noisy port. Out Karori way, I thought, where country acres were now being cleared. A neat cottage with a proper coal stove. A vegetable garden out the back (with Liddy managing it!). I would not wash for my guests; just the tablecloths and napkins. A dream perhaps. It might not suit Huw. But in this country one can dream.

Liddy made sure to take every seed and shoot she could garner from the Harrisons' garden — fruit, vegetable and flower — to plant and bring to life again elsewhere, in a garden of her own.

She now helped me with the washing most days, and planted a little garden in amongst Bryn's building activities. Bryn couldn't face going back up the Hutt, see. He would shake his head when I asked what his plans were or what was happening to his land.

'I will only see her screaming all over again, Martha. Every time the river rises it will be the same.' His poor shaggy head hanging as he asked could he just stay until he sorted his matters. Mostly Liddy looked after little Sarah; Bryn had no idea what to do with a child, unless it was a song at bedtime, or a sharp word if she cried.

Huw would have been gone months down at the Wairau, not one word from him, when Bryn announced he would shortly go back to the Hutt to collect his tools, salvage whatever he could and then try to make his way as a blacksmith at Port Nicholson. He still had some money, he said, might pick up a cheap piece of land. Or lease some. I noticed he was saying all this more to Liddy than to me. Naturally the thought had occurred to me. Liddy and Bryn. A solution for both of them.

'Do you fancy him, then?' I asked Liddy one day as we hung out the sheets and shirts. 'Could you make a go of it? He is not your most cheerful nowadays, I have to say.'

Liddy leapt to his defence. 'That's just his manner, Martha. He is kindness itself. Look what he has built me and the girls.'

Wasn't *I* kindness itself to have allowed all these huts on our land? What would Huw say when he came home to this? But I kept that thought to myself. Truth is, I was feeling out of sorts. Huw gone, Liddy blossoming, and Alfie still peaky and listless no matter what I did to feed him up.

Liddy stopped with an armful of sheet, dropped it back in the basket and came over to me. She could always read what was in your mind. 'Sit down, Martha dear, sit down. You are not yourself today.'

To my surprise I let her seat me. Felt the hot tears flow. I tried to dash them away, but they came in a torrent, willy-nilly, until my fresh collar was soaked. 'Oh, don't mind me,' I sobbed, 'I must be tired. Sorry, Liddy.' It was her concern and her kindness as much as anything that set me off.

'You are missing Huw,' she said, stroking my arm.

'And Alfie not well!' I howled. 'And . . .'

'Say it,' she said. 'Say what is bothering you.'

But I couldn't. How to say that I suspected Hineroa's child — Waewae — might be Huw's? She had said Waewae should learn to speak Welsh; why would she say that unless the baby had Welsh blood? The fear had been eating away at me.

Liddy had a different answer to my tears, though. 'Can you be expecting? Have your monthlies been coming?'

That took me aback. All these months — years, now — we had been here and no sign of another child. I had thought that maybe all the change — the new land, the strangeness — had made me barren. I tried to think.

Now the cascading tears held a different meaning. 'Liddy, Liddy, you have hit on it! I can't think when my last monthly was.' I touched my breast where it had been tender this past month. 'Oh, I believe you are right. Wait till I tell Huw!'

We hugged and laughed, the washing lying forgotten in the basket, making plans for a wee one in this new place. It was like an omen, see, a sign that we might survive all this hardship. That children might prosper here and grow up different, away from the dark future that faced them back in Wales.

'How could I have missed it?' I said to Liddy. 'Haven't I longed for another?'

'Well, sister,' (Liddy liked to call me sister when she was in a brighter mood) 'you have had other worries. Huw away. Alfie sick.' She picked at a weed lying in the middle of our little path. Rolled it in her fingers and smelled it, as was her way with all living plants. 'And I have a bit of news, too. Bryn has asked me to marry him. I am of a mind to say yes.'

Her quick glance in my direction was anxious. I knew what she was thinking. Was she being disloyal to my brother? Or was Bryn asking too quickly after Arial's death? Maybe I would have thought so if we were back home. But here all sorts of rules were broken, with no family tradition to stick to; no older generations to disapprove. And none of those elders — the grandmothers — to help out a mother or a father who had no husband or wife.

'I think you will make a bonny couple,' I said, all my misery forgotten. 'Bryn is a fine man. Mind you, he is a fortunate one, too, if you say yes.'

She giggled then, like a young courting maid, and the shadows that had blighted her prettiness during those months of the voyage out and of working off her passage quite disappeared. I had noticed the way she was taking trouble with her hair again, washing it in the spring water and adding a dash of vinegar, if we had it, so it shone; the lovely, shining tresses falling loose down her back. I had offered to plait it for her, but she shook her head. Plain to see now that it was all for Bryn.

So we hung out our washing and fed the children and delivered the folded dry linen. 'Huw, Huw, come home quick, you wretched man,' I muttered as I staggered over the muddy paths and knocked on the back doors and pocketed the precious coins.

---

Dr Dorset told me that 'my friend' (that is, Hineroa, but I hadn't mentioned her by name for fear he would scorn me) was right and the stream down the valley at the foot of Ahumairangi Hill was indeed foul. 'The new outhouses at the barracks are too close to the stream,' he said, 'and I am afraid that many settler families simply deposit their night soil directly into the fresh running water.' He felt Alfie's tummy and checked his tongue. 'You should keep him away from the stream,' he said. 'And give him plenty of good hot soups.'

'You are the senior doctor here,' I told him. 'Can't you put a stop to what's going on?'

He simply shook his head and took my money. 'I have no control over the natives and their habits. Alfie needs rest and warmth. You should not let him run wild.'

He is well respected, Dr Dorset, but I left his little office near the beach fuming. Hineroa is right: it is we settlers who foul up the rivers. But neither the doctor's advice nor Hineroa's potions seemed to be doing any good. Alfie had lost all his spirit. I wondered if he was missing Huw. When Holly and Meg urged him to come down to the beach, he simply shook his head and sat drooping on the bench, watching as we boiled and wrung and hung day after day.

The news from the Wairau was alarming, to say the least. Hineroa read pieces from the *Gazette* to us. 'Thirty dead,' she said. 'Colonel Wakefield's brother Arthur dead.' No mention of a Pengellin dead.

'Check again! Let me see!' I cried.

Sometimes I could pick out the words, which gave me the wildest pleasure. Liddy, too. We had swallowed our pride and allowed Hineroa to teach us. Alfie was going on six and should have been learning with us, but he didn't have the strength to concentrate.

Most days as Hineroa walked back from the Mission to Gareth's, she would stop by, and in her queer, grave way point out a new word or a new letter for us to learn. She was a strict teacher; insisted we practise every day. She brought us each a slate from the Mission and a piece of chalk — goodness knows if they knew what she was up to. Each afternoon, I found myself looking forward not just to the lessons but to spending more time with Hineroa and her bright little girl, who might one day be a friend for my new baby. I determined to surprise Huw with my new skill — and the new baby — when he returned, which must surely be soon. Though I couldn't help but worry that there had been no news from him. Surely I'd have heard if he were among the dead? Had they sent him off on a new survey task over there? Or (but surely not?) had he gone off on his own into the wild?

Was it the baby — which now began to show — or the lessons that made me easier with Hineroa? Who knows? But one day, after she had actually smiled at my reading and pronounced it 'very creditable', I broached the subject of Waewae.

'Is Huw Waewae's father?' I asked straight out, almost surprising myself at the bluntness of my words.

She turned to look at that beautiful daughter, who was sitting at her feet scratching on a broken piece of slate, trying to make marks or pictures. 'I think so, don't you?' she said, no hint of shame or alarm. 'She has a look of him.'

Even though I had expected this, it still took my breath away. I sat there silent, fiddling with my chalk. I wanted to hate Hineroa, but the honesty with which she had answered somehow disarmed me.

'Yes, I believe so,' she said. 'I cannot think of anyone else at that time.' Then she looked me in the eye and said with great fierceness: 'But I will not give her away to you. Not even if Alfie dies.'

Dear God, the things she would come out with! If Alfie dies!

She saw my shock. Took the chalk from my hand and wrote on my slate. *Alfie might die.* I could read *Alfie* and *die*, but not the word in between. She told me. 'He is very sick,' she said. 'You should be prepared.'

We both went inside to look at him where he lay on the little bed beside ours. It was early evening; normally he would be out playing still. In his hands was the toy horse Bryn had carved him from a fallen branch. Over and over he turned it, running his fingers across the raised head and the four galloping legs. He looked up at us and smiled, but just as quickly closed his eyes again while his hands went on with their exploration.

Hineroa beat her hands against the dress she wore now that she was back teaching at the Mission. I was surprised to see her distress. Usually you could not tell what she might be thinking. She laid her hand on poor, quiet Alfie's head. 'If only I could remember,' she whispered. 'If only my mother were still alive.'

I had never heard her talk about her family. Huw had told me when we first arrived that both of her parents were dead long ago. We sat now on our bed, Huw's and mine, and watched Alfie sink into sleep. Waewae ran in, and Hineroa lifted her up onto her lap. I should have been angry with Hineroa. Why didn't I ask her to leave with the baby Huw had fathered? Why did I let her sit on our bed — *our bed!* — as if she were part of the family? I can't tell you. I don't understand myself these days. We sat together and watched my Alfie and talked.

'Waewae will need him,' she said. 'Alfie is her only family. We must find a way.' She told me that her mother had great knowledge of healing plants, but that she herself only remembered a few names. She had tried to learn from Ngāti Toa custom, but they were not interested in sharing their secrets with a slave. Sometimes she saw a plant or tree that reminded her of her mother's knowledge, but she could never be sure. The memory could be a warning *not* to pick, she said.

As she was about to leave, she said, 'I thought you might be angry that Huw is the father.'

My wretched tears started up again. 'I might well be at some stage, Hine. At the moment Alfie is too sick.' Was there anger under all the fear and worry? I could not tell, but I did know I needed Hineroa's friendship.

She nodded. 'We will find a way to save him. You should understand this: I have been brought up in a different way to you. I was often sent to give comfort — as a woman does to a man — to a visitor who arrived with no woman. Also— But you do not need to know about those times which are better forgotten. With Huw it was before you arrived. I gave him comfort in that same way. Except that this time I chose to. He did not ask or force me. I saw his need . . .' Her quick smile was almost mischievous. 'He said he was not used to seeing so much of a woman uncovered and apologised. Also, he was not rude or rough. Just a little ashamed, I think.'

At the door she paused, looking out, down to the beach. 'I wonder if it is the pipi. Liddy's girls often bring them.'

There could well be some truth in that. The pipi were often the only meat we had to flavour our stew. Eggs and pork were in short supply and usually found their way to wealthier tables. But we all ate the shellfish.

'I don't understand white people's illnesses,' she said, tucking her sleeping daughter into a sling, 'but there have been other deaths among the children. At the pā, too. And the dirt in the stream flows into the sea. Perhaps that illness Alfie had earlier on weakened him in some way.'

She picked up my slate and wrote *pipi shellfish*. 'No more pipi,' she said firmly. And offered to bring me an egg or two from the Mission.

I could have hugged this woman. She who had lain with my husband! Perhaps living at the bottom of the world turns our habits and feelings topsy-turvy. Would she have welcomed a hug? I had no idea. But something about Hineroa was different. Her calm assurance — her distance — what I often called her lofty manner, seemed to be weakening. I wondered suddenly if Gareth was behaving himself.

# SECRETS AND OTHER TROUBLES

## HUW PENGELLIN

*PORT NICHOLSON, WINTER 1843*

What a homecoming! You would think I had been away a year not a few months. My nice little quarter of a town acre crowded with shacks; half of Wales settled on it. Liddy and Bryn both smiling again, and my poor Alfie lying pale as Martha's sheets on his bed, hardly an inch of flesh on his bones.

Martha full of secrets. 'Well, if you will stay away from your family you must expect changes,' she said. But her step had a spring in it, and her bonny smile, which had dimmed even before I left, was in full bloom again. 'No, Alfie is getting better,' she said, 'thank the good Lord. He is eating again. But, Huw, we must take better care of him. Hine says he has a weak constitution.'

It was all too much for me to take in. The chatter and bustle. Tall Hineroa coming and going with her daughter. It was as if they had all learned to take care of themselves without me. Wasn't I the earner in the family, the one who had paid for the precious plot of land with my own sweat? To be honest, I was out of sorts. The pay for my months of surveying was not, so far, forthcoming. And the time spent waiting for a boat back from Nelson had left me out of pocket to Tuckett. The Colonel said the pay would come but I had to be patient. But I had my doubts. This is the last time I will work for the Company, I said to him. Word is that the Company owes plenty of others besides me.

So when Bryn asked me to help recover his tools of trade and what bits and pieces had survived the flood, I was eager to set out again.

'Not before we have a quiet word together,' said my dear Martha, dragging at my sleeve. She led me away from the activity of the evening meal to where a log I had felled was still lying. It made a fine seat for viewing the comings and goings on the harbour. We sat. I feared some recriminations were coming. I had seen her watching Waewae; or maybe she had caught me doing the same. It was hard to drag your eyes away: so lively, already chattering in two languages; easy to see she had her mother's wit (and her father's tidy looks, I was tempted to think).

Martha took my hand and my mind eased. It was a loving gesture. 'Have you not noticed something about me?' she said, her voice gentle as she played with my fingers.

I looked at her. She wore no bonnet, and I spotted a grey hair or two among the brown. Surely I should not mention those? The hand that fondled mine was rough and cracked from all the washing and wringing. The hem of her skirt, scuffed beyond repair a year ago and restitched at a shorter level, was again in need of repair. What was I expected to find? Something she was proud of by the smile and the light in her eyes.

Those eyes led me to it. She looked down at her belly, and there — oh, there I could see it! A new curve; her apron stretched. My Martha was with child! I kissed her, brushing away her tears and my own. 'I had given up hope of another.'

We sat watching the hills on the far side of the harbour turn purple — range upon range, each higher than the last, each a different darkening shade. The sun had long set for us, but their flanks still glowed.

I suppose she saw a shadow cross my face, for she laughed. Martha always knew what I thought, even before I could put words to the feeling. 'No, you ninny, it is yours. I am four months at least.' Then, a little more tartly: '*I* have been faithful.'

Here it comes, I thought, to spoil my joy. But to my amazement there was no anger. She knew that Waewae was mine. Hineroa had explained. Martha had accepted her explanation.

'Has she asked for assistance?' I asked, fearful that another child would be a burden.

Martha shook her head. 'The opposite really, Huw. She has been a help to us and to Alfie. She thinks of Alfie as Waewae's only family. I find it hard to understand her; she is fiercely independent and yet comes here often. Look!'

She took from her apron pocket a folded piece of the *Gazette*. She stared at the page for a while and then, hesitantly, read a few words. Then another line. Then stopped.

She let out a curse that I never thought my proper Martha would ever use. 'God be dammed! I had hoped to impress you, but now I am stuck!'

We laughed together. It felt so good. But Martha reading! Who would have thought! It was hard enough for me to learn all those years ago when it was in a language we did not speak. And here was Martha. A certain shame, to be honest, in me. If she was so determined to read that she would learn on her own without my instruction . . .

But here she was surprising me on a new tack. She demanded I read aloud the rest of the article. 'It's to do with that chief over in the Hutt. Dog Ear. You should know about this if you are heading that way with Bryn.'

I had not even heard this news. True, I was back from Nelson only a few days, but I did not expect Martha to keep *me* up with political events. My quiet, dependable wife was changing. I picked up the paper. 'You've changed,' I said.

'For the better, I hope.'

Well, see, I was not entirely sure. It was unsettling.

The *Gazette* reported that the chief Taringa Kurī — 'Dog Ear' for his extremely sharp sense of hearing — was threatening to hack a line through the bush halfway up the Hutt Valley and pronounced that all of the land north of this line belonged to his tribe, Ngāti Tama. Settlers were being warned off. Clearly trouble was brewing. Martha was right. If we were to retrieve Bryn's blacksmithing tools (assuming they were still there and intact), we would have to be careful. Taringa Kurī had always spoken against the sale of land. He was a smart old fellow, and I liked him. Perhaps we could succeed if we were diplomatic. But best warned.

---

Bryn wanted to use my dog-cart as far as we could get up the valley, and then, when the tracks were too narrow, perhaps persuade a settler to take us upriver in his boat. Better a native waka, I suggested, though the practicalities of that were questionable. Ngāti Tama were not friendly with Te Āti Awa, who occupied the lower part of the valley.

The first part of the trip passed quietly enough. Me in a sunny mood because of the baby, Bryn the same over his betrothal to Liddy. Gareth, who had insisted on coming along to provide 'military support', stalking darkly ahead with his musket at the ready. I was not happy to see him there, but Bryn had agreed to the offer. 'We should try to heal the rift,' he said in his genial way. Well, true enough, we were a small community, we Welsh, and my brother was part of it.

'At least leave your gun in the cart,' I said to Gareth. 'We will only succeed if we show a peaceful front.'

But he wouldn't. I tried to impress on him that I should do any talking with the natives, but I doubt he was listening. My brother's mood was as stony as mine was soft. Martha said he had confronted Liddy in a fury when he heard about her betrothal to Bryn, accusing her of shaming him; insisting his had been the first offer; demanding to know why she would choose an adulterer ahead of himself. And so on. In the end it had been Hineroa who spoke sternly to him and led him away. Martha said her strong words had quietened him. He had left off his ranting and went with her. Interesting.

It was the first time I had been up the valley for some months. There were more whare along the banks of the river, and more patches of cleared ground. My Muka trotted along easy enough on our second day, in and out of bush over a track she could manage with ease. Several wheat fields were looking green and promising; vegetable patches the same. We even came upon a small flock of sheep grazing on a lovely green field surrounded by bush. I began to wonder if we had chosen wisely, coming to live at Lambton Harbour. Obviously the soil here, being river flat, was fertile.

We stopped to talk to a settler — James Brown his name — a big, strong fellow guiding his horse and plough over a newly cleared patch.

He nodded over at Gareth and his firearm. 'Best put that away, son. Show that further up the valley and you might not come back in one piece.'

Gareth scowled, but put the musket down. Don't ask me how he had the gun in the first place. He didn't own one. The muskets for our weekly drills were locked away back in the barracks.

Bryn knew James. 'Are we safe to continue on up to my old place? What about this line Dog Ear is threatening to cut?'

James slapped at a sandfly. 'Hard to say. Nothing's really safe these days. One week you might find the natives friendly; help you thatch a roof or sell you a side of pork. Next week a corner of your potato patch is dug up in the night and the crop stolen.'

His horse pawed at the loamy soil, ready to keep going, but James was on for a chat. 'You'll see the line soon enough. Dog Ear can be perfectly friendly if you treat him right. I reckon old Te Rangihaeata is goading him on. Wants to make trouble for that tribe downriver who are in the settlers' pocket. Anyways,' he pointed to where the track disappeared into the bush, 'you won't get much further with the cart. Bridle track only, half an hour yonder. But it will get you right up, I reckon, on foot . . . if the natives allow it.'

He told us, laughing, of an epic journey a few months back, to get a cart upriver and over some hill to a settler farm. 'Don't know what he'd do with a cart up there — not a drivable track in sight. They paid me to dismantle the cart and carry the wheels separately through the river and up over the hill. Another big feller carried the axle and then the tray. Five days it took, to get all the bits up there. But there you are. That settler was easy with the natives and they with him. You never know.'

He would have chatted all day. Easy to see he was lonely. But Gareth was fidgeting and Bryn on edge, too. No doubt reminded of Arial's dreadful death as we came closer. So we set out again, Gareth insisting on walking ahead with musket at the ready. Sure enough, half an hour on, the track narrowed just where the beginning of the native line was clear to see: east to west, freshly cut in the bush. Two tall, spiked poles set in the ground either side of the track. A warning. We unhitched Muka. Me anxious now that I might lose my precious cart. But Gareth would not stay to guard it. He as skittery as a newborn lamb, starting at every noise.

'For pity's sake, Gareth,' I said, 'settle down with that musket or it's us will be dead.'

So then. We crossed the line, see, with no fuss. No sign of anyone

— settler or native — just dark bush and the birds in fine voice. I touched my little medal for luck but was alarmed to discover I could not for the life of me remember the name of our god of forests. Were our ancient ones forsaking me? I looked over in alarm at Bryn, but he plodded on, head down.

We came to a branch in the track, and Bryn, very sombre now, pointed out which way we should turn. The place where his home once was, now a muddy bank with uprooted trees lying all around. His shed, further back from the river, still standing. That treacherous river placid and crystal-clear — why wouldn't you build close to the banks of such a beautiful view? Now we were here, Bryn wanted to get this over quick-smart. He went to open the shed while I brought Muka up. Gareth circled the clearing with his gun pointed. Hoping for trouble, it would seem.

Then the circus began. First, there was a bloodcurdling war cry. Then out from the bushes leaped two natives, feathers in hair, bare but for loincloths, prancing and yelling, muskets held high as if they were spears.

Gareth let out a scream to rival theirs, dropped his gun and tore off back the way we came.

I raised my hands and shouted 'Kāti! Kāti!', which I fervently hoped was some kind of begging them to stop, not having had cause to use the word before.

Bryn turned slowly, empty hands held up in surrender; then stopped with a grin.

One of the natives stopped mid-prance. 'Pine! Pine!' he roared out — his name for Bryn. The savage challenge dissolved suddenly into laughter and back-slapping. Turned out he had helped Bryn build his house, and had also dragged Bryn and Sarah from the river on that dreadful day. So it was all sunshine again. They walked Bryn down to the river, and all three stood where the house had once stood. Te Kāhui — Bryn's friend — broke off a spray of kawakawa leaves, waded into the water and cast the branch in. He chanted in a low voice while Bryn stood, head hanging. They hongied, sadly.

Then it was back to business. The natives helped us fill our sacks with Bryn's tools, and then made a clever kind of sledge with poles so that Muka could drag the anvil out.

Gareth still nowhere in sight.

'Would you have hurt us?' I asked in their tongue, curious whether their dance was all for show or in earnest.

Te Kāhui shrugged. 'Maybe. Taringa Kurī — our chief — wants us to scare the Pākehā. We will cut this line all the way across the valley. He thinks if we lie down with you in peace you will take all the land. I think he is right, don't you?'

He grumbled about some settler who had planted crops on cleared land that was his hapū's potato patch. 'So of course we take some of their crop. That is fair, eh?'

The other fellow, who had worked in silence so far, joined in. 'But the big chief, Te Rangihaeata, says we should fight. Not just take the food that is owed us. We Ngāti Tama are allied with him, so if he says fight we will.'

When we came finally upon Gareth, half-hidden in the bushes to the side of the track, Te Kāhui and his friend started up all over again with their war dance, but this time it was obviously in jest, with much laughter and jeering. Bryn laughing, too. Poor Gareth dreadfully embarrassed.

He glowered. Demanded his gun, which was resting over Te Kāhui's shoulder. But the demand was either not understood or ignored. When we came to our cart, the two men dumped the sacks of tools into it, slapped Bryn's back and offered a warning. 'Don't come up this way again, friend. There will be trouble soon. The chiefs are angry.'

And in a moment they had disappeared, silently blending into the bush. If there is war between us, surely they will have the upper hand. They know how to fight here. Our British garrison will have no idea, with their marching four abreast and their wheeling and lining up.

Gareth turned on me in a fury. 'You let him take my musket! Why didn't you explain it was mine?' He grabbed me by the arm. 'It's gone now, you fool!'

Bryn, who was as tall as my brother and stronger, spun him around. Shoved him in the direction of the track. 'So, you are brave when your brother is smaller, you coward. We saw you run. We heard your scream. Saw you throw away government property. Wait till they hear this back in Port Nic.'

Martha had told me about the Ceffyl Pren back in our village in Wales, when Gareth had targeted Bryn, rolling him in mud and accusing him of dallying with another's wife. Clearly no love lost between these two.

As we walked, I had a strange feeling. 'Eh, Bryn, do I look smaller to you?'

He looked sideways at me with a half smile but said nothing.

'No, but. Am I shrinking, do you think?'

Bryn laughed out loud. 'Huw, my friend, it's the tall trees all around. You planning to join your elves and sprites, are you?'

But it wasn't a joke to me. My gods or the native ones were angry. I could feel it. And the only name I could remember to call on was their god — Tane Māhuta.

# A DUET

## HINEROA

*TE WHANGANUI A TARA, SPRING 1843*

That year, near the end of 1843, Reverend Aldred became — what word can I use? — 'embarrassed', perhaps, with my presence at the Mission. And Minarapa was not so friendly with either me or the Reverend. For one thing I did not attend the church service on Sunday. For another there were more white settlers than natives at those services. And for a third I was a better teacher and more loved by the children than the Pākehā teacher. This was obvious to all. Miss Emily Entwhistle could not control the little ones in the Sunday School, and her knowledge of the Bible stories was quite limited.

Also I myself was not particularly happy with the way I was being treated. Or paid. Miss Entwhistle received three shillings for her daily classes in writing and reading. My pay was one shilling and sixpence, even though I taught the older children, included what I knew of counting, and taught them to write in both languages no matter what colour their skin. (This last was frowned upon.)

If it had not been for the situation at home (by 'home' I mean Gareth's cottage, though try as I might it never felt homely to me), I might have left the Mission. But I needed to keep Waewae and myself away from Gareth's (I should say 'Hamish', for it only annoyed him further if I called him Gareth) increasingly wild moods. After the trip up to the Hutt Valley, Gareth was often at home during the day. To escape the laughter, I guessed.

Reverend Aldred believed that Hamish and I were married. A small untruth that was necessary to secure my work and payment.

I told them that we had married elsewhere and that he had adopted Waewae, which was also untrue. But this allowed me to bring her with me to join in the classes even though she was younger than most of the children there.

I do not remember this time as happy. If it were not for Ripeka, the chief's former third wife, I might have walked away. (To where, though?) Huw and Martha and Liddy were busy with wedding plans. Gareth drank every night and was rough with me if I refused to lie with him. Sometimes I would do this just to have a peaceful night's sleep and to keep Waewae safe. But his demands were increasingly unacceptable. I felt as if my old life as a slave had returned to haunt me.

Often after teaching the children I would sit with Ripeka outside her whare, for company and to delay the walk back to Gareth's place. Ripeka understood my problem, and we discussed what solutions might be available.

'If only,' she said, laughing, 'the Pākehā had many wives. Then you could be Huw's second wife and all would be well. They say he is a good enough man. I wonder why Christians don't?'

True enough. In the Bible there are men who have more than one wife. Also terrible wars and much persecution. Why do the missionaries say there must be peace between tribes here? And yet they send out soldiers when our people claim food from gardens that used to be tribal land? This is hard to understand.

Ripeka had a new baby to her breast — another boy, so she was in high standing with the hapū, even though not officially a wife anymore. 'What about Kumutoto pā?' she said. 'They would take you in. You are a skilled flax-scraper.'

'But I would still be a slave, even though we no longer have slaves. You know that.'

She sighed and sat the baby on her knee to bring up his wind. 'True. You cannot undo that, no matter what they say. It is a pity,

Hineroa, that you were born so clever. But surely there must be people of your tribe somewhere?'

One day, I thought, Muaūpoko will come together again. And stand proudly. But it will take a generation or maybe two before we are not considered a beaten and enslaved people. Not in my time.

Ripeka found a biscuit for Waewae and another for me. 'You will think of something. You always do. But be careful of that Hamish Scott. They say everyone is laughing because he ran away from a couple of Ngāti Tama over the other side. Laughing at a warrior is dangerous.'

Waewae tugged at my missionary skirt. She was eager to move on, even if I was not.

'If there is too much trouble,' said Ripeka, 'come to my whare. But quietly.' She giggled. 'I might have a visitor.'

---

Two days before the wedding, I came home to find Gareth singing. He had a lovely voice, though this was the first time I had heard it. The words strange. I knew enough by now to understand it was in the Welsh language. As I cut slices of bread and bacon and boiled up carrots with pūhā, I listened. It is a hard language to piece together. Something to do with a young woman. Sad, I thought.

But Gareth was in good spirits, so I left him to it. Every now and then he stopped and went back. I think he was trying to remember. On and on he went until I called him to his meal. For once he was not drunk.

I complimented him on his singing and asked what the song was about.

'Oh, nothing to interest you,' he said, eating away. 'A song for the wedding.'

'It is a lovely tune,' I said. 'Maybe if I learned some of the words I could join in singing a second part to it? Like they do in church.'

He looked at me — an odd, thoughtful stare. 'Well, maybe you could hum. The words are difficult. It is a long story.' He sang a verse.

'About a poor young woman?' I guessed.

'How can you tell that?'

He seemed annoyed, which was the last thing I wanted. I shrugged and remained silent.

As he sang the verse again, I joined in with a harmony part, low and quiet beneath his tune.

For once he seemed pleased with me. Perhaps singing would bring him out of his moods. 'Again,' he said. This time when he sang I joined in with the words, though I didn't understand their meaning. He was surprised. 'What about this, then?' Another verse followed. I copied him. We sounded good together — his rich voice and my softer one beneath.

Waewae tried to join in, waving her arms, delighted with the sound. 'She likes the Welsh,' I said. 'She will learn it more quickly than me.'

'Why would she need to learn our language? Put her to bed,' he said. 'She's messing it up.'

For hours that night we practised. It was maddening not to know the meaning, but Gareth would not translate. 'It's an old Welsh folk song about a young girl in love.' That is all he would say. From what I had learned from Martha and Liddy, I could piece a few words. Definitely there was a sad tinge to it.

'Does she die?'

'Never you mind.'

'A death would not be suitable for a wedding, surely?'

'You heard me. Come to bed now.'

Because he had been pleasant and because I liked his beautiful voice, I went with him. That night he was not rough. Still there was something in his manner that made me uneasy. What was it? His easy mood had an edge to it.

# A WELSH WEDDING

## MARTHA PENGELLIN

*THORNDON FLAT, SPRING 1843*

The wedding day began happily enough. There were a surprising number of Welshmen and women in the settlement by now, some of them soldiers with the garrison who came in their dress uniform, which brightened the scene. Liddy wore her Sunday dress, which was white with green embroidery around the bodice and waist. She had worn it at her wedding to Dai, too, but it had to do: she had nothing better. Bryn very handsome in a dark suit and tie. His cap was not as smart as the minister's hat, but they were a very good-looking couple. And happy.

The three girls, Meg, Holly and little Sarah, took their role as 'bridesmaids' very seriously, attending to Liddy every few minutes, smoothing her dress and her hair, which was brushed out and bedecked with flowers that Liddy had grown — little cream roses, blue forget-me-nots and sprigs of green mint, which the girls had woven into a crown. Liddy showed me the love spoon that Bryn had carved her from a piece of wood — so beautiful and silky-smooth I had to lay it against my cheek. A tear in my eye. Huw had carved me mine out of a branch of oak that grew on his father's farm. But this, I had to admit, was more beautiful. Bryn was a lovely craftsman. Between the bowl of the spoon and the top of the handle was a clever entwining of strands, which is usual for a love spoon, but he had added the delicate fronds of a fern to the carving. Old country and new life joined together. A small thing, that love spoon, but full of hope, I thought.

I wore my Sunday dress, but over it a lovely yellow smock I had sewn especially as the baby was now large, and nothing fitted me unless I undid all the buttons and laced the two gaping sides together.

The ceremony at the Chapel went smoothly. There was, of course, an undercurrent of sadness because of Arial and the baby, but also a determined mood of moving forward. You had to be proud of the way we sang our hymns. Minarapa smiling and applauding in his top hat, quite the smartest fellow in the congregation. Gareth would not sit up with the family at the front; he was still nervous of being caught and sent back to prison. He sat with his cap pulled low over his forehead and his head down. Hine and Waewae sat with him, which was decent of her.

Then I was hurrying back home to make sure all was ready for the feast. We had twenty-three guests, mostly Welsh. Dora and her family, who were now flourishing, Russ in charge of maintenance at Mr Molesworth's mill over on the Hutt River, came in their own cart, pulled by their own horse, and presented us with two roasted chickens for the feast. Huw had invited the chiefs and their wives from Pipitea pā and Kumutoto pā where he had had his flax business, and Dr Dorset. Colonel Wakefield himself did not come, though Huw had invited him.

Two long slabs of wood formed the tables, which were laid out under the trees beside our house. What were left of the blessed rātā trees on the hill above us had flowered in time. I had picked a basket of them and laid the beautiful red sprays all down the centre amidst the bowls and trays of food. Wooden benches for the guests. There was a leg of ham, and the Southeys' chickens, dishes of potatoes, and a bowl of boiled eggs for good fortune. Liddy had been urging her leeks to grow fast, and there they were — a steaming bowl of them to make us all feel homesick. Smoked eel from Pipitea pā. Shellfish from Kumutoto. Cool watercress from the spring under

Ahumairangi. My beautiful fruitcake, and apple pies with cream, the apples coming from trees that had been planted up north by the early missionaries. All the guests had brought their own plate, mug and fork as was the custom.

My Alfie, so much livelier these days and resplendent in his yellow waistcoat embroidered in green leeks, and Liddy's girls, flowers in their hair, passed around dishes. I looked for Gareth to lead us in the grace, but he had disappeared. We had to make do with Huw, whose voice is not so strong, but we sang the feast proud like good Welsh and sat down to eat.

Then came the surprise. Some tall fellow arrived dressed in Ceffyl Pren garb: in a long, pale dress, beribboned bonnet and face blackened with soot. My heart sank. This was surely Gareth up to no good.

'Ho, ho!' he called out in our native language, touching the top of Huw's head. 'Who have we here? A Welshman who speaks three languages! Give us a toast then in the native tongue!'

Everyone applauded and laughed, and Huw obeyed very creditably. But his eyes met mine in alarm.

'Ho, ho!' cried the black-faced fellow, rapping Dr Dorset on his fine hat. 'Here is a man who charges a pretty penny even when he has no cure to offer. Lay a shilling on the table in honour of the bride!'

The laughter continued as the doctor laid down the shilling. And so it went. One of the garrison lads had to stand, come to attention and salute. Alfie had to walk down the table without touching a dish. Perhaps it would all be in good humour. But I hardly dared hope.

Finally, when all were enjoying this Welsh playacting, Gareth roared out: 'Ho, ho! I see a pretty bride. A kiss please in honour of Ceffyl Pren!' And stood in front of her.

Dear Liddy, what a trooper. I saw her recoil. But then she rose to her feet, smiling, and blew him a kiss. What must she have been thinking? He who had stolen her land. But she would not spoil the fun.

Quickly Huw led a round of applause for the Rebecca Man and began his speech to the bride and groom. Gareth, alias Hamish alias Ceffyl Pren, retired and sat at the far end of the table next to Hine.

If only the day had ended after Huw's speech. Everyone was so happy; even Gareth, I thought. Well, I was wrong. I had thought that perhaps Hine in her quiet, reserved way was doing him some good. I should have remembered that he had wanted — needed somehow — to marry Liddy. To make amends.

Huw greeted the chiefs in their own tongue, then spoke in English, with some parts in Welsh. He said how happy he was to see Bryn and Liddy together after their trials, and wished them all the best in their life from now on.

Before Bryn could speak in reply, Gareth rose again, Hine with him. 'A song,' he announced in his booming vice, 'for the bride and groom.' At first everyone smiled and some sang along. Or tapped spoons on the table. Hine sang a second part beneath the tune, more in the New Zealander manner, but very lovely. I was marvelling that she could sing in our Welsh language, so didn't pay attention at first to the song. Then the penny dropped, as they say. Dear sweet Jesus, he was singing 'Yr Eneth Gadd ei gwrthod'!

As the song unfolded, those in the crowd who understood Welsh grew quiet. Then stony-faced. Gareth sang on, a sly, triumphant grin on his face. I doubt Hine understood the words, which told the story of a girl pregnant out of wedlock who drowned herself out of shame for her wicked ways. Suddenly, in the middle of a verse, Bryn stood, his face white, his hands shaking.

'Thank you, Gareth. That will do!'

He used Gareth's real name. No doubt deliberately.

Those who understood applauded loudly. 'Enough!' they shouted, not in any friendly way.

But Gareth sang on, raising his voice over the hubbub. His eyes shone darkly, fixed on Bryn's. He was singing his revenge. Most were puzzled; but the family understood only too well, and were furious.

Hine was quick to understand there was a problem. She took hold of Gareth's arm, clapped a hand over his mouth and turned him away from the crowd. She is remarkably strong. But so is he. He ripped her hand away, planted a fierce blow to her face and continued to sing over the uproar, his voice now high and triumphant as he reached the end. Then he pointed a finger at Bryn and shouted at the top of his voice: 'Adulterer! Stealer of another man's wife!'

And off he strode, down to the beach, skirt flapping, bonnet ribbons streaming, pausing every now and then to turn, finger raised to heaven, his awful black face shouting 'Adulterer!' again.

Hine, blood streaming from her nose, crept up to me. 'I don't understand the song's words. I am so sorry. Please forgive me.'

And she walked away, holding Waewae in her arms, everyone staring. No one offering help.

# ADULTERY

---

## HINEROA

*TE WHANGANUI A TARA, SPRING 1843*

I swore that afternoon of the wedding that I would never go back to Gareth's whare. But I did, shame on me. By nightfall I needed shelter for Waewae. Rain drove in from the south, coming swiftly and cold, as if it, too, would drive away the joy of the wedding. I walked along to Ripeka's hut, but could hear voices inside. Waewae was whimpering. We were both in summer clothes. I thought of my precious belongings back in Gareth's house. Any of the pā would take me in, I knew, but in my stubbornness — perhaps pride — I would not go back to a life of servitude.

Gareth was drunk. Singing that song all over again, keeping time with a thumping of his mug on the table.

I looked at him sitting there. 'Are you not ashamed to spoil the wedding?' What I would like to have added was spoiling my friendship with Huw and Martha and Liddy. In my anger I had no inclination to curb my famous sharp tongue. 'Those were your family and your people. Your tribe. Because Liddy would not marry you, you must spoil her happiness and Bryn's. Your Jesus would not praise you for taking revenge. Shame, Gareth!'

He grinned and went on singing. The words garbled now, even I could tell that, his eyes rolling loose. I walked past him, holding on tight to Waewae, who was sleeping now. I tucked her down in her box-bed, wrapped warmly in a piece of blanket. I quietly gathered my possessions — one dress (the other still on Gareth's drunken frame), my flax cloak, Waewae's clothes, a kettle and a pan, a knife, a stirring spoon and a tomahawk. Years ago, I would have considered these few pieces riches beyond my wildest dreams; most would fit into my kete. All the rest belonged to Gareth. I made a bundle in one of his blankets and added a mug — his, but surely I was owed a mug for cooking for him these past months? In the morning, I would leave. Meantime I lay on the floor beside my daughter, keeping her and myself in the darkest corner. Soon, I hoped, Gareth would fall asleep.

Whatever had we sung? And why would that fine man Bryn, who had been so unlucky, and so loving to his first wife, be an adulterer? My understanding of that word was unclear. It nagged and nagged at me. Surely nothing to do with being an adult. We all become adults.

During that long night, another thought troubled me. I believed that I was carrying Gareth's child. I tried to make a plan. No doubt Huw and Martha would have nothing to do with me now. I had seen people toiling up the track beside our whare carrying saws and axes. They said there were lush valleys away up there, past Ahumairangi Hill — land which they had bought from Te Āti Awa. Perhaps I could make a life up there where my past was not known? But I had very little. Gareth took what I earned for my food and lodging. Five shillings was all I had managed to secrete away. I had thought, before the wedding, that perhaps he was growing to like me. Was there any way I could manage to live with Gareth? Or Hamish, as he insisted I call him. For a few months anyway? In my desperation and out of poor judgement, I decided to try one last time.

The next morning, I cooked him some bacon and our last egg. He woke to a fine smell of frying and the table laid ready for him as he liked. 'Good morning,' I said quietly, as if nothing unusual had happened the day before, and laid the food in front of him. He, still in my dress, his face still blackened, my lovely bonnet hanging by its ribbons down his back, dirty and crumpled. I wanted to snatch it away, but with difficulty held my peace.

He would not look at me. Drank his tea in great gulps; wolfed down the food and rose. In a moment he would change into his suit and leave. It was a Sunday and usually he went to Chapel. But I could not let him go without knowing. It was my need to understand that was my undoing that day. And perhaps his.

'Please tell me, Hamish. I didn't understand yesterday. What does "adulterer" mean? Why is Bryn an adulterer?' I spoke in what I hoped was a pleasant, enquiring manner, not attaching blame to my words.

He picked up his Bible. I thought he would not answer, but then he spoke directly — fiercely — to me. 'A man who sleeps with another man's wife. It is a sin.'

I thought about this. Christians have so many rules! 'Was Arial . . . ?'

'Yes, back in Wales. Another man's wife. They ran away — Bryn and Arial — from him.'

'But then, is it acceptable for you to lie with me even though we are not married?'

'That is the point: you are not another man's wife.'

He said this almost with a smile, so I felt bold enough to tell him that I thought I was expecting his child.

He sat down heavily. The liquor from the night before was still in him, I think. 'My child? It is mine?'

I swear there was not a shred of anger in the way he spoke. More of wonder, which gave me courage to continue. A foolish, foolish mistake. Perhaps I spoke too sternly. I told him that I would like to stay with him, but that he must be gentler with me and Waewae. And not drink too much. I told him that I would like this child of his to grow up in the Welsh community here and speak his language as well as mine and English.

'Waewae is learning, too,' I said, 'as she also is half-Welsh.'

He was not thinking very clearly, I think. For a long moment he looked at me. 'Waewae?'

I smiled. At that time I did not know how dangerous I was being. 'She is Huw's child, yes. Didn't you know? Huw knows this and so does Martha.'

He dropped his head into his hands. Picked up his Bible, and then laid it down again. I could not read his mood. Was he not pleased that these two children would be related? 'My child,' he said, each word dropping like a stone into the morning air, 'is growing in the same *adulterous* womb as my brother's *adulterous* child? These are children of Satan!'

I began to feel fear. Clearly, I was not understanding. 'You have just said I am not an adulterer.'

He threw the Bible at me. It caught me just where he had slapped me the day before. Waewae cried out and ran to me as I staggered. Hamish threw her out of the way and came at me with his knife. 'I will cut it out! You whore!' And lunged. I dodged around the table, keeping a chair between him and me, but it was no use. He was in a rage.

'Run away, Waewae!' I screamed, but she would not; stayed behind the bedroom curtain, whimpering. Next time he lunged, cutting through cloth to the flesh, I grasped his knife arm, twisting his wrist away from me, back towards him. Again he lunged, this time onto his own knife. I heard him grunt. But my bone was broken.

I felt the crack. Any further battle was hopeless. I threw the chair at him and tipped the table over, hoping to delay him. Then grabbed Waewae from the bedroom with my one good arm, preparing to run. At the door I glanced back. Was he going to come after me? He stood stock-still, staring. Not at me. As if some monster had entered the room.

'Sweet Jesus, help me!' he cried.

I ran.

# MY BROTHER

---

## HUW PENGELLIN

*GARETH'S HUT, LATER THE SAME DAY*

I could not let him go back to the penal colony. His fear of that place still gnawed at him, worse than a cancer. Any mention of New South Wales and he would walk away.

When we grew up together on the farm in the Preseli Hills, he was not so bad, see. We shared good times together down by the little stream; staged mock battles together, rolling on the grass among the great standing stones. Sometimes he protected me from the other boys. I was ever the smallest; quick, mind, but light and short-limbed. It was later, when he became a man, that his mood darkened. He should have been happy — he was the one to inherit the farm. So, when Bryn, in his anger, said he was going to report Gareth to the magistrate as an escaped convict, and also said, clenching his big fists, that he would teach him a lesson he would not forget, I went up to warn my brother.

I found him sitting on the floor, still in his Ceffyl Pren garb. Table overturned, chairs likewise, a mess of bacon-rind and crusts on his lap. In his hand a knife. Blood on the floor. Dear God, those dark eyes staring out of his black-smeared face! As if he were staring at death itself.

I forgot the warning, fear rising in me at the sight of that blood. 'Where is she?' I shouted. 'And Waewae? What have you done?'

He answered not one word. I dashed aside the canvas curtain. They were not in the bedroom. But more drops of blood made a trail in and back out.

Still he did not move. His eyes followed me. He picked up a scrap of bacon and slowly put it in his mouth. I knelt beside him and tried to shake some sense into him. 'Are they dead? Oh, Gareth, what have you done with her? With Waewae? They will deport you for sure now.'

He would not speak. So I left him there and ran into the bush, fearing what I might find.

A trail of blood led me uphill behind the whare and then into the bush. The undergrowth was thick here and the trees close together. Hard to make any headway. The thorns of bush lawyer grabbing me as if determined to keep her hidden. 'Hine!' I shouted. 'Waewae!' But there was no sound at all. Even the chattering of the green parrots silenced. 'Hine!' Surely if she could hear she would answer?

After an hour of this, I gave up. If I could make no progress, surely she would not, hurt as she must be and with the child? I scrambled back down, rocks sliding with me, my Sunday suit and shoes a sorry mess.

Bryn was there. Standing in the doorway of the whare looking down at my brother. Who sat, propped against a fallen chair, in the same position on the floor. Bryn, hands clenched by his side, brows stormy, just standing.

He turned to see me and nodded a greeting. 'I think your brother is dead.' Said in a wooden voice, neither pity nor anger in the words. He spread his hands towards me — an odd pleading gesture. They were clean of blood or bruising.

Oh, dear Lord, true it was. My difficult, brawling brother dead. His eyes staring, face blackened from his wretched Ceffyl Pren carry-on, mouth open and still holding that piece of bacon-rind on his tongue.

I had supposed that the blood was all Hine's.

We looked at each other, Bryn and me, neither asking the question that surely must be in our thoughts. He thinking it might be me; I the opposite, but dreading that it might be Hineroa.

I knelt to close those staring eyes. 'God rest you, brother,' I said, meaning it, too. He was ever a troubled soul, but in the end couldn't manage life in this new land. Couldn't let the past go. His guilt over Liddy's land, yes. And then his treatment in the penal colony had driven him, perhaps, further into his darker self. They say a bully cannot survive the punishment he is used to imposing on others. Would he have lived a useful or satisfied life back in Wales? God knows. Not here, though. Not here. Gareth liked a neat and tidy world run by his own rigid rules. The leaders of this new town of Wellington might try to organise the settlers and the natives into a world Gareth would have enjoyed. But I don't think they will succeed. In the end I hope that this wild country — its rugged landscapes and tempestuous storms and ancient stories full of mysteries — will bend us to its tune. I am drawn to all of it. Not my brother, though; it frightened him, I think.

Well, so be it. Strange thoughts as I crouched beside my dead brother.

After a long while I stood. Bryn had not moved from his spot in the doorway. 'Well, Bryn, we must do something about this, I'm thinking. Are you with me?'

# THE HANGING MAN

## MARTHA PENGELLIN

*THORNDON FLAT, THE SAME DAY*

I had no inkling that morning, the day after the blessed wedding, that by sunset I would be labelled — and avoided, given the strangeness of it all — as weird, some kind of witch, even an accomplice to murder. The sun shone on Thorndon Flat, the stench from the stream rose as usual, the blasted green parrots swooped down with threats to sully my washing. Liddy in our little garden, rooting up plants to take with her, dear soul, singing to them as she dug. She and Bryn were moving up over the hill to the Karori Valley. The children were still asleep after the big day, and the men away — who knows where? How is a body to keep track of them all these days?

I called out a greeting to Mrs Barton across the way, just to annoy her. She couldn't abide the fact that her washerwoman lived so close in a hut of her own, instead of around the back of the Bartons' large house in respectable but hidden servants' quarters. Out of sight. It was a good drying day, so despite its being Sunday the wash would be done (another affront to Mrs Barton).

By the middle of the afternoon I had most of the wash drying nicely, strung out on the lines which criss-crossed the lower part of our front garden: adding further annoyance. Mrs Barton naturally thought washing should hang out the back, not in full view of her so-called 'rose garden'. But the alternative was to do the work herself, so she bit her tongue.

Tommy's screeching was not at first out of the ordinary. You

could hear the lad shouting from across the valley. 'Marta! Marta!'
My name, the best he could do with it. Little Tommy Titch could not
say half his words properly, but the high scrape of his voice would
cut through a brick wall at the best of times. When he was upset, I
swear it would rupture an eardrum. He was often upset, poor lad;
his mind was not right. Sometimes I paid him a ha'penny to scare the
parrots off my washing, so he could be useful.

Down he came running, across the native gardens, past the
barracks, still screaming my name. 'Marta! Marta!' Crossed the
stinking stream in his bare feet, three leaps and he was over. Dodged
between the new butcher's and the big house on Tinakori Track. I
could see him then, his shirt flapping, face contorted: a perfect mask
of misery. Right through Mrs Barton's smart garden, scattering filth
from the stream over her new lawn — no use telling him it was
private property, though she had tried many a time in a voice near
as loud as Tommy's — and here he was, standing in front of me,
gasping. His heart would tear itself out of his skinny body.

I threw my wet sheet over the line and sighed. Some new disaster.
A bee-sting or a dead bird was the end of the world to Tommy Titch.
But something in his face told me there was more to this.

'Tell me then, lad, what is it?'

He grabbed my skirt with his dirty hand and pulled. Wanted me
to go with him.

'Get your breath, Tommy. Then tell me.' Mrs Titch next door
was poorly with the stomach cramps, so it was no use hoping for
her intervention.

The boy pointed up to the hill and tugged at me again. Tears
were tracking through the grime on his face and he trembled. But
he would not say, which was not at all like him. Usually, his odd,
garbled words rolled out unchecked.

So I called to Liddy to see to our Alfie, and went with Tommy, stepping out through my poor rickety gate, just as I was, in my washerwoman's apron and boots. It is different here. Back home, what decent woman would step out into the road without coat on and bonnet firmly in place? In Thorndon Flat no one will turn to stare. Well, I tell a lie; Mrs Barton and Mrs Sinclair would disapprove. And others. But we of the labouring classes are freer here.

Tommy wanted me to go up the hill, which my Huw calls Ahumairangi. Others call it McCleverty's after the farmer who is clearing land beyond there. That tall hill — mountain to my eyes — was a glory when we arrived; covered in the thickest bush you could imagine, red flowers and white here and there, and birds singing in the morning. Now it is a mess of fallen branches and muddy slides. When it rains, half the hill comes down to the flat.

We headed up a track, Tommy moaning and racing ahead, then scrambling back to cling onto my skirt again. Me, in my condition, straining and puffing. I wished then that I had brought Liddy with me or waited for Huw, wherever he had got to. But it seemed we had arrived, for Tommy stopped at a place where the great trees still stood, and pointed into the darkness. His feet were rooted.

Catching my breath, I peered in. 'Well, show me, Tommy. What is all this fuss, then?' I was cross with him, calling me out on a wash day and making me climb up. I could see nothing but tree trunks and vines and the track winding through ferns. Tommy covered his eyes with his hands, whining in that strange, high way of his.

Then I saw a skirt hanging in the gloom beneath a branch. Dear sweet Jesus. Not just a skirt. There was a body inside it; a pair of boots hanging below the dress. A bonneted head with a blackened face and a rope around the neck. Tucked into the pocket of the skirt was a bouquet of red rātā flowers. And strangest of all, perched on those pretty shoulders, four green parrots staring down at me. Three on the right side, one on the left. Like that picture of Saint Francis of

Assisi, except the saint's hands are outstretched and his face joyful. Here, the hands hung down and the face showed nothing beneath its daubing of black.

I must have shouted out in my fear and horror, for suddenly a flock of parrots, including those perched on the hanging body, burst from the trees screeching and clattering into the sky, leaving me staring alone at — at who? Even Tommy, his task over, had run away back into the sunlight.

There was a rustle behind me, in the darkness of the trees. Someone was watching. I thought of Hineroa and called out her name, but no reply. Perhaps just a dog or a pig, then.

I knew what this was. Ceffyl Pren. The body will be a Welshman, not a despairing woman. He would once have likely been a Rebecca Man. Of course, after yesterday I could hazard a guess. Surely not, though? But whoever was hanging there, Gareth would be involved. Who had he hounded now? It couldn't be Bryn, who was so angry last night he could have strung the wretched man up himself. That gave me pause for thought. But though punishment and hilarity by Ceffyl Pren are handed out, it is never death. Never.

But who could he be? The blackened face and bonnet gave no clue. I reached up to touch the skirt. Not mine. So this hanging and silent man would not be my Huw. The boots were too big, the ankles too thick. Not Huw. Not Huw. Of course not. Not for one minute could I imagine that my lovely, lively, bright-eyed man would take his own life. But then . . . Was the dress Hineroa's?

I should have run to the barracks or the magistrate but dared not. Lord, Lord, what was the connection? After the trouble the day before yesterday at the wedding they were asking questions of the Welsh. Already the preacher (not a Welshman) who had married Bryn and Liddy was asking about the accusation of adultery. My first thought — to run, crying for help down to the settlement —

quickly faded. Should I just walk quietly away? But then Tommy
had made such a fuss, someone was bound to ask what he was on
about. I couldn't take my eyes away from the body. The little one
in my belly kicked hard; did he or she catch my fright? I held tight
to that lovely swelling curve. Stay calm, rest easy, little one. I stood
there, unmoving, until my breath steadied. Not even a shred of
birdsong to break the silence.

Then a cough from above in the dark bush had me poised to run.

Out crept Hineroa, not in her missionary dress but in her old
native cloak, Waewae clutching a handful of the frayed matting and
solemn for once.

'I've been waiting,' said Hineroa, her voice almost too low to
hear, 'until someone came. I could not leave him alone.' She looked
pale. 'Thank goodness it was you, Martha.'

She sat down suddenly, as if her legs could not hold her. 'I'm
afraid I need help.' Waewae sat, too, watching her mother, her eyes
round, and her little fingers stroking Hineroa's hand. 'Oh, Martha, I
am no good at asking for help. It is something I have never learned.
What should I do?'

If the situation were not so grave, I would have smiled. True
enough, I had never heard Hineroa ask for help. Plenty of times
offered it, and plenty of times given not necessarily welcome advice.

'It is Gareth,' she said, 'in my dress.'

I sat down beside her. Gareth. The man was clearly dead. No
need to rush.

'I made a mistake. I'm sorry, Martha. This is your Huw's brother.
My words to him were in some way wrong. I still don't understand.'

We talked. She apologised for the wedding song. 'I didn't
understand the words. What were they?'

'"Yr Eneth gaddei grw thod." It is about a girl who becomes
pregnant out of wedlock, then out of shame drowns herself. Bryn

and Arial escaped from Arial's old husband and came here. It's more or less the same story. No one knew, except a few family and friends.'

'But why was Gareth so angry?'

'It's a long story, Hine, to do with land back in Wales and Liddy. And — well — just Gareth.'

She was nursing one arm. I wondered if she was hurt. Also I wanted to discuss what we should do now. But Hineroa kept on with her questions. She always had to know. Had to understand.

'I understand he was angry. I also understand utu. The righting of wrongs. But I thought that maybe I could have one last try to . . . to tame him, Martha. Does that sound stupid?'

I had never heard Hineroa suggest anything she did might be stupid! 'Taming Gareth is not a path I would attempt. How did you go about this great task?'

'This morning I told him I was pregnant with his child. That if he would live a life more gentle, I would stay with him and marry him in the Pākehā manner and we could bring up his child and Huw's together.'

'Oh dear.'

'Yes. A mistake. I thought perhaps he knew. I told him Huw knew about Waewae, and you also knew this and accepted it.'

'Oh *dear*, Hine. Gareth would hate to think we accepted it. His life is full of rules.'

'Yes.' She frowned at me as if I were to blame. 'Christian rules? Not all Christians are so . . . rigid. Huw was not. And Gareth himself was happy to lie with me.'

'Gareth's rules applied to other people, not himself.'

'I have known plenty of people like that. My mistake was thinking white people might be different. Reverend Aldred is always talking about bringing civilisation to us. Peaceful ways.'

She reached out to pick something from a row of ferns. Stopped, with a cry. 'Please, Martha, could you pick that small inner part and give it to Waewae? She's hungry.'

'And you are hurt.'

Waewae came forward and brushed the hairs from a tiny, curled frond and chewed on it.

'Yes, I am hurt. Which is a problem. He would have hurt Huw, too, I think. To punish him for lying with me. Oh, Martha, I am not thinking very well.'

She closed her eyes, and I feared she might faint.

Little Waewae stood up. 'Hine,' she said. And then looked at me with those dark eyes, so like Huw's. 'Hine is hurt.' Spoken in our Welsh tongue. She would be a bright one like her mother — and her father, I had to admit. Whereas I was the practical one, relied on to find the solutions.

Hineroa's left arm was broken. No bone protruding, but a painful swelling and a big bruise already spreading down to her wrist. She asked me to support it with small branches, one each side and tied together with a strip of cloth.

'I have my bundle behind me in the bush. You can tear up my dress.'

But I would do no such thing. A piece of my apron would not be missed. More serious, though, was the cut just below her breast, which was stuffed with some sort of moss. A little blood still leaking through. She would not let me touch it.

'But it may need stitching,' I said.

'We can do that later, Martha. The moss will keep it clean.'

Well, I had to trust to her; their ways are different, but they survive same as us. Or some of them do. These days there is much sickness.

All this time the body above us was turning this way and that as the breeze came and went. Flies gathering, too, I noticed.

'Gareth did this to you?'

She nodded. 'When he heard his child was growing in the same womb as Waewae. He kept saying the same word as at the wedding. *Adulterer.* Is the black face and lady's clothes a strange kind of revenge dress? Or punishment? I thought at the wedding it was meant for a game.'

'Yes. Usually it is. Just not when Gareth is involved.'

'We fought. He attacked me with a knife. Said he would destroy the womb that produced children of Satan. I think in the fight he was cut, too. Perhaps badly.'

Waewae watched as I tore strips of apron and bound her mother's arm. Seeing my splints, she gathered a few more and presented them with a smile. The little dear. I had to ask it. 'You didn't kill him and then string him up?' I wouldn't have put it past her. She is as tall as a man. And fierce.

'I did not. But I would have if he came near Waewae.' She looked up at his body. 'I am surprised he would do that. Also, if I wounded him deeply, he would find climbing up difficult. Impossible maybe.'

Her questioning unsettled me. She would try to work everything out; best to just accept he hanged himself.

But she would continue her puzzling. 'And the flowers in the pocket up there. Why? He would not do that, would he? At first I thought it was blood from my stabbing him. Are they a message? Like our kawakawa leaves for the dead?'

I looked down at the ground below the body, and there was the blood, a small pool of it. Using one of Waewae's sticks I scuffed the ground until there was no sign, Waewae joining in with her sticks; all a game to her.

Hineroa nodded. 'Thank you. Martha, just before I ran I saw the blood drain from his face. Surely not pain from the wound. Some terrible realisation. "Sweet Jesus, help me!" he said. What did he mean, do you think?'

Well, I have never been party to Gareth's strange thoughts.
Perhaps he was always a little mad? His bullying a screen to hide a
deep fear? That he might be sent back to the penal settlement? Huw
might have a theory. Meantime the sun was setting, this matter of a
hanging man to be reported and a sensible story to go with it.

'Can you walk? Shall we go back now?'

Such an odd look came over her. Most people I can tell what they
are on about. I could never make out Hineroa. 'Go where?' she said.
'Not back to the settlement. They will take Waewae away. And your
family might demand utu for Gareth. But Martha, I have nothing.
How could I pay?'

She said she had hidden in the bush for some time. Heard Huw
calling but stayed hidden, then, later, crept back to the whare to
pick up her bundle. Gareth was not there. Seems she was heading
away up the Karori track and into the bush or God knows where
when she found him hanging and so waited with the body.

It took some persuading to get her to go back to Gareth's shack
and wait there. Clearly she had no confidence at all in our magistrate
or our laws. 'I am of no importance. I have no tribe to stand up for
me. I will win no argument.'

'Huw will not demand any settlement,' I said firmly. 'Every flock
has its black sheep. Gareth was ours.' I helped her up. It was high
time I reported the death. With me carrying her bundle, and Waewae
attached like a burr to her cloak, we managed to steer Hineroa to the
whare. Fortunately, it was close by. The table overturned, crockery
smashed, bedding on the floor, not to mention blood. Useful evidence
of the fight, so best leave it untouched. Nothing for it but that we
head back into town, all three, to our little Welsh Corner, as I liked
to call it.

# A VERDICT

## MARTHA PENGELLIN

### *THORNDON FLAT, LATE 1843*

I read the article out loud to the family. Only once did I falter. Alfie offered to help, the scamp, but I wouldn't let him. Start to finish I made it out:

> N. Z. Journal, 14ᵗʰ December 1843
>
> The body of the man found hanging in proximity of the Karori track on 27th November has been identified as Mr Gareth Pengellin, known in Port Nicholson as Hamish Scott. The reason for the female garb in which the body was encased when discovered and which afforded much gossip among the curious has been explained by his brother Mr Huw Pengellin (arr. Tory, 1839). Some readers may recall events in Wales just prior to the first emigrant ships arriving in these blessed isles. To wit the burning of Welsh toll gates by Rebecca Men and the violent clash in Newport between those loyal to the Mother Country and a band of hot-headed Welsh Chartists. During the toll-gate atrocities, Welshmen adopted female garb and blackened faces in order to escape detection.
>
> Mr G. Pengellin was a ringleader in both insurrections, arrested, tried for treason and sentenced to death, later commuted to deportation. The N.Z.

*Journal has ascertained that Mr G. Pengellin was
an escaped convict from the New South Wales
penal colony who has been living among us without
detection for approximately three and a half years.
While it is understandable that his brother, Mr Huw
Pengellin, might desire to protect his brother from the
deservedly harsh prison conditions across the Tasman
Sea, we consider that it is every settler's duty to uphold
the law, be the perpetrator family or foe. However,
Colonel Wakefield has generously interceded on behalf
of the brother, recognising his loyal service to himself
during the Peninsular War in Spain.*

*We can only surmise that the frenzied attack prior
to the suicide on his companion, Hineroa, wife in
the manner of native custom, unhinged the convict;
or perhaps brought him to a sense of shame. This
unhappy incident is the third death by suicide this
month. Mr McDonagh, Police Magistrate for Port
Nicholson and Dr Dorset acting as Coroner cleared
the body for burial (not within Church or Mission
grounds). The penal settlement in New South Wales
has been informed.*

*Some members of the Lodge expressed the opinion
that many settlers may be downhearted, nay even
fearful, after the questionable judgement of Land
Commissioner Spain over the Wairau massacre, and
that further self-inflicted deaths might be expected.
Other more sanguine landowners, this writer among
them, pointed to the enthusiastic plans for the
upcoming Anniversary Celebrations in January. More
on those plans in the next issue.*

# SAFE HARBOURS

## HINEROA

*THORNDON FLAT, JANUARY 1844*

After the many questions by the magistrate and the curious bystanders, native and Pākehā, Martha and Huw and I were left in peace to live our lives.

As my arm and my body healed and our babies grew inside us, Martha and I would sit on the bench in front of Huw's whare on the Hill Street and talk. (Waewae and I occupied the whare Bryn had built.) She is an unusual woman, Martha. I believe that learning to read has changed her; also this life away from her own tribe back in Wales. She soaks up new thoughts like dry moss in wet weather.

'Why did you leave?' I asked her. 'Did another tribe drive you out?'

She thought about this for a while. 'Maybe the English took away some of our land. I don't know if that is true or how it happened. But in Wales the English are wealthy and we Welsh are mostly poor.'

'They conquered you.'

'Perhaps. I think there were wars in the old days. Huw says that once the kings of England were Welsh. I suppose the English conquered us by wealth. They had more of everything than us.'

'More guns?'

'Oh, yes. And everything else.'

'More guns. As Te Rauparaha and the Taranaki tribes conquered us. And,' I said, 'as the settlers overcome us here by wealth. Greed, I would say.'

She smiled. 'Do you think me greedy, Hine? To want a better life for my children?'

'Not you, not you, Martha. The Wakefields. The Company. The rich investors who come here to buy land and sell at a profit. And who bring people like you to serve them.'

We often talk like this while Huw is away surveying. He cannot sit at home for long. He loves to find unknown pathways through mountains, or discover where rivers end up. Martha is the homemaker.

One time I asked her: 'I don't understand how you could leave your family and come so far, if there was no war to force you.'

She looked out over the harbour. It was a beautiful day when this conversation took place. No wind; clear sky. This was before they moved over the hill. 'My parents were dead,' she said. 'Huw's, too.'

'But your hapū? Your aunts and uncles? Your cousins? You left them all? That seems strange to me.'

She sighed. 'Poor harvests, large families, the need for work. These were all driving us apart, scattering us to different places. No, it is more the land that I miss. Our beautiful valley. We talk of *hiraeth*, a longing for the place you call home.'

'We would call it tūrangawaewae. The place where your feet belong. But you left it.'

'Well, yes, we left it. This is where my hearth lies now. The fire-place here contains a stone that came with me from my mother's and my grandmother's hearth. I will take it with me over the hill.' She stood, smoothed down her apron. 'But now there is washing to be boiled.'

A practical woman, Martha. But strong, too. She is the centre of her small family and seems contented to have so few relatives in this land. That is strange to me.

Later, when the washing was done and she was stirring the stew over the fire for our dinner, she said — as if the conversation of the morning had been developing in her head all day: 'We were desperate, see; hungry. The roof over our head leaked. We were cold and very poor. Huw had to work at something he hated.'

This was easier to understand. 'Oh! You were slaves like me? You were owned by . . . ? Was it the English?'

She laughed. 'No, Hine, we weren't slaves. The factory boss was English, yes, but he didn't own us. We were free to go.'

I wanted to argue this point, but I am learning to be more careful. My mother would approve. Go where? I wanted to say. You say you were desperate. You had *nowhere* to go. It seems to me that many labourers who arrive here are not free at all. They must work for the landowners or the Company who have paid their passage. Does that not make them slaves? I suppose, like me, they believe they can free themselves. In time. Or at least give their children a chance.

It was Martha's idea to move. Thorndon Flat is not healthy, she said, and Alfie not strong. Also she finds the town of Wellington too rowdy — public hotels and trading posts and warehouses all along the Lambton Quay. Settlers still arrive by the shipload every month or two. Trading cutters queue to tie up at the three jetties; horses and carts come and go. Settlers now outnumber our people. The pā are shrinking; every day I see Te Āti Awa from Pipitea carrying their bundles, heading north.

The days are filled with the noise of sawing and hammering. Martha says that, of course, it is not like the belching manufactories of Newport and their rat-ridden hovel there, but also it no longer reminds her of the gentle Preseli Hills and their family farm. Her dream is to run a small hotel at the crossroads up on the hill, serving travellers on their way to Karori Valley or Ōhāriu or the sea at Mākara. She hopes that Bryn and Liddy and the girls will join them. And me and Waewae.

But Waewae and I will not be joining them. I have work here at the Anglican Mission which I enjoy. Something about the bustle and energy of this town draws me. We will of course stay connected with the Pengellins; they are family now. But it is time for me to make my own free way.

---

Last week, as I stood among the piles of potatoes and vegetables and all manner of goods for sale at Pipitea market, an unfamiliar man caught my eye. I know most of the traders, native and settler. This fellow was tall — almost my height — dark-skinned and burly. He stared at me in a way I found unsettling. Something about him. He nodded towards me in an easy, friendly way, then turned to take up his full kete. After a few steps, he stopped. For a few moments he stood there with his back to me. Then slowly, carefully, his eyes on the ground, he picked his way back towards me, never once looking up. Waewae tugged at my cloak. She had noticed, too.

He spoke quietly. 'I remember a girl who was tall. A chief's daughter. I imagine she might have grown to look like you.'

'I am Muaūpoko,' I said.

He glanced around quickly, but no one was paying attention to us. 'Then this is a happy day for me. I know who you are. I knew your brother.' He smiled. 'I remember you as very outspoken, like your mother.'

'They say that is still the case.'

He said that, like me, he had been captured and bonded. But that now he lived freely with a Muaūpoko hapū further north.

'Oh! They welcomed you?'

'Āe. They would welcome you, too. They follow the new ways. Do you have your mother's healing skills? If so, they are sorely needed among our people.'

Good news. We talked a little, then he went on his way. A coastal cutter was waiting for him.

Waewae, who notices more than she should, tugged at my skirt. 'But we will stay here, won't we?'

I looked out over the sea. The sun was setting. The hills to the east, the sky above them turning rosy; the harbour below luminous. I will always love this beautiful place, long ago a home to my tribe.

'Yes, Waewae,' I said. 'I think we will stay.'

# HISTORICAL NOTE

The main characters in the novel are imaginary — the Pengellin family, Welsh settlers, Hineroa and Rere. Others are mainly historical. Their actions and movements are as accurate as I could (or should, being a novelist) make them. Once or twice I have moved dates slightly, but never significantly.

The interpreter Te Whaiti, described variously as Nahiti, Nayti, Neti and Ngaiti in other accounts, was a real person. He was Ngāti Toa, a nephew of Te Rauparaha and first cousin to Te Rangihaeata. He died, probably of consumption, two years after arriving back in New Zealand. His wife, Te Rongopamamao, then became a wife of Te Rangihaeata. Her death during the confrontation at Tuamarina, Wairau Valley, was a central event in that conflict.

Minarapa, a Ngāti Mutunga chief and a Christian preacher, was also a real person. Once bonded to Ngā Puhi he was trained by Wesleyan missionaries in the north then sent down to Te Aro pā, to build a Mission house and to preach.

# THE PURCHASE OF WELLINGTON

The following is the approximate cost of Wellington to the New Zealand Land Company. In some cases the amounts are doubtful, but the available information makes it clear that the total must have been very close to this figure:

| | £ | s. | d. |
|---|---|---|---|
| 120 only muskets at 15/- each | 90 | 0 | 0 |
| 2 tierces tobacco | 50 | 7 | 7 |
| 48 only iron pots | 3 | 4 | 3 |
| 2 cases soap | 8 | 4 | 10 |
| 4 only fowling pieces at 15/- each | 3 | 0 | 0 |
| 11 only fowling pieces at 18/- each | 9 | 18 | 0 |
| 1 cask ball cartridges | 0 | 7 | 0 |
| 1 case for fowling pieces | 0 | 8 | 6 |
| 1 keg lead slabs | 6 | 0 | 0 |
| 1 keg for lead | 0 | 4 | 0 |
| 100 only cartouche boxes at 3/6 each | 17 | 10 | 0 |
| 100 only tomahawks at 1/- each | 5 | 0 | 0 |
| 1 case for tomahawks | 0 | 10 | 0 |
| 40 only pipe tomahawks at 4/- each | 8 | 0 | 0 |
| 10 gross pipes at 2/3 per gross | 1 | 2 | 6 |
| 1200 only fishhooks at £1/0/6 per thousand | 1 | 4 | 8 |
| 12 only bullet moulds at 1/- each | 0 | 12 | 0 |
| 6 doz. shirts at 21/6 per doz. | 6 | 9 | 0 |
| 6 doz. shirts at 25/6 per doz. | 7 | 13 | 0 |
| 20 only jackets at 7/4 each | 7 | 6 | 8 |
| 20 pairs trousers at 3/9 per pair | 3 | 15 | 0 |
| 300 yards cotton duck at 4 ½d. per yard | 5 | 12 | 6 |

| | | | |
|---|---|---|---|
| 100 yards check at 4 ½d. per yard | 1 | 17 | 6 |
| 2 doz. slates at 3/10 per doz. | 0 | 7 | 8 |
| 200 only pencils at 4/6 per thousand | 0 | 0 | 11 |
| 10 doz. pocket knives at 4/3 per doz. | 2 | 2 | 6 |
| 4 doz. pairs scissors at 2/6 per doz. | 0 | 10 | 0 |
| 6 doz. pairs scissors at 9/6 per doz. | 2 | 17 | 0 |
| 1 doz. umbrellas at £1/9/6 per doz. | 1 | 9 | 6 |
| 2 lbs. beads at 2/9 per lb | 0 | 5 | 6 |
| 1 gross iron jew's harps at 5/- per gross | 0 | 5 | 0 |
| 1 doz. razors at 3/6 per doz. | 0 | 3 | 6 |
| 1 doz. shaving boxes and brushes at 2/4 per doz. | 0 | 2 | 4 |
| 1 doz. sticks sealing wax at 8/3 per doz. | 0 | 8 | 3 |
| 100 only red blankets at 11/5 each | 57 | 1 | 8 |
| 21 kegs gunpowder at 21/- each | 22 | 1 | 0 |
| 21 kegs for gunpowder at 1/6 each | 1 | 12 | 6 |
| 2 doz. spades at 28/- per doz. | 2 | 16 | 0 |
| 50 only steel axes at 2/- each | 5 | 0 | 0 |
| 60 only red night-caps at 8/- per doz. | 2 | 0 | 0 |
| 200 yards calico at 3½d. per yard | 2 | 18 | 4 |
| 10 doz. looking glasses at 5/- per doz. | 2 | 10 | 0 |
| 1 doz. pairs shoes at 67/6 per doz. | 3 | 7 | 6 |
| 1 doz. hats at 9/- per doz. | 0 | 9 | 0 |
| 100 yards ribbon (price per yard not given) | 2 | 3 | 11 |
| 10 doz. dressings combs at 3/- per doz. | 1 | 10 | 0 |
| 6 doz. hoes at 15/- per doz. | 4 | 10 | 0 |
| 2 only suits of clothes at 80/- each | 8 | 0 | 0 |
| 2 doz. adzes at 20/- per doz. | 2 | 0 | 0 |
| 2 doz. handkerchiefs at 6/- per doz. | 0 | 12 | 0 |
| | — | | |
| | £365 | 11 | 1 |

It was agreed by the New Zealand Company that Colonel William Wakefield would be allotted an allowance of £500 plus fit-out for leading the enterprise.

## ACKNOWLEDGEMENTS

Thanks to Paul Diamond (Ngāti Hauā, Te Rarawa, Ngāpuhi) for reading the manuscript and making very useful observations.

Also to Hilary and the late Maui John Mitchell (Ngāti Tama, Ngāti Atiawa, Ngāti Toa), whose research uncovered valuable information about the identity of the New Zealand Company interpreter Te Whaiti.

Gillian Johnston allowed me to use her extensive family research into early settlers in Wellington and the Hutt Valley. I am very grateful for her generosity.

Books lent by Vicky Ellis and Tim Barlow were invaluable, as was the wealth of information in our libraries and on the internet.

As always, Harriet Allan, Fiction Publisher for all my ten novels, was great to work with, as was the team at Penguin Random House.

Laughton Pattrick heard me read aloud Part One of this novel before he died. His enthusiasm gave me the courage to continue. We have both lived our long lives in Wellington, Te Upoko o te Ika.